DOVER · THRIFT · EDITIONS

Civil War Short Stories and Poems

EDITED BY

BOB BLAISDELL

DOVER PUBLICATIONS, INC.
Mineola, New York

DOVER THRIFT EDITIONS

GENERAL EDITOR: MARY CAROLYN WALDREP

EDITOR OF THIS VOLUME: SUSAN L. RATTINER

Copyright

Bibliographical Note

Civil War Short Stories and Poems, first published by Dover Publications, Inc., in 2011, is a new anthology of short stories and poems reprinted from standard sources. A new introductory Note has been specially prepared for this edition.

Library of Congress Cataloging-in-Publication Data

Civil War short stories and poems / edited by Bob Blaisdell.
    p. cm. — (Dover thrift editions)
  Includes bibliographical references.
  ISBN-13: 978-0-486-48226-2
  ISBN-10: 0-486-48226-X
  1. United States—History—Civil War, 1861–1865—Fiction. 2. United States—History—Civil War, 1861–1865—Poetry. 3. Historical fiction, American.
4. Historical poetry, American. I. Blaisdell, Robert.
  PS648.C54C535 2011
  813'.0108358737—dc22

2011010011

Manufactured in the United States by Courier Corporation
48226X01
www.doverpublications.com

Note

A hundred and fifty years ago the war was all the rage! Not only were the politicians and leaders beating the drums for (and against) secession, for (and against) union, for (and against) war, they and the millions of Americans, North and South, were in the war's midst, in its grip, and it can seem now that everyone who could write did write about their experiences and opinions at home and on the battlefields. Literacy was the day's latest technology; the North, with more money, more social dynamism, had more of it. In the South, with its millions of slaves who were for the most part denied that technology, literacy was owned and operated by the same men who owned the slaves. The soldiers were all "home" in the land that had been everyone's (slaves notwithstanding), and whenever periodicals and personal letters could be sent and delivered, they were. Though the land was being torn apart, mostly in the South, news of the movements and battles traveled fast, and the cries for justice or for revenge and the cries of grief and pride were expressed every day, every week, and every month in the hundreds of local and regional newspapers and magazines.

For this anthology I was inclined toward poems and short stories of not only typical or obsessional attitudes and demonstrations of feelings but ones that stood conventional feelings upside down and surprised their readers. For instance, the Elizabethan-inspired "L-E-G on My Leg," published on September 26, 1863, in *Harper's Weekly* by an anonymous soldier who had lost his leg at the Battle of Fair Oaks, must have given its amused readers pause:

> Good leg, thou wast a faithful friend,
>   And truly hast thy duty done;
> I thank thee most that to the end
>   Thou didst not let this body run.

Strange paradox! that in the fight
  Where I of thee was thus bereft,
I lost my left leg for "the Right,"
  And yet the right's the one that's left!

But while the sturdy stump remains,
  I may be able yet to patch it,
For even now I've taken pains
  To make an L-E-G to match it.

Readers of Civil War literature have always been struck by the countless allusions to amputated limbs—how many amputations were there? (At least 40,000!) Count four in "The Case of George Dedlow," wherein the great American neurologist S. Weir Mitchell imagines the first-person story of a quadruple amputee who has plenty of time to reflect on his war experiences and his identity. Who is he, limbless?

> At times the conviction of my want of being myself was overwhelming and most painful. It was, as well as I can describe it, a deficiency in the egoistic sentiment of individuality. About one half of the sensitive surface of my skin was gone, and thus much of relation to the outer world destroyed. As a consequence, a large part of the receptive central organs must be out of employ, and, like other idle things, degenerating rapidly. Moreover, all the great central ganglia, which give rise to movements in the limbs, were also eternally at rest. Thus one half of me was absent or functionally dead. This set me to thinking how much a man might lose and yet live.

Citizens could have wondered, having taken in Mitchell's amazing story, how many limbs *America* "might lose and yet live"?

The most useful works I found for ready material were edited by Frank Moore (1828–1904), who assembled the colossal multivolume *Rebellion Record* over the course of the war. He collected and arranged so much material that for the next twenty years he continued to make little thematic anthologies of his work, particularly of the poems and anecdotes he had collected from the magazines, journals, newspapers and personal correspondence of the time. In 1886, introducing his *Songs and Ballads of the Southern People: 1861–1865*, he explained: "This collection has been made with the view of preserving in permanent form the opinions and sentiments of the Southern people." That is, "their Songs and Ballads . . . better than any other medium, exhibit the temper of the times and popular feeling. The historical value of the productions is admitted. Age will not impair it." Meanwhile,

Kathleen Diffley's scholarly, relatively recent *To Live and Die: Collected Stories of the Civil War, 1861–1876* pointed me to at least a half-dozen of the eighteen short stories included here that I might otherwise have overlooked.

The most historically interesting of the stories were composed during the war—with life, death, and dismemberment being transformed into public entertainment. The most famous story included here is the "newest," Ambrose Bierce's "An Occurrence at Owl Creek Bridge" (1890). Another famous story, Mark Twain's "A True Story, Repeated Word for Word As I Heard It," was published only nine years after the conclusion of the war. Its *veracity*, as Huck Finn might say, may be doubted. But the emotional "truth" of the stories and poems, being written as they were in the midst of the conflict, is deep and real. The truth was that the South felt persecuted by the economically and politically more powerful North, while the North felt outraged not only by the audacity of the South's desire for separation but the obtuseness of fellow Christians believing in the right to enslave human beings. The truth is that more than 600,000 people died as a result of the war, and there were, naturally, bad and hard feelings about that. The truth is that America's idea of itself was being argued about with bayonets, guns, and cannonballs. The truth is that slavery, which the Founding Fathers unhappily accepted for the sake of union, was moral and economic poison, which infected the entire country and had to be treated. The truth was that the South, defeated, refused to concede, and that the North, in victory, was not itself transformed into a more moral or tolerant society. It is hard to think about the Civil War and not feel that however horrible it was, it was also inevitable.

In the introductory notes I have explained little about the authors or events described, sometimes simply from lack of information but usually from anxiety about distracting the reader's attention from the raw and clear sentiments and plainly described occurrences. Among my favorite selections of verse, besides the witty, were those by or about the women back home: mothers, sisters, and wives. For one thing, except for the occasional firebrand oaths against the enemy, the outpourings seem indistinguishable. I have tried to arrange the poems and stories chronologically or, absent chronological clues, thematically. As we read through the years of the war, we witness the variety and development of feelings and experiences that very few people in America could have believed would have been possible.

Before the war, the abolitionist John Brown was the subject of enthusiastic poetry; mad with anger to the death, he became, for many, the war's symbol and martyr. As secession erupted in December 1860 and spread throughout the South in the winter and spring of 1861, the rhetoric justifying secession, often by asserting the State's "freedom" from the tyranny of the North but never doubting its right to take away the *real* freedom of fellow human beings, continues to be remarkably galling and appalling. As the war moved into actual battles, with Bull Run in July 1861 proving to be not the last but among the first of hundreds of battles, the rhetoric shifts. We hear the changes in the voices of the people of the time as they, astounded by the carnage, fearfully wonder at it all. The year 1862 gave hope to the South and doubt to the North, while 1863, with the Emancipation Proclamation and the shocking death of the most admired figure of the war, the Confederate General Stonewall Jackson, brought a terrible acceptance of what seemed an interminable struggle. Then in 1864, as Ulysses S. Grant, William T. Sherman, and Abraham Lincoln pushed the Federal onslaught to its limits, we feel the eyes of the people begin to lift toward the horizon. In 1865, the end comes—with relief, sadness, and finally bewilderment that such a manmade disaster could have happened at all.

—BOB BLAISDELL
New York City, 2011

Contents

1862

1864

1865

POST-WAR

BEFORE THE WAR

How Old Brown Took Harper's Ferry

EDMUND CLARENCE STEDMAN

Stedman tells the story of John Brown (1800–1859), the militant abolitionist whose guerilla-band captured the arsenal at Harper's Ferry in Virginia on October 16, 1859. This act put the issue of slavery at the forefront of the national consciousness, as he intended. He and his men were all killed or taken prisoner. He was put on trial for murder and treason. Stedman ends the ballad, which he completed in November 1859, with a prophecy of the coming war. On December 2, Brown was hanged.

John Brown in Kansas settled, like a steadfast Yankee farmer,
    Brave and godly, with four sons, all stalwart men of might.
There he spoke aloud for freedom, and the Border-strife grew
      warmer,
    Till the Rangers fired his dwelling, in his absence, in the night;
        And Old Brown,
          Osawatomie Brown,
Came homeward in the morning—to find his house burned down.

Then he grasped his trusty rifle and boldly fought for freedom;
    Smote from border unto border the fierce, invading band;
And he and his brave boys vowed—so might Heaven help and
      speed 'em!—
    They would save those grand old prairies from the curse that
      blights the land;
        And Old Brown,
          Osawatomie Brown,
Said, "Boys, the Lord will aid us!" and he shoved his ramrod down.

And the Lord *did* aid these men, and they labored day and even,
   Saving Kansas from its peril; and their very lives seemed charmed,
Till the ruffians killed one son, in the blessed light of Heaven,—
   In cold blood the fellows slew him, as he journeyed all unarmed;
         And Old Brown,
         Osawatomie Brown,
Shed not a tear, but shut his teeth, and frowned a terrible frown!

Then they seized another brave boy,—not amid the heat of battle,
   But in peace, behind his ploughshare,—and they loaded him with
      chains,
And with pikes, before their horses, even as they goad their cattle,
   Drove him cruelly, for their sport, and at last blew out his brains;
         And Old Brown,
         Osawatomie Brown,
Raised his right hand up to Heaven, calling Heaven's vengeance
   down.

And he swore a fearful oath, by the name of the Almighty,
   He would hunt this ravening evil that had scathed and torn
      him so;
He would seize it by the vitals; he would crush it day and night; he
   Would so pursue its footsteps, so return it blow for blow.
         That Old Brown,
         Osawatomie Brown,
Should be a name to swear by, in backwoods or in town!

Then his beard became more grizzled, and his wild blue eye grew
      wilder,
   And more sharply curved his hawk's-nose, snuffing battle from afar;
And he and the two boys left, though the Kansas strife waxed milder,
   Grew more sullen, till was over the bloody Border War,
         And Old Brown,
         Osawatomie Brown,
Had gone crazy, as they reckoned by his fearful glare and frown.

So he left the plains of Kansas and their bitter woes behind him,
   Slipt off into Virginia, where the statesmen all are born,
Hired a farm by Harper's Ferry, and no one knew where to find
      him,
   Or whether he'd turned parson, or was jacketed and shorn;
         For Old Brown,
         Osawatomie Brown,
Mad as he was, knew texts enough to wear a parson's gown.

He bought no ploughs and harrows, spades and shovels, and such
　　trifles;
　　But quietly to his rancho there came, by every train,
Boxes full of pikes and pistols, and his well-beloved Sharp's rifles;
　　And eighteen other madmen joined their leader there again.
　　　　　　Says Old Brown,
　　　　　　Osawatomie Brown,
"Boys, we've got an army large enough to march and take the town!

"Take the town, and seize the muskets, free the negroes and then arm
　　them;
　　Carry the County and the State, ay, and all the potent South.
On their own heads be the slaughter, if their victims rise to harm
　　them—
　　These Virginians! who believed not, nor would heed the warning
　　mouth."
　　　　　　Says Old Brown,
　　　　　　Osawatomie Brown,
"The world shall see a Republic, or my name is not John Brown."

'Twas the sixteenth of October, on the evening of a Sunday:
　　"This good work," declared the captain, "shall be on a holy night!"
It was on a Sunday evening, and before the noon of Monday,
　　With two sons, and Captain Stephens, fifteen privates—black
　　and white,
　　　　　　Captain Brown,
　　　　　　Osawatomie Brown,
Marched across the bridged Potomac, and knocked the sentry down;

Took the guarded armory-building, and the muskets and the cannon;
　　Captured all the county majors and the colonels, one by one;
Scared to death each gallant scion of Virginia they ran on,
　　And before the noon of Monday, I say, the deed was done.
　　　　　　Mad Old Brown,
　　　　　　Osawatomie Brown,
With his eighteen other crazy men, went in and took the town.

Very little noise and bluster, little smell of powder made he;
　　It was all done in the midnight, like the Emperor's *coup d'etat*.
"Cut the wires! Stop the rail-cars! Hold the streets and bridges!" said he.
　　Then declared the new Republic, with himself for guiding star,—
　　　　　　This Old Brown,
　　　　　　Osawatomie Brown;
And the bold two thousand citizens ran off and left the town.

Then was riding and railroading and expressing here and thither;
  And the Martinsburg Sharpshooters and the Charlestown
    Volunteers,
And the Shepherdstown and Winchester militia hastened whither
  Old Brown was said to muster his ten thousand grenadiers.
        General Brown,
        Osawatomie Brown!
Behind whose rampant banner all the North was pouring down.

But at last, 'tis said, some prisoners escaped from Old Brown's
    durance,
  And the effervescent valor of the Chivalry broke out.
When they learned that nineteen madmen had the marvellous
    assurance—
  Only nineteen—thus to seize the place and drive them straight
    about;
        And Old Brown,
        Osawatomie Brown,
Found an army come to take him, encamped around the town.

But to storm, with all the forces I have mentioned, was too risky;
  So they hurried off to Richmond for the Government Marines,
Tore them from their weeping matrons, fired their souls with
    Bourbon whiskey,
  Till they battered down Brown's castle with their ladders and
    machines;
        And Old Brown,
        Osawatomie Brown,
Received three bayonet stabs, and a cut on his brave old crown.

Tallyho! the old Virginia gentry gather to the baying!
  In they rushed and killed the game, shooting lustily away;
And whene'er they slew a rebel, those who came too late for slaying,
  Not to lose a share of glory, fired their bullets in his clay;
        And Old Brown,
        Osawatomie Brown,
Saw his sons fall dead beside him, and between them laid him down.

How the conquerors wore their laurels; how they hastened on the trial;
  How Old Brown was placed, half dying, on the Charlestown
    court-house floor;
How he spoke his grand oration, in the scorn of all denial;
  What the brave old madman told them,—these are known the
    country o'er.

> "Hang Old Brown,
> Osawatomie Brown,"
Said the judge, "and all such rebels!" with his most judicial frown.

But, Virginians, don't do it! for I tell you that the flagon,
  Filled with blood of Old Brown's offspring, was first poured by
    Southern hands;
And each drop from Old Brown's life-veins, like the red gore of
    the dragon,
  May spring up a vengeful Fury, hissing through your slave-worn
    lands!
> And Old Brown,
> Osawatomie Brown,
May trouble you more than ever, when you've nailed his coffin
    down!

★　★　★

Glory Hallelujah! or John Brown's Body

ANONYMOUS

"John Brown's Body" in its various versions, including Southern parodies, was the most popular marching song in the war. The author of this version is said to be Charles Sprague Hall.

> John Brown's body lies a–mould'ring in the grave,
> John Brown's body lies a–mould'ring in the grave,
> John Brown's body lies a–mould'ring in the grave.
> His soul is marching on!
>
> *Chorus*—Glory! Glory Hallelujah!
> Glory! Glory Hallelujah!
> Glory! Glory Hallelujah!
> His soul is marching on.
>
> He's gone to be a soldier in the army of the Lord!
> His soul is marching on.
>
> John Brown's knapsack is strapped upon his back.
> His soul is marching on.
>
> His pet lambs will meet him on the way.
> And they'll go marching on.

They'll hang Jeff Davis on a sour apple tree,
As they go marching on.

Now for the Union let's give three rousing cheers.
As we go marching on.

Hip, hip, hip, hip, Hurrah!

★　★　★

Ye Men of Alabama!

JOHN D. PHELAN

The author, seized by a Herculean image, was from Montgomery, the first capital of the Confederacy, where this poem was published in October 1860 in the Montgomery Advertiser.

Ye men of Alabama,
　Awake, arise, awake!
And rend the coils asunder
　Of this Abolition snake.
If another fold he fastens
　If this final coil he plies
In the cold clasp of hate and power
　Fair Alabama dies.

Though round your lower limbs and waist
　His deadly coils I see,
Yet, yet, thank Heaven! your head and arms
　And good right hand, are free;
And in that hand there glistens—
　O God! what joy to feel!—
A polished blade, full sharp and keen,
　Of tempered State Rights steel.

Now, by the free-born sires
　From whose brave loins ye sprung!
And by the noble mothers
　At whose fond breasts ye hung!
And by your wives and daughters,
　And by the ills they dread,

Drive deep that good Secession steel
　　Right through the Monster's head.

This serpent Abolition
　　Has been coiling on for years;
We have reasoned, we have threatened,
　　We have begged almost with tears:
Now, away, away with Union,
　　Since on our Southern soil
The only union left us
　　Is an anaconda's coil.

Brave, little South Carolina
　　Will strike the self-same blow,
And Florida, and Georgia,
　　And Mississippi, too;
And Arkansas and Texas;
　　And at her death, I ween,
The head will fall beneath the blows
　　Of all the brave Fifteen.

In this our day of trial,
　　Let feuds and factions cease,
Until above this howling storm
　　We see the sign of Peace.
Let Southern men, like brothers,
　　In solid phalanx stand,
And poise their spears and lock their shields
　　To guard their native land.

The love that for the Union
　　Once in our bosoms beat,
From insult and from injury
　　Has turned to scorn and hate;
And the banner of Secession
　　Today we lift on high,
Resolved, beneath that sacred flag,
　　To conquer or TO DIE!

Arise

C. G. POYNAS

This blustering war-call was published in the Charleston Mercury.

This call for
Carolinians! who inherit
   Blood which flowed in patriot veins!
Rouse ye from lethargic slumber,
   Rouse and fling away your chains!
From the mountain to the seaboard,
   Let the cry be—Up! Arise!
Throw our pure Palmetto banner
   Proudly upward to the skies.

Fling it out! its lone star beaming
   Brightly to the nation's gaze;
Lo! another star arises!
   Quickly, proudly it emblaze!
Yet another! Bid it welcome
   With a hearty "three times three";
Send it forth, on boom of cannon,
   Southern men will *dare be free.*

Faster than the cross of battle
   Summoned rude Clan Alpine's host,
Flash the news from sea to mountain—
   Back from mountain to the coast!
On the lightning's wing it fleeth,
   Scares the eagle in his flight,
As his keen eye sees arising
   Glory, yet shall daze his sight!

Cease the triumph—days of darkness
   Loom upon us from afar:
Can a woman's voice for battle
   Ring the fatal note of war?
Yes—when we have borne aggression
   Till submission is disgrace—
Southern women call for *action*;
   Ready would the danger face!

Yes, in many a matron's bosom
   Burns the Spartan spirit now;
From the maiden's eye it flashes,
   Glows upon her snowy brow;
E'en our infants in their prattle
   Urge us on to *risk our all*—
"Would we leave them, as a blessing.
   The oppressor's hateful thrall?"

No!—then up, true-hearted Southrons,
   Like bold "giants nerved by wine";
Never fear! The cause is holy—
   It is sacred—yea, divine!
For the Lord of Hosts is with us,
   It is *He* has cast our lot;
Blest our homes—from lordly mansion
   To the humblest negro cot.

God of battles! hear our cry—
   Give us nerve to *do* or *die!*

1861

A Poem for the Times

JOHN R. THOMPSON

The Southern position on secession was that each state had the right to decide to belong or not to the Union. That the arguments linked to this position asserted a state's "freedom" from "tyranny" while defending or ignoring the existence of slavery was pathetic. This poem was published in the Charleston Mercury. *Thompson was an editor of the* Southern Literary Messenger.

Who talks of Coercion? Who dares to deny
   A resolute people their right to be free?
Let him blot out forever one star from the sky,
   Or curb with his fetter one wave of the sea.

Who prates of Coercion? Can love be restored
   To bosoms where only resentment may dwell;
Can peace upon earth be proclaimed by the sword,
   Or good-will among men be established by shell?

Shame! shame that the statesman and trickster, forsooth,
   Should have for a crisis no other recourse,
Beneath the fair day-spring of Light and of Truth,
   Than the old *brutum fulmen* of Tyranny,—Force.

From the holes where Fraud, Falsehood, and Hate slink away;
   From the crypt in which Error lies buried in chains;
This foul apparition stalks forth to the day,
   And would ravage the land which his presence profanes.

Could you conquer us, Men of the North, could you bring
   Desolation and death on our homes as a flood;

Can you hope the pure lily, Affection, will spring
   From ashes all reeking and sodden with blood?

Could you brand us as villeins and serfs, know ye not
   What fierce, sullen hatred lurks under the scar?
How loyal to Hapsburg is Venice, I wot;
   How dearly the Pole loves his Father, the Czar!

But 'twere well to remember this land of the sun
   Is a *nutrix leonum,* and suckles a race
Strong-armed, lion-hearted, and banded as one,
   Who brook not oppression and know not disgrace.

And well may the schemers in office beware
   The swift retribution that waits upon crime,
When the lion, Resistance, shall leap from his lair,
   With a fury that renders his vengeance sublime.

Once, men of the North, we were brothers, and still,
   Though brothers no more, we would gladly be friends;
Nor join in a conflict accurst, that must fill
   With ruin the country on which it descends.

But if smitten with blindness, and mad with the rage
   The gods give to all whom they wished to destroy,
You would act a new *Iliad* to darken the age,
   With horrors beyond what is told us of Troy:

If, deaf as the adder itself to the cries,
   When Wisdom, Humanity, Justice implore,
You would have our proud eagle to feed on the eyes
   Of those who have taught him so grandly to soar:

If there be to your malice no limit imposed,
   And your reckless design is to rule with the rod
The men upon whom you have already closed
   Our goodly domain and the temples of God:

To the breeze then your banner dishonored unfold,
   And at once let the tocsin be sounded afar;
We greet you, as greeted the Swiss Charles the Bold,
   With a farewell to peace and a welcome to war!

For the courage that clings to our soil, ever bright,
   Shall catch inspiration from turf and from tide;
Our sons unappalled shall go forth to the fight,
   With the smile of the fair, the pure kiss of the bride;

And the bugle its echoes shall send through the past,
  In the trenches of Yorktown to waken the slain
    While the sods of King's Mountain shall heave at the blast,
And give up its heroes to glory again.

★ ★ ★

A Word for the Hour

JOHN GREENLEAF WHITTIER

The firmament breaks up. In black eclipse
Light after light goes out. One evil star,
Luridly glaring through the smoke of war,
As in the dream of the Apocalypse,
Drags others down. Let us not weakly weep
Nor rashly threaten. Give us grace, to keep
Our faith and patience; wherefore should we leap
On one hand into fratricidal fight,
Or, on the other, yield eternal right,
Frame lies of law, and good and ill confound?
What fear we? Safe on freedom's vantage ground
Our feet are planted: let us there remain
In unrevengeful calm, no means untried
Which truth can sanction, no just claim denied,
The sad spectators of a suicide!
They break the links of Union: shall we light
The fires of hell to weld anew the chain
On that red anvil where each blow is pain?
Draw we not even now a freer breath,
As from our shoulders falls a load of death
Loathsome as that the Tuscan's victim bore
When keen with life to a dead horror bound?
Why take we up the accursed thing again?
Pity, forgive, but urge them back no more
Who, drunk with passion, flaunt disunion's rag
With its vile reptile blazon. Let us press
The golden cluster on our brave old flag
In closer union, and, if numbering less,
Brighter shall shine the stars which still remain.

Jefferson D.

H. S. CORNWELL

Davis (1808–1889), a former Secretary of War and Senator from Mississippi, was inaugurated as president of the Confederate States of America on February 18, 1861. He announced, to the derision of the poem's author: "All we want is to be let alone."

You're a traitor convicted, you know very well!
       Jefferson D., Jefferson D.!
You thought it a capital thing to rebel, Jefferson D.!
    But there's one thing I'll say:
    You'll discover some day,
When you see a stout cotton cord hang from a tree,
There's an accident happened you didn't foresee, Jefferson D.!

What shall be found upon history's page?
       Jefferson D., Jefferson D.!
When a student explores the republican age! Jefferson D.!
    He will find, as is meet.
    That at Judas's feet
You sit in your shame, with the impotent plea.
That you hated the land and the law of the free, Jefferson D.!

What do you see in your visions at night,
       Jefferson D., Jefferson D.?
Does the spectacle furnish you any delight, Jefferson D.?
    Do you feel in disgrace
    The black cap o'er your face,
While the tremor creeps down from your heart to your knee,
And freedom, insulted, approves the decree, Jefferson D.?

Oh! long have we pleaded, till pleading is vain,
       Jefferson D., Jefferson D.!
Your hands are imbrued with the blood of the slain, Jefferson D.!
    And at last, for the right,
    We arise in our might,
A people united, resistless, and free,
And declare that rebellion no longer shall be! Jefferson D.!

Rebels

ANONYMOUS

Rebels! 'tis a holy name!
  The name our fathers bore,
When battling in the cause of Right,
Against the tyrant in his might,
  In the dark days of yore.

Rebels! 'tis our family name!
  Our father, Washington,
Was the arch-rebel in the fight,
And gave the name to us—a right
  Of father unto son.

Rebels! 'tis our given name!
  Our mother, Liberty,
Received the title with her fame,
In days of grief, of fear, and shame,
  When at her breast were we.

Rebels! 'tis our sealed name!
  A baptism of blood!
The war—aye, and the din of strife—
The fearful contest, life for life—
  The mingled crimson flood.

Rebels! 'tis a patriot's name!
  In struggles it was given;
We bore it then when tyrants raved,
And through their curses 'twas engraved
  On the doomsday-book of heaven.

Rebels! 'tis our fighting name!
  For peace rules o'er the land,
Until they speak of craven woe—
Until our rights receive a blow,
  From foe's or brother's hand.

Rebels! 'tis our dying name!
  For, although life is dear,
Yet, freemen born and freemen bred,
We'd rather live as freemen dead,
  Than live in slavish fear.

Then call us rebels, if you will—
  We glory in the name;
For bending under unjust laws,
And swearing faith to an unjust cause,
  We count a greater shame.

* * *

The Bonnie Blue Flag

Harry Macarthy

By the end of May 1861, the Confederacy was complete: eleven states had seceded from the Union; they rallied under "the Bonnie Blue Flag."

We are a band of brothers, and natives to the soil,
Fighting for the property we gained by honest toil,
And when our rights were threatened, the cry rose near and far:
Hurrah for the bonnie Blue Flag that bears a single star!

Chorus—Hurrah! hurrah! for the bonnie Blue Flag
    that bears a single star.

As long as the Union was faithful to her trust,
Like friends and like brothers, kind were we and just;
But now when Northern treachery attempts our rights to mar,
We hoist on high the bonnie Blue Flag that bears a single star.

First, gallant South Carolina nobly made the stand;
Then came Alabama, who took her by the hand;
Next, quickly, Mississippi, Georgia, and Florida—
All raised the flag, the bonnie Blue Flag that bears a single star.

Ye men of valor, gather round the banner of the right;
Texas and fair Louisiana join us in the fight.
Davis, our loved President, and Stephens, statesmen are;
Now rally round the bonnie Blue Flag that bears a single star.

And here's to brave Virginia! the Old Dominion State
With the young Confederacy at length has linked her fate.
Impelled by her example, now other States prepare
To hoist on high the bonnie Blue Flag that bears a single star.

Then here's to our Confederacy; strong we are and brave,
Like patriots of old we'll fight, our heritage to save;
And rather than submit to shame, to die we would prefer;
So cheer for the bonnie Blue Flag that bears a single star.

Then cheer, boys, cheer, raise the joyous shout,
For Arkansas and North Carolina now have both gone out;
And let another rousing cheer for Tennessee be given,
The single star of the bonnie Blue Flag has grown to be eleven!

★   ★   ★

Reply to the Bonnie Blue Flag

ISAAC M. BALL

We're fighting for our Union,
    We're fighting for our trust;
We're fighting for that happy land,
    Where sleeps our father's dust.
It cannot be dissevered,
    Though it cost us bloody wars,
We ne'er can give up the land
    Where float the Stripes and Stars.

Chorus—Hurrah! hurrah!
        For equal rights, hurrah!
        Hurrah for the good old flag
        That bears the Stripes and Stars.

We treated you as brothers,
    Until you drew the sword,
With wrong impious hand at Sumter
    You cut the silver cord,
So now you hear our bugles,—
    We come, the sons of Mars;
We'll rally round that brave old flag,
    Which bears the Stripes and Stars.

We do not want your cotton,
    We care not for your slaves,
But rather than divide this land,
    We'll fill your Southern graves.

With Lincoln for our Chieftain,
   We'll wear our country's scars;
We'll rally round that brave old flag,
   Which bears the Stripes and Stars.

We deem our cause most holy,
   We know we're in the right;
And twenty millions of free men
   Stand ready for the fight.
Our bride is fair Columbia,
   No stain her beauty mars;
O'er her we'll raise that brave old flag,
   Which bears the Stripes and Stars.

And when this war is over,
   We'll each resume our homes,
And treat you still as brothers,
   Wherever you may roam.
We'll pledge the hand of friendship
   And think no more of wars;
But dwell in peace beneath that flag
   Which bears the Stripes and Stars.
      Hurrah! hurrah!
      For equal rights, hurrah!
      Hurrah for that brave old flag
      Which bears the Stripes and Stars.

★ ★ ★

Secession

ANONYMOUS

The Union author mockingly dedicates the poem to the Louisiana native General P. G. T. Beauregard, who commanded the Confederate troops at Fort Sumter, South Carolina, and then at First Bull Run in Virginia.

RESPECTFULLY DEDICATED TO GENERAL BEAUREGARD.

The sun's hot rays were falling fast,
As through a Southern city passed
A man who bore, 'midst rowdies low,

A banner with the strange motto—
        Secession!

His brow was sad; his mouth beneath
Smelt strong of fire at every breath:
And like a furious madman sung
The accents of that unknown tongue—
        Secession!

In happy homes he saw the light
Of household fires gleam warm and bright;
Above, the spectral gallows shone,
And from his lips escaped a groan—
        Secession!

"Try not that game!" Abe Lincoln said,
"Dark lower the thunders overhead;
The mighty North has been defied."
But still that drunken voice replied—
        Secession!

"Oh! pause!" the Quaker said, "and think
Before thee leaps from off the brink!"
Contempt was in his drunken leer;
And still he answered, with a sneer—
        Secession!

"Beware the pine-tree's bristling branch!
Beware the Northern avalanche!"
And that was Scott's restraining voice;
But still this was the traitor's choice—
        Secession!

At close of war, as toward their homes
Our troops as victors hurried on,
And turned to God a thankful prayer,
A voice whined through the startled air—
        Secession!

A traitor by a soldier keen,
Suspended by the neck was seen,
Still grasping in his hand of ice
That banner, with this strange device—
        Secession!

There, to the mournful gibbet strung,
Lifeless and horrible he hung;
And from the sky there seemed to float
A voice like angel's warning note —
    Secession!

★ ★ ★

Dirge: For One Who Fell in Battle

THOMAS WILLIAM PARSONS

Among the first Union soldiers to die in battle was Major Theodore Winthrop on June 10, 1861.

Room for a Soldier! lay him in the clover;
He loved the fields, and they shall be his cover;
Make his mound with hers who called him once her lover:
    Where the rain may rain upon it,
    Where the sun may shine upon it,
    Where the lamb hath lain upon it,
    And the bee will dine upon it.

Bear him to no dismal tomb under city churches;
Take him to the fragrant fields, by the silver birches.
Where the whippoorwill shall mourn, where the oriole perches:
    Make his mound with sunshine on it,
    Where the bee will dine upon it,
    Where the lamb hath lain upon it,
    And the rain will rain upon it.

Busy as the busy bee, his rest should be the clover;
Gentle as the lamb was he, and the fern should be his cover;
Fern and rosemary shall grow my soldier's pillow over:
    Where the rain may rain upon it,
    Where the sun may shine upon it,
    Where the lamb hath lain upon it,
    And the bee will dine upon it.

Sunshine in his heart, the rain would come full often
Out of those tender eyes which evermore did soften;

He never could look cold, till we saw him in his coffin:
    Make his mound with sunshine on it,
    Where the wind may sigh upon it,
    Where the moon may stream upon it,
    And Memory shall dream upon it.

"Captain or Colonel,"—whatever invocation
Suit our hymn the best, no matter for thy station,—
On thy grave the rain shall fall from the eyes of a mighty nation!
    Long as the sun doth shine upon it
    Shall grow the goodly pine upon it,
    Long as the stars do gleam upon it
    Shall Memory come to dream upon it.

★　★　★

The Battle-Cry of Freedom

George Frederick Root

The composer George Frederick Root said he was inspired to write the words and music of this famous song when he read President Lincoln's call for troops in June 1861.

Yes, we'll rally round the flag, boys, we'll rally once again,
    Shouting the battle-cry of freedom,
We will rally from the hill-side, we'll gather from the plain,
    Shouting the battle-cry of freedom.

Chorus—The Union forever, hurrah! boys, hurrah!
        Down with the traitor, up with the star,
          While we rally round the flag, boys, rally once again,
           Shouting the battle-cry of freedom.

We are springing to the call of our brothers gone before.
    Shouting the battle-cry of freedom,
And we'll fill the vacant ranks with a million freemen more.
    Shouting the battle-cry of freedom.

We will welcome to our numbers the loyal, true, and brave.
    Shouting the battle-cry of freedom,
And altho' they may be poor, not a man shall be a slave.
    Shouting the battle-cry of freedom.

So we're springing to the call from the East and from the West,
    Shouting the battle-cry of freedom,
And we'll hurl the rebel crew from the land we love the best.
    Shouting the battle-cry of freedom.

★ ★ ★

Dixie All Right

ANONYMOUS

Sunny South we trust will be—hurrah! hurrah! hurrah!
Ere long from Northern rulers free—hurrah! hurrah! hurrah!
With lead and powder, sword and gun, they will him to the
      —— run!
They will him to the —— run! Hurrah! hurrah! hurrah!

    Then hang the fiddle on the wall,
    With fife and drumsticks lead the ball;
    We'll teach them dancing fine and neat
    With cannon, sword, and bayonet.

    We bought the dry goods from the North,
    Now all our clerks are going forth
    To do the job of measuring—
    With swords, not yards, they do the thing.

    Our doctors found a remedy
    For every Northern malady;
    They cure all fevers, pains and chills,
    With bombshells and with leaden pills.

    Thus men throughout the South are armed.
    Their hearts by freedom steeled and warmed;
    And should one man refuse to fight,
    The ladies will their courage slight.

Bull Run: A Parody

ANONYMOUS

At Bull Run when the sun was low,
Each Southern face grew pale as snow,
While loud as jackdaws rose the crow
    Of Yankees boasting terribly!

But Bull Run saw another sight,
When at the deepening shades of night,
Towards Fairfax Court-House rose the flight
    Of Yankees running rapidly.

Then broke each corps with terror riven.
Then rushed the steeds to battle driven,
The men of battery Number Seven
    Forsook their red artillery!

Still on McDowell's farthest left,
The roar of cannon strikes one deaf,
Where furious Abe and fiery Jeff
    Contend for death or victory.

The panic thickens—off, ye brave!
Throw down your arms! your bacon save!
Waive, Washington, all scruples waive,
    And fly, with all your chivalry!

★ ★ ★

The March into Virginia: Ending in the First Manassas

HERMAN MELVILLE

Melville reflects on the same disastrous battle as the previous two Confederate poems.

(*July, 1861*)

Did all the lets and bars appear
  To every just or larger end,
Whence should come the trust and cheer?
  Youth must its ignorant impulse lend—

Age finds place in the rear.
   All wars are boyish, and are fought by boys,
The champions and enthusiasts of the state:
   Turbid ardors and vain joys
     Not barrenly abate—
Stimulants to the power mature,
     Preparatives of fate.

Who here forecasteth the event?
What heart but spurns at precedent
And warnings of the wise,
Contemned foreclosures of surprise?

The banners play, the bugles call,
The air is blue and prodigal.
   No berrying party, pleasure-wooed,
No picnic party in the May,
Ever went less loth than they
   Into that leafy neighborhood.
In Bacchic glee they file toward Fate,
Moloch's uninitiate;
Expectancy, and glad surmise
Of battle's unknown mysteries.
All they feel is this: 'tis glory,
A rapture sharp, though transitory,
Yet lasting in belaureled story.
So they gayly go to fight,
Chatting left and laughing right.

But some who this blithe mood present,
   As on in lightsome files they fare,
Shall die experienced ere three days are spent—
   Perish, enlightened by the vollied glare;
Or shame survive, and, like to adamant,
   The throe of Second Manassas share.

The War Fever in Baldinsville

ARTEMUS WARD (CHARLES FARRAR BROWNE)

The comic letters and stories of Charles Farrar Browne (1834–1867), written under the pen name of "Artemus Ward," amused Abraham Lincoln to no end. These two stories, published in July of 1861, relate Artemus's attempt to recruit a volunteer company of Union soldiers, "composed excloosively of offissers," in the fictional backwater of Baldinsville, Ohio.

As soon as I'd recooperated my physikil system, I went over into the village. The peasantry was glad to see me. The skoolmaster sed it was cheerin to see that gigantic intelleck among 'em onct more. That's what he called me. I like the skoolmaster, and allers send him tobacker when I'm off on a travelin campane. Besides, he is a very sensible man. Such men must be encouraged.

They don't git news very fast in Baldinsville, as nothin but a plank road runs in there twice a week and that's very much out of repair. So my nabers wasn't much posted up in regard to the wars. Squire Baxter sed he'd voted the dimicratic ticket for goin on forty year, and the war was a dam black republican lie. Jo. Stackpole, who kills hogs for the Squire, and has got a powerful muscle into his arms, sed he'd bet $5 he could lick the Crisis in a fair stand-up fight, if he wouldn't draw a knife on him. So it went—sum was for war, and sum was for peace. The skoolmaster, however, sed the Slave Oligarky must cower at the feet of the North ere a year had flowed by, or pass over his ded corpse. "Esto perpetual," he added. "And sine qua non also!" sed I, sternly, wishing to make a impression onto the villagers. "Requiescat in pace!" sed the skoolmaster. "Too troo, too troo!" I anserd, "it's a scanderlus fack!"

The newspapers got along at last, chock full of war, and the patriotic fever fairly bust out in Baldinsville. Squire Baxter sed he didn't b'lieve in Coercion, not one of 'em, and could prove by a file of Eagles of Liberty in his garrit, that it was all a Whig lie got up to raise the price of whisky and destroy our other liberties. But the old Squire got putty riley when he heard how the rebels was cuttin up, and he sed he reckoned he should skour up his old muskit and do a little square fitin for the Old Flag, which had allers bin on the ticket he'd voted and he was too old to Bolt now. The Squire is all right at heart, but it takes longer for him to fill his venerable Biler with steam than it used to when he was young and frisky. As I previsly informed you, I am Captin of the Baldinsville Company. I riz gradooally but majesticly from drummer's Secretary to my present position. But I found the ranks wasn't full by no means, and commenced for to recroot. Havin notist a ginral desire on the part of young men who are into the Crisis to wear eppylits, I determined to have my company composed excloosively of offissers, everybody to rank as Brigadeer-Ginral. The follerin was among the varis questions which I put to recroots:

Do you know a masked battery from a hunk of gingerbread?

Do you know a eppylit from a piece of chalk?

If I trust you with a real gun, how many men of your own company do you speck you can manage to kill durin the war?

Hav you ever heard of Ginral Price of Missouri, and can you avoid simler accidents in case of a battle?

Hav you ever had the measles, and if so, how many?

How air you now?

Show me your tongue, &c., &c. Sum of the questions was sarcusstical.

The company filled up rapid, and last Sunday we went to the meetin house in full uniform. I had a seris time gittin into my military harness, as it was bilt for me many years ago; but I finally got inside of it, tho it fitted me putty clost. Howsever, onct into it, I lookt fine—in fact, aw-inspirin. "Do you know me, Mrs. Ward?" sed I, walkin into the kitchin.

"Know you, you old fool? Of course I do."

I saw to onct she did.

I started for the meetin house, and I'm afraid I tried to walk too strate, for I cum very near fallin over backards; and in attemptin to recover myself my sword got mixed up with my legs, and I fell in among a choice collection of young ladies, who was standin near the church door a-seein the sojer boys come up. My cockt hat fell off, and sumhow my coat tales got twisted round my neck. The young ladies put their handkerchers to their mouths and remarked: "Te he," while my ancient female single friend, Sary Peasley, bust out into a loud larf. She exercised her mouth so vilently that her new false teeth fell out onto the ground.

"Miss Peasley," sed I, gittin up and dustin myself, "you must be more careful with them store teeth of your'n or you'll have to gum it agin!"

Methinks I had her. I'd bin to work hard all the week, and I felt rather snoozy. I'm fraid I did git half asleep, for on hearin the minister ask, "Why was man made to mourn?" I sed, "I giv it up," havin a vague idee that it was a conundrum. It was a onfortnit remark, for the whole meetin house lookt at me with mingled surprise and indignation. I was about risin to a pint of order, when it suddenly occurd to me whare I was, and I kept my seat, blushin like the red, red rose—so to speak.

The next mornin I 'rose with the lark (N. B.—I don't sleep with the lark, tho. A goak.)

My little dawter was execootin ballids, accompanyin herself with the Akordeon, and she wisht me to linger and hear her sing: "Hark, I hear a angel singin, a angel now is onto the wing."

"Let him fly, my child!" said I, a-bucklin on my armer, "I must forth to my Biz."

We air progressin pretty well with our drill. As all air commandin offissers, there ain't no jelusy; and as we air all exceedin smart, it tain't worth while to try to outstrip each other. The idee of a company composed excloosively of Commanders-in Chiefs, orriggernated, I spose I skurcely need say, in these Brane. Considered as a idee, I natter myself it is putty hefty. We've got all the tackticks at our tongs' ends, but what we particly excel in is restin muskits. We can rest muskits with anybody.

Our corpse will do its dooty. We go to the aid of Columby—we fight for the stars!

We'll be chopt into sassige meat before we'll exhibit our coat tales to the foe.

We'll fight till there's nothin left of us but our little toes, and even they shall defiantly wiggle!

> "Ever of thee,"
> A Ward

★　★　★

The Draft in Baldinsville

If I'm drafted I shall *resign*.

Deeply grateful for the onexpected honor thus confered upon me, I shall feel compeld to resign the position in favor of sum more worthy person. Modesty is what ails me. That's what's kept me under.

I meanter-say, I shall hav to resign if I'm drafted everywheres I've bin inrold. I must now, furrinstuns, be inrold in upards of 200 different towns. If I'd kept on travelin I should hav eventooaly becum a Brigade, in which case I could have held a meetin and elected myself Brigadeer-ginral quite unanimiss. I hadn't no idee there was so many of me before. But, serisly, I concluded to stop exhibitin, and made tracks for Baldinsville.

My only dawter threw herself onto my boosum and said, "It is me, fayther! I thank the gods!"

She reads the *Ledger.*

"Tip us yer bunch of fives, old faker!" said Artemus, Jr. He reads the *Clipper.*

My wife was to the sowin circle. I knew she and the wimin folks was havin a pleasant time slanderin the females of the *other* sowin circle (which likewise met that arternoon, and was doubtless enjoyin theirselves ekally well in slanderin the fustnamed circle), and I didn't send for her. I allus like to see peple enjoy theirselves.

My son Orgustus was playin onto a floot.

Orgustus is a ethereal cuss. The twins was bildin cob-houses in a corner of the kitchin.

It'll cost some postage stamps to raise this famly, and yet it 'ud go hard with the old man to lose any lamb of the flock.

An old bachelor is a poor critter. He may have hearn the skylark or (what's nearly the same thing) Miss Kellogg and Carlotty Patti sing; he may have hearn Ole Bull fiddle, and all the Dodworths toot, an yet he don't know nothin about music—the real, ginuine thing—the music of the laughter of happy, well-fed children! And you may ax the father of sich children home to dinner, feelin werry sure there'll be no spoons missin when he goes away. Sich fathers never drop tin five-cent pieces into the contribution box, nor palm shoe-pegs off onto blind hosses for oats, nor skedaddle to British sile when their country's in danger—nor do anything which is really mean, I don't mean to intimate that the old bachelor is up to little games of this sort—not at all—but I repeat, he's a poor critter. He don't live here; only stays. He ought to pologize, on behalf of his parients, for bein here at all. The happy marrid man dies in good stile at home, surrounded by his weeping wife and children. The old bachelor don't die at all—he sort of rots away, like a pollywog's tail.

My townsmen were sort o' demoralized. There was a evident desine to ewade the Draft, as I obsarved with sorrer, and patritism was below Par—and *Mar,* too. I hadn't no sooner sot down on the piazzy of the tarvun than I saw sixteen solitary hossmen, ridin four abreast, wendin their way up the street.

"What's them? Is it calvary?"

"That," said the landlord, "is the stage. Sixteen able-bodied sitterzens has lately bot the stage line tween here and Scotsburg. That's them. They're stage-drivers. Stage-drivers is exempt!"

I saw that each stage-driver carried a letter in his left hand.

"The mail is hevy, to-day," said the landlord. "Ginrally they don't have more'n half a dozen letters tween em. To-day they've got one apiece! Bile my lights and liver!"

"And the passengers?"

"There ain't any, skacely, nowdays," said the landlord, "and what few there is, very much prefier to walk, the roads is so rough."

"And how ist with you?" I inquired of the editer of the *Bugle-Horn of Liberty,* who sot near me.

"I can't go," he sed, shakin his head in a wise way. "Ordinarily I should delight to wade in gore, but my bleedin country bids me stay at home. It is imperatively necessary that I remain here for the purpuss of announcin, from week to week, that *our Govment is about to take vigrous measures to put down the rebellion!*"

I strolled into the village oyster-saloon, where I found Dr. Schwazey, a leadin sitterzen, in a state of mind which showed that he'd bin histin in more'n his share of pizen.

"Hello, old Beeswax," he bellered. "How's yer grandmams? When you goin to feed your stuffed animils?"

"What's the matter with the eminent physician?" I pleasantly inquired.

"This," he said; "this is what's the matter. I'm a habitooal drunkard! I'm exempt!"

"Jes so."

"Do you see them beans, old man?" and he pinted to a plate before him. "Do you see em?"

"I do. They are a cheerful fruit when used tempritly."

"Well," said he, "I hain't eat anything since last week. I eat beans now *because* I eat beans *then.*"

"It's quite proper you should eat a little suthin once in a while," I said. "It's a good idee to occasionally instruct the stummick that it mustn't depend excloosively on licker for its sustainance."

"A blessin," he cried; "a blessin onto the hed of the man what inwented beans. A blessin onto his hed!"

"Which his name is Gilson! He's a first family of Bostin," said I.

This is a speciment of how things was goin in my place of residence.

A few was true blue. The skoolmaster was among em. He greeted me warmly. He said I was welkim to those shores. He said I had a massiv mind. It was gratifyin, he said, to see that great intelleck stalkin in their midst onct more. I have before had occasion to notice this skoolmaster. He is evidently a young man of far more than ordnary talents.

The skoolmaster proposed we should git up a mass meetin. The meetin was largely attended. We held it in the open air, round a roarin bonfire.

The skoolmaster was the first orator. He's pretty good on the speak. He also writes well, his composition bein seldom marred by ingrammatticisms. He said this inactivity surprised him. "What do you expect will cum of this kind of doins? *Nihil fit—*"

"Hooray for Nihil!" I interrupted. "Feller sitterzens, let's giv three chears for Nihil, the man who fit!"

The skoolmaster turned a little red, but repeated— *"Nihil fit."*

"Exactly," I said. "Nihil *fit*. He wasn't a strategy feller."

"Our venerable frend," said the skoolmaster, smilin pleasantly, "isn't posted in Virgil."

"No, I don't know him. But if he's a able-bodied man he must stand his little draft."

The skoolmaster wound up in eloquent style, and the subscriber took the stand.

I said the crisis had not only cum itself, but it had brought all its relations. It has cum, I said, with a evident intention of makin us a good long visit. It's goin to take off its things and stop with us. My wife says so too. This is a good war. For those who like this war, it's just such a kind of war as they like. I'll bet ye. My wife says so too. If the Federal army succeeds in takin Washinton, and they seem to be advancin that way pretty often, I shall say it is strategy, and Washinton will be safe. And that noble banner, as it were—that banner, as it were—will be a emblem, or rather, I should say, that noble banner—*as it were.* My wife says so too. (I got a little mixed up here, but they didn't notice it.) Feller sitterzens, it will be a proud day for this Republic when Washinton is safe. My wife says so too.

There's money enough. No trouble about *money*. They've got a lot of first-class bank-note engravers at Washinton who turn out two or three cords of money a day—good money, too.

Then it isn't money we want. But we do want *men,* and we must have them. We must carry a whirlwind of fire among the foe. We must crush the ungrateful rebels who are poundin the Goddess of Liberty over the hed with slung-shots, and stabbin her with stolen knives! We must lick em quick. We must introduce a large number of first-class funerals among the peple of the South. Betsy says so too.

This war hain't been too well managed. We all know that. What then? We are all in the same boat—if the boat goes down, we go down with her. Hence we must all fight. It ain't no use to talk now about who *caused* the war. That's played out. The war is upon us—upon us all—and we must all fight. We can't "reason" the matter with the foe. When, in the broad glare of the noonday sun, a speckled jackass boldly and maliciously kicks over a peanut-stand, do we "reason" with him? I guess not. And why "reason" with those other Southern people who are tryin to kick over the Republic? Betsy, my wife, says so too.

   The meetin broke up with enthusiasm. We shan't draft in Baldinsville if we can help it.

★ ★ ★

Melt the Bells

F. Y. ROCKETT

"These lines were written when General Beauregard appealed to the people of the South to contribute their bells, that they might be melted into cannon," noted the editor Frank Moore. The South had many more limitations in its ability to produce weaponry than the North. See the following poem, "What the Village Bell Said," as well.

> Melt the bells, melt the bells,
> Still the tinkling on the plain,
> And transmute the evening chimes
> Into war's resounding rhymes,
> That the invaders may be slain
>   By the bells.
>
> Melt the bells, melt the bells,
> That for years have called to prayer,
> And, instead, the cannon's roar
> Shall resound the valleys o'er,
> That the foe may catch despair
>   From the bells.
>
> Melt the bells, melt the bells,
> Though it cost a tear to part
> With the music they have made,
> Where the friends we love are laid,
> With pale cheek and silent heart,
>   'Neath the bells.
>
> Melt the bells, melt the bells,
> Into cannon, vast and grim,
> And the foe shall feel the ire
> From the heaving lungs of fire,

And we'll put our trust in Him,
　　And the bells.

Melt the bells, melt the bells,
And when foes no more attack,
And the lightning cloud of war
Shall roll thunderless and far,
We will melt the cannon back
　　Into bells.

Melt the bells, melt the bells,
And they'll peal a sweeter chime,
And remind of all the brave
Who have sunk to glory's grave,
And will sleep through coming time
　　'Neath the bells.

★　★　★

"What the Village Bell Said"

John G. M'Lemore

M'Lemore was from South Carolina; the year after he wrote this poem, he was mortally wounded on May 31, 1862, at the Battle of Seven Pines.

Full many a year in the village church,
　　Above the world have I made my home;
And happier there, than if I had hung
　　High up in air in a golden dome;
　　　　For I have tolled
　　　　When the slow hearse rolled
　　Its burden sad to my door;
　　　　And each echo that woke,
　　　　With the solemn stroke,
　　Was a sigh from the heart of the poor.

I know the great bell of the city spire
　　Is a far prouder one than such as I;
And its deafening stroke, compared with mine,
　　Is thunder compared with a sigh;
　　　　But the shattering note
　　　　Of his brazen throat,

As it swells on the Sabbath air,
　　Far oftener rings
　　For other things
Than a call to the house of prayer.

Brave boy, I tolled when your father died,
　And you wept when my tones pealed loud;
And more gently I rung when the lily-white dame
　Your mother dear lay in her shroud:
　　　And I rang in sweet tone
　　　The angels might own,
　When your sister you gave to your friend;
　　　Oh! I rang with delight,
　　　On that sweet summer night,
　When they vowed they would love to the end!

But a base foe comes from the regions of crime,
　With a heart all hot with the flames of hell;
And the tones of the bell you have loved so long
　No more on the air shall swell:
　　　For the people's chief,
　　　With his proud belief
That his country's cause is God's own,
　　　Would change the song,
　　　The hills have rung
　To the thunder's harsher tone.

Then take me down from the village church,
　Where in peace so long I have hung;
But I charge you, by all the loved and lost,
　Remember the songs I have sung.
　　　Remember the mound
　　　Of holy ground
Where your father and mother lie
　　　And swear by the love
　　　For the dead above
To beat your foul foe, or die.

Then take me; but when (I charge you this)
　You have come to the bloody field,
That the bell of God, to a cannon grown,
　You will ne'er to the foeman yield.
　　　By the love of the past,

Be that hour your last,
When the foe has reached this trust;
And make him a bed
Of patriot·dead,
And let him sleep in this holy dust.

★ ★ ★

The Little Drummer: A Soldier's Story

RICHARD H. STODDARD

In August of 1861, at the Battle of Wilson's Creek in Missouri, the Union's Nathaniel Lyon was the first general to die in battle in the Civil War. The little drummer served "out in the West with Lyon."

I.

'Tis of a little drummer,
  The story I shall tell;
Of how he marched to battle,
  And all that there befell.
Out in the West with Lyon,
  (For once the name was true,)
For whom the little drummer beat
  His *rat-tat-too.*

II.

Our army rose at midnight,
  Ten thousand men as one,
Each slinging on his knapsack,
  And snatching up his gun:
"Forward!" and off they started,
  As all good soldiers do,
When the little drummer beats for them
  The *rat-tat-too.*

III.

Across a rolling country,
  Where the mist began to rise;
Past many a blackened farm-house,
  Till the sun was in the skies:
Then we met the Rebel pickets,

Who skirmished and withdrew,
While the little drummer beat and beat
   The *rat-tat-too.*

IV.

Along the wooded hollows
   The line of battle ran,
Our center poured a volley,
   And the fight at once began;
For the Rebels answered shouting,
   And a shower of bullets flew;
But still the little drummer beat
   His *rat-tat-too.*

V.

He stood among his comrades,
   As they quickly formed the line,
And when they raised their muskets
   He watched the barrels shine!
When the volley rang, he started!
   For war to him was new;
But still the little drummer beat
   His *rat-tat-too.*

VI.

It was a sight to see them,
   That early autumn day,
Our soldiers in their blue coats,
   And the Rebel ranks in gray:
The smoke that rolled between them,
   The balls that whistled through,
And the little drummer as he beat
   His *rat-tat-too.*

VII.

His comrades dropped around him,—
   By fives and tens they fell,
Some pierced by Minnie bullets,
   Some torn by shot and shell;
They played against our cannon,
   And a caisson's splinters flew;
But still the little drummer beat
   His *rat-tat-too.*

VIII.

The right, the left, the center—
    The fight was everywhere:
They pushed us here,—we wavered,—
    We drove and broke them there.
The gray-backs fixed their bayonets,
    And charged the coats of blue,
But still the little drummer beat
    His *rat-tat-too.*

IX.

"Where is our little drummer?"
    His nearest comrades say,
When the dreadful fight is over,
    And the smoke has cleared away.
As the Rebel corps was scattering
    He urged them to pursue,
So furiously he beat and beat
    The *rat-tat-too!*

X.

He stood no more among them,
    For a bullet as it sped
Had glanced and struck his ankle,
    And stretched him with the dead!
He crawled behind a cannon,
    And pale and paler grew:
But still the little drummer beat
    His *rat-tat-too!*

XI.

They bore him to the surgeon,
    A busy man was he:
"A drummer boy—what ails him?"
    His comrades answered, "See!"
As they took him from the stretcher,
    A heavy breath he drew,
And his little fingers strove to beat
    The *rat-tat-too!*

XII.

The ball had spent its fury:
  "A scratch," the surgeon said,
As he wound the snowy bandage
  Which the lint was staining red!
"I must leave you now, old fellow."
  "O take me back with you,
For I know the men are missing me,
  And the *rat-tat-too!*"

XIII.

Upon his comrade's shoulder
  They lifted him so grand,
With his dusty drum before him,
  And his drum-sticks in his hand!
To the fiery front of battle,
  That nearer, nearer drew,—
And evermore he beat, and beat,
  His *rat-tat-too!*

XIV.

The wounded as he passed them
  Looked up and gave a cheer:
And one in dying blessed him,
  Between a smile and tear!
And the gray-backs—they are flying
  Before the coats of blue,
For whom the little drummer beats
  His *rat-tat-too!*

XV.

When the west was red with sunset,
  The last pursuit was o'er;
Brave Lyon rode the foremost,
  And looked the name he bore!
And before him on his saddle,
  As a weary child would do,
Sat the little drummer fast asleep,
  With his *rat-tat-too.*

All Quiet Along the Potomac

ETHEL LYNN BEERS

*"There was no poem written during the war that had a wider popularity than this,"
claimed H. M. Wharton, the Confederate veteran who edited* War Songs of the
Confederacy. *Beers's own fascinating note on its publishing history follows the poem.*

> "All quiet along the Potomac," they say,
>   "Except, now and then, a stray picket
> Is shot, as he walks on his beat to and fro,
>   By a rifleman hid in the thicket.
> 'Tis nothing—a private or two now and then
>   Will not count in the news of the battle;
> Not an officer lost—only one of the men
>   Moaning out, all alone, the death-rattle."

★ ★ ★

> All quiet along the Potomac tonight,
>   Where the soldiers lie peacefully dreaming;
> Their tents, in the rays of the clear autumn moon
>   Or the light of the watch-fire, are gleaming.
> A tremulous sigh of the gentle night-wind
>   Through the forest-leaves softly is creeping,
> While stars up above, with their glittering eyes,
>   Keep guard, for the army is sleeping.
>
> There's only the sound of the lone sentry's tread
>   As he tramps from the rock to the fountain,
> And thinks of the two in the low trundle-bed
>   Far away in the cot on the mountain.
> His musket falls slack; his face, dark and grim,
>   Grows gentle with memories tender
> As he mutters a prayer for the children asleep—
>   For their mother; may Heaven defend her!
>
> The moon seems to shine just as brightly as then,
>   That night when the love yet unspoken
> Leaped up to his lips—when low-murmured vows
>   Were pledged to be ever unbroken.
> Then drawing his sleeve roughly over his eyes,
>   He dashes off tears that are welling,

And gathers his gun closer up to its place,
    As if to keep down the heart-swelling.

He passes the fountain, the blasted pine tree,
    The footstep is lagging and weary;
        Yet onward he goes through the broad belt of light,
    Toward the shade of the forest so dreary.
Hark! was it the night-wind that rustled the leaves?
    Was it moonlight so wondrously flashing?
It looked like a rifle—"Ha! Mary, good-bye!"
    The red life-blood is ebbing and plashing.

All quiet along the Potomac tonight,
    No sound save the rush of the river;
While soft falls the dew on the face of the dead—
    The picket's off duty forever!

Note: In All Quiet Along the Potomac and Other Poems, *Beers explains:*

"In the fall of 1861 'All Quiet along the Potomac' was the familiar heading of all war-despatches. So when this poem appeared in the columns of Harper's Weekly, *Nov. 30th, it was quickly republished in almost every journal in the land. As it bore only the initials E. B., the poem soon became a nameless waif, and was attributed to various pens.*

"The London Times *copied it as having been written by a Confederate soldier and found in his pocket after death. (It seems to have been a dangerous thing to copy it, as it has so often been found in dead men's pockets.) An American paper quoted it, saying that it was written by a private soldier in the United States service, and sent home to his wife. This statement was met by another, asserting that it was written by Fitz-James O'Brien. As the soul of that true poet and gallant soldier had gone out through a ragged battle-rift won at Ball's Bluff, this was uncontradicted until an editorial paragraph appeared in* Harper's Weekly, *July 4th, 1863, saying it had been written for that paper by a lady contributor.*

It appeared in a volume of War-Poetry of the South, *edited by Wm. Gilmore Sims, as a Southern production, and was set to music by a Richmond music-publisher in 1864, with "Words by Lamar Fontaine" on its title-page. A soldier-cousin, who went with Sherman to the sea, found in a deserted printing-office at Fayetteville a paper containing a two-column article on the poem, with all the circumstances under which "Lamar Fontaine composed it while on picket-duty."*

It appeared in the earlier editions of Bryant's Library of Poetry and Song *over Mrs. Howland's name, which was afterward corrected by Mr. Bryant.*

Within the last year a Mr. Thaddeus Oliver claims its authorship for his deceased father, being no doubt misled by a wrong date, as he fixes an earlier time than its first appearance in Harper's Weekly.

I have been at some pains to gather up these dates and names as one of the curiosities of newspaper-waif life. To those who know me, my simple assertion that I wrote the poem is sufficient, but to set right any who may care to know, I refer to the columns of the old ledger at Harper's, on whose pages I saw but the other day the business form of acceptance of, and payment for, "The Picket-Guard," among other contributions.

Fortunately, I have two credible witnesses to the time and circumstances of its writing. A lovely lady sitting opposite me at the boarding-house table looked up from her morning paper at breakfast-time to say, " All quiet along the Potomac, as usual," and I, taking up the next line, answered back, " Except a poor picket shot." After breakfast it still haunted me, and with my paper across the end of my sewing-machine I wrote the whole poem before noon, making but one change in copying it, reading it aloud to ask a boy's judgment in reference to two different endings, and adopting the one he chose. Nothing was ever more vivid or real to me than the pictures I had conjured up of the picket's lonely walk and swift summons, or the waiting wife and children. A short sojourn in Washington had made me quite familiar with the routine of war-time and soldier-life. The popularity of the poem was perhaps due more to the pathos of the subject than to any inherent quality.

*   *   *

Thinking of the Soldiers

ANONYMOUS

The poem is dated November 24, 1861.

We were sitting around the table,
    Just a night or two ago,
In the little cozy parlor,
    With the lamp-light burning low,
And the window-blinds half opened,
    For the summer air to come,
And the painted curtains moving
    Like a busy pendulum.

Oh! the cushions on the sofa,
    And the pictures on the wall,
And the gathering of comforts,
    In the old familiar hall;
And the wagging of the pointer,
    Lounging idly by the door,

And the flitting of the shadows
   From the ceiling to the floor.

Oh! they wakened in my spirit,
   Like the beautiful in art,
Such a busy, busy thinking—
   Such a dreaminess of heart,
That I sat among the shadows,
   With my spirit all astray;
Thinking only—thinking only
   Of the soldiers far away;

Of the tents beneath the moonlight,
   Of the stirring tattoo's sound,
Of the soldier in his blanket,
   In his blanket on the ground;
Of the icy winter coming,
   Of the cold bleak winds that blow,
And the soldier in his blanket,
   In his blanket on the snow.

Of the blight upon the heather,
   And the frost upon the hill,
And the whistling, whistling ever,
   And the never, never still;
Of the little leaflets falling,
   With the sweetest, saddest sound—
And the soldier—oh! the soldier,
   In his blanket on the ground.

Thus I lingered in my dreaming,
   In my dreaming far away,
Till the spirit's picture-painting
   Seemed as vivid as the day;
And the moonlight faded softly
   From the window opened wide,
And the faithful, faithful pointer
   Nestled closer by my side.

And I knew that 'neath the starlight,
   Though the chilly frosts may fall,
That the soldier will be dreaming,
   Dreaming often of us all.
So I gave my spirit's painting

Just the breathing of a sound,
For the dreaming, dreaming soldier,
In his slumber on the ground.

★ ★ ★

Only One Killed

JULIA L. KEYES

Keyes was from Montgomery, Alabama.

Only one killed in Company B,
　'Twas a trifling loss—one man!
A charge of the bold and dashing Lee,
While merry enough it was, to see
　The enemy, as he ran.

Only one killed upon our side—
　Once more to the field they turn.
Quietly now the horsemen ride,
And pause by the form of the one who died,
　So bravely, as now we learn.

Their grief for the comrade loved and true
　For a time was unconcealed;
They saw the bullet had pierced him through;
That his pain was brief—ah! very few
　Die thus on the battle-field.

The news has gone to his home, afar—
　Of the short and gallant fight;
Of the noble deeds of the young La Var,
Whose life went out as a falling star
　In the skirmish of the night.

"Only one killed! It was my son,"
　The widowed mother cried;
She turned but to clasp the sinking one,
Who heard not the words of the victory won,
　But of him who had bravely died.

Ah! death to her were a sweet relief,
   The bride of a single year.
Oh! would she might, with her weight of grief,
Lie down in the dust, with the autumn leaf,
   Now trodden and brown and sere!

But no, she must bear through coming life
   Her burden of silent woe,
The aged mother and youthful wife
Must live through a nation's bloody strife,
   Sighing and waiting to go.

Where the loved are meeting beyond the stars,
   Are meeting no more to part,
They can smile once more through the crystal bars—
Where never more will the woe of wars
   O'ershadow the loving heart.

1862

Battle-Hymn of the Republic

Julia Ward Howe

Howe (1819–1910) wrote the most famous marching poem in American history in 1861 and published it in The Atlantic Monthly *in February 1862. The "Hallelujah" chorus was subsequently added in April when the verses were accompanied by music.*

Mine eyes have seen the glory of the coming of the Lord:
He is trampling out the vintage where the grapes of wrath are stored;
He hath loosed the fateful lightning of his terrible swift sword:
　　His truth is marching on.

I have seen Him in the watch-fires of a hundred circling camps;
They have builded Him an altar in the evening dews and damps;
I can read His righteous sentence by the dim and flaring lamps.
　　His day is marching on.

I have read a fiery gospel, writ in burnished rows of steel:
"As ye deal with my contemners, so with you my grace shall deal;
Let the Hero, born of woman, crush the serpent with his heel,
　　Since God is marching on."

He has sounded forth the trumpet that shall never call retreat;
He is sifting out the hearts of men before his judgment-seat:
Oh! be swift, my soul, to answer Him! be jubilant, my feet!
　　Our God is marching on.

In the beauty of the lilies Christ was born across the sea,
With a glory in his bosom that transfigures you and me:
As He died to make men holy, let us die to make men free,
　　While God is marching on.

Song of the Irish Legion

JAMES DE MILLE

As many as 150,000 Irish natives and descendents fought for the Union in the Civil War. ("Erin go Bragh!" is a vow of "Ireland forever!")

E Pluribus Unum! Erin go Bragh!

Ye boys of the sod, to Columbia true,
Come up, lads, and fight for the Red, White, and Blue!
Two countries we love, and two mottoes we'll share,
And we'll join them in one on the banner we bear:
　　Erin, mavourneen! Columbia, agra!
　　E pluribus unum! Erin go bragh!

Upon them, my lads! and the Rebels shall know
How Erin can fight when she faces the foe;
If they can't give us arms, sure, we needn't delay;
With a sprig of shillalah we'll open the way.
　　Erin, mavourneen! Columbia, agra!
　　E pluribus unum! Erin go bragh!

"Blood-Tubs" and "Plug-Uglies," and others galore,
Are sick for a thrashing in sweet Baltimore;
Be Jabers! that same I'd be proud to inform
Of the terrible force of an Irishman's arm.
　　Erin, mavourneen! Columbia, agra!
　　E pluribus unum! Erin go bragh!

Before you the tyrant assembles his band,
And threatens to conquer this glorious land;
But it wasn't for this that we traversed the sea,
And left the Green Isle for the land of the free.
　　Erin, mavourneen! Columbia, agra!
　　E pluribus unum! Erin go bragh!

Go forth to the tyrant, and give him to know
That an Irishman holds him his bitterest foe;
And his sweetest delight is to meet him in fight,
To battle for freedom, with God for the right!
　　Erin, mavourneen! Columbia, agra!
　　E pluribus unum! Erin go bragh!

Come List, My Boys, Enlist

ANONYMOUS

This rallying poem, one of many encouraging enlistment, was published in Chester County's Philadelphia Press.

Hurrah! the boys are moving—the fife and drum speak war;
A Quaker's son is captain, and numbers up his score.
And harvest past, right well we know, he'll drill his eighty more.
 For it must be done, the people say;
 It must be done, and now's the day;
 It must be done, and this the way—
  Come list, my boys, enlist.

The fields stand rough in stubble, the wheat is under roof;
What are you made of, country boys? come, give your mother
  proof:
Your comrades fight, and cowards you if you shall stand aloof.

 For it must be done, the people say, etc.

Up change the rake for rifle—the companies recruit;
Come, out with arms all brawn, and learn the secret how to
  shoot;
Your sisters, in the cider-time, will gather in the fruit.

 For it must be done, the people say, etc.

Good tidings for the telegraph, swift let the message run:
Old Chester sends her greeting proud along to Washington;
Each farm-house pours its treasures free, and consecrates a son.

 For it must be done, the people say, etc.

Hurrah I hurrah! old farmer, shout from your brown-tanned
  throat;
Pish! for each home-found man, today, who wears moustache
  or goat;
For every male who well might go, but stays, a *petticoat*.

 For it must be done, the people say, etc.

Hurrah! hurrah! old farmer's wife, you'll see the whole thing
  done;

The maidens will be weaving it—you'll see the worsted spun;
The coward's be the *petticoat*—but it will not be your son.
    For it must be done, the people say;
    It must be done, and now's the day;
    It must be done, and this the way—
        Come list, my boys, enlist.

★ ★ ★

Army-Hymn: "Old Hundred"

OLIVER WENDELL HOLMES

Holmes, Sr. (1809–1894), was a doctor and well-known author who published this prayer in 1862. His son served in the Union Army and later became a Supreme Court Justice.

O Lord of Hosts! Almighty King!
Behold the sacrifice we bring!
To every arm Thy strength impart,
Thy spirit shed through every heart!

Wake in our breasts the living fires,
The holy faith that warmed our sires;
Thy hand hath made our Nation free:
To die for her is serving Thee.

Be Thou a pillared flame to show
The midnight snare, the silent foe;
And when the battle thunders loud,
Still guide us in its moving cloud.

God of all nations! Sovereign Lord!
In thy dread name we draw the sword,
We lift the starry flag on high
That fills with light our stormy sky.

From Treason's rent, from Murder's stain
Guard Thou its folds till Peace shall reign,—
Till fort and field, till shore and sea
Join our loud anthem, PRAISE TO THEE!

On Board the *Cumberland*

GEORGE HENRY BOKER

The Confederacy's ironclad Merrimack *(known also as the* Virginia) *rammed and destroyed the blockading U.S.S.* Cumberland *in Hampton Roads, Virginia, on March 7, 1862, but not before the* Cumberland *inflicted some damage on the ironclad. (On March 9, the Union sent out its ironclad, the* Monitor, *to battle the* Merrimack.)*

"Stand to your guns, men!" Morris cried.
    Small need to pass the word;
Our men at quarters ranged themselves,
    Before the drum was heard.

And then began the sailors' jests:
    "What thing is that, I say?"
"A long-shore meeting-house adrift
    Is standing down the bay!"

A frown came over Morris' face;
    The strange, dark craft he knew;
"That is the iron *Merrimac,*
    Manned by a Rebel crew.

"So shot your guns, and point them straight;
    Before this day goes by,
We'll try of what her metal's made."
    A cheer was our reply.

"Remember, boys, this flag of ours
    Has seldom left its place;
And where it falls, the deck it strikes
    Is covered with disgrace.

"I ask but this: or sink or swim,
    Or live or nobly die,
My last sight upon earth may be
    To see that ensign fly!"

Meanwhile the shapeless iron mass
    Came moving o'er the wave,
As gloomy as a passing hearse,
    As silent as the grave.

Her ports were closed; from stem to stern
　　No sign of life appeared.
We wondered, questioned, strained our eyes,
　　Joked—everything but feared.

She reached our range. Our broadside rang,
　　Our heavy pivots roared;
And shot and shell, a fire of hell,
　　Against her sides we poured.

God's mercy! from her sloping roof
　　The iron tempest glanced,
As hail bounds from a cottage-thatch,
　　And round her leaped and danced;

Or when against her dusky hull
　　We struck a fair, full blow,
The mighty, solid iron globes
　　Were crumbled up like snow.

On, on, with fast increasing speed,
　　The silent monster came;
Though all our starboard battery
　　Was one long line of flame.

She heeded not, no gun she fired,
　　Straight on our bow she bore;
Through riving plank and crashing frame
　　Her furious way she tore.

Alas! our beautiful keen bow,
　　That in the fiercest blast
So gently folded back the seas,
　　They hardly felt we passed!

Alas! alas! my *Cumberland,*
　　That ne'er knew grief before,
To be so gored, to feel so deep
　　The tusk of that sea-boar!

Once more she backward drew a space,
　　Once more our side she rent;
Then, in the wantonness of hate,
　　Her broadside through us sent.

The dead and dying round us lay,
　　But our foemen lay abeam;

Her open portholes maddened us;
  We fired with shout and scream.

We felt our vessel settling fast,
  We knew our time was brief,
"The pumps, the pumps!" But they who pumped,
  And fought not, wept with grief.

"Oh! keep us but an hour afloat!
  Oh! give us only time
To be the instruments of Heaven
  Against the traitors' crime!"

From captain down to powder-boy,
  No hand was idle then;
Two soldiers, but by chance aboard,
  Fought on like sailor-men.

And when a gun's crew lost a hand,
  Some bold marine stepped out,
And jerked his braided jacket off,
  And hauled the gun about.

Our forward magazine was drowned;
  And up from the sick bay
Crawled out the wounded, red with blood,
  And round us gasping lay.

Yes, cheering, calling us by name,
  Struggling with failing breath,
To keep their shipmates at the post
  Where glory strove with death.

With decks afloat, and powder gone,
  The last broadside we gave
From the guns' heated iron-lips
  Burst out beneath the wave.

So sponges, rammers, and handspikes—
  As men-of-war's-men should—
We placed within their proper racks,
  And at our quarters stood.

"Up to the spar-deck! save yourselves!"
  Cried Selfridge. "Up, my men!

God grant that some of us may live
   To fight yon ship again!"

We turned—we did not like to go;
   Yet staying seemed but vain,
Knee-deep in water; so we left;
   Some swore, some groaned with pain.

We reached the deck. There Randall stood:
   "Another turn, men—so!"
Calmly he aimed his pivot-gun:
   "Now, Tenny, let her go!"

It did our sore hearts good to hear
   The song our pivot sang,
As rushing on from wave to wave
   The whirring bomb-shell sprang.

Brave Randall leaped upon the gun,
   And waved his cap in sport;
"Well done! well aimed! I saw that shell
   Go through an open port."

It was our last, our deadliest shot;
   The deck was overflown;
The poor ship staggered, lurched to port,
   And gave a living groan.

Down, down, as headlong through the waves
   Our gallant vessel rushed,
A thousand gurgling, watery sounds
   Around my senses gushed.

Then I remember little more;
   One look to heaven I gave,
Where, like an angel's wing, I saw
   Our spotless ensign wave.

I tried to cheer. I cannot say
   Whether I swam or sank;
A blue mist closed around my eyes,
   And everything was blank.

When I awoke, a soldier-lad,
   All dripping from the sea,
With two great tears upon his cheeks,
   Was bending over me.

I tried to speak. He understood
    The wish I could not speak.
He turned me. There, thank God! the flag
    Still fluttered at the peak!

And there, while thread shall hang to thread,
    Oh! let that ensign fly!
The noblest constellation set
    Against our northern sky.

A sign that we who live may claim
    The peerage of the brave;
A monument, that needs no scroll,
    For those beneath the wave!

★ ★ ★

The Turtle

ANONYMOUS

This poem makes light of the Confederacy's terribly destructive Merrimack *(the* Virginia*). See Boker's "On Board the* Cumberland*," above.*

Caesar, afloat with his fortunes!
    And all the world agog,
Straining its eyes
At a thing that lies
    In the water, like a log!
It's a weasel! a whale!
I see its tail!
    It's a porpoise! a polywog!

Tarnation! it's a *turtle!*
    And blast my bones and skin,
My hearties, sink her,
Or else you'll think her
    A regular terror—pin!

The frigate poured a broadside!
    The bombs they whistled well,
But—hit old Nick
With a sugar stick!
    It didn't phase her shell!

Piff, from the creature's larboard—
    And dipping along the water
A bullet hissed
From a wreath of mist
    Into a Doodle's quarter!

Raff, from the creature's starboard—
    Rip, from his ugly snorter,
And the *Congress* and
The *Cumberland*
    Sunk, and nothing—shorter.

Now, here's to you, *Virginia,*
    And you are bound to win!
By your rate of bobbing round
    And your way of pitchin' in—
For you are a cross
Of the old sea-horse
    And a regular terror—pin.

★　★　★

Stonewall Jackson's Way

ANONYMOUS

"These verses were found written on a small piece of paper, all stained with blood, in the bosom of a dead soldier of the old Stonewall Brigade, after one of Jackson's battles in the Shenandoah Valley," writes editor H. M. Wharton. More believably, Wharton adds: "It is well known that [Jackson] was a man of prayer. His servant man, a faithful negro, would sometimes go out early in the morning to the officer's camp and say: 'Gentleman, there's gwine to be hard fightin' today; Mars Tom was on his knees praying all night long.'"

Come, men, stack arms! Pile on the rails—
    Stir up the camp-fire bright;
No matter if the canteen fails.
    We'll make a roaring night
Here Shenandoah crawls along,
Here burly Blue Ridge echoes strong,
To swell the brigade's rousing song,
    Of "Stonewall Jackson's way."

We see him now—the old slouched hat,
 Cocked o'er his eye askew—
The shrewd, dry smile—the speech so pat,
 So calm, so blunt, so true,
The "Blue Light Elder" knows 'em well;
Says he, "That's Banks, he's fond of shell;
Lord save his soul! we'll give him ———" Well!
 That's "Stonewall Jackson's way."

Silence! ground arms! kneel all! caps off!
 Old Blue Light's going to pray;
Strangle the fool that dares to scoff!
Attention! It's his way!
Appealing from his native sod,
 "Hear us, Almighty God!
Lay bare thine arm, stretch forth thy rod,
 Amen!" That's Stonewall Jackson's way.

He's in the saddle now! Fall in!
 Steady! The whole brigade!
Hill's at the ford, cut off; we'll win
 His way out, ball and blade.
What matter if our shoes are worn?
What matter if our feet are torn?
Quick step! we're with him ere the dawn!
 That's Stonewall Jackson's way.

The sun's bright lances rout the mists
 Of morning—and, by George!
Here's Longstreet struggling in the lists,
 Hemmed in an ugly gorge.
Pope and his Yankees, whipped before,
"Bayonets and grape!" hear Stonewall roar.
"Charge, Stuart! pay off Ashby's score,"
 Is Stonewall Jackson's way."

Ah! maiden, wait, and watch, and yearn,
 For news of Stonewall's band!
Ah! widow, read with eyes that burn,
 That ring upon thy hand!
Ah! wife, sew on, pray on, hope, and pray!
Thy life shall not be all forlorn;
The foe had better ne'er been born
 That gets in Stonewall's way.

Shiloh: A Requiem

HERMAN MELVILLE

(April, 1862)

Skimming lightly, wheeling still,
  The swallows fly low
Over the field in clouded days,
  The forest-field of Shiloh—
Over the field where April rain
Solaced the parched ones stretched in pain
Through the pause of night
That followed the Sunday fight
  Around the church of Shiloh—
The church so lone, the log-built one,
That echoed to many a parting groan
    And natural prayer
  Of dying foemen mingled there—
Foemen at morn, but friends at eve—
  Fame or country least their care:
(What like a bullet can undeceive!)
  But now they lie low,
While over them the swallows skim,
  And all is hushed at Shiloh.

★ ★ ★

Epigram: "Whilst Butler plays his silly pranks"

ANONYMOUS

First published in the Charleston Mercury, *1862*

Whilst Butler plays his silly pranks
And closes up New-Orleans banks,
Our Stonewall Jackson, with more cunning,
Keeps Yankee Banks forever running.

The Drummer-Boy of Tennessee

MINNIE HART

When called the fife and drum at morn
    The soldier from his rest,
And those to higher honors born
    With softer couches blest,
There came, a captain brave to seek,
    Deep in her mourning clad,
By loss made sad, and journeying weak,
    A mother and a lad—
And they had come from Tennessee,
Waiting the beat of reveille.

But, penniless and widowed,
    Her story soon she told:
The hand of traitor had not spared
    Her husband's life nor gold;
And now she brought her only son
    To fill the drummer's place;
Thus young his daily bread to earn,
    His country's foes to face:
For he had learned, in Tennessee,
To beat the call of reveille!

The boy upturned his eager gaze,
    And, with a beating heart,
He read upon the captain's face
    Both kindliness and doubt;
For he had marked his tender years,
    His little fragile form—
"Don't be afraid," he boldly cried,
    "For, captain, I can drum!
And I have come from Tennessee,
To sound for you the reveille!"

"Well, call the fifer!—bring the drum,
    To test this noble youth!"
And well his part he did perform,
    A "drummer-boy," in truth!
"Yes, madam, I will take your boy,"
    The captain kindly said.

"Oh! bring him back," her quick reply,
   "Unnumbered with the dead!
And Eddie Lee, of Tennessee,
Shall play for you the reveille!"

'Twas many a weary march was made,
   To sound of drum and fife,
And well the "drummer-boy" essayed
   To play the march of life;
Each soldier loved and sought to share
   Their part of good with him;
The fifer on his back did bear
   Across each swollen stream
This "drummer-boy" from Tennessee,
Who beat with him the reveille!

But came the battle-shock, and doom
   Of one great "Lyon" heart,
The victor's shout—the victim's groan,
   Fulfilled their fearful part!
And, on that blood-stained field of woe
   The darkness threw its pall!
The morning dawned on flying foe;
   When, list!—the "morning call!"
Our "drummer-boy" from Tennessee,
Beating for help the reveille!

Upon the valley sod he lay
   Beside a lifeless foe,
Whose dying hand had sought to stay
   The life-blood's ebbing flow:
The quivering drum yet echoing
   The beating of his heart—
The encamping angel beckoning
   From drum and fife to part!
And Eddie Lee, of Tennessee,
Awaits the final reveille!

The Hero of the Drum

George W. Bungay

The drummer with his drum,
Shouting, "Come! heroes, come!"
Forward marched, nigher, nigher;
When the veterans turned pale,
And the bullets fell like hail;
In that hurricane of fire,
Beat his drum,
Shouting, "Come!
Come! come! come!
And the fife
In the strife
Joined the drum, drum, drum—
And the fifer with his fife and the drummer with his drum,
Were heard above the strife and the bursting of the bomb;
The bursting of the bomb,
Bomb, bomb, bomb.

Clouds of smoke hung like a pall
Over tent, and dome, and hall;
Hot shot and blazing bomb
Cut down our volunteers,
Swept off our engineers;
But the drummer beat his drum—
And he beat
"No retreat!"
With his drum;
Through the fire,
Hotter, nigher,
Throbbed the drum, drum, drum,
In that hurricane of fame, and the thunder of the bomb!
Braid the laurel-wreath of flame for the hero of the drum.
The hero of the drum,
Drum, drum, drum.

Where the Rappahannock runs,
The sulphur-throated guns
Poured out hail arid fire;
But the heroes in the boats

Heeded not the sulphur-throats,
 For they looked up higher, higher;
  While the drum,
  Never dumb,
   Beat, beat, beat,
    Till our oars
    Touch the shores,
   And the feet, feet, feet,
Of the soldiers on the shore, with the bayonet and gun,
Though the drum could beat no more, made the dastard rebels run,
  The dastard rebels run,
   Run, run, run.

★ ★ ★

"The Yankee hosts with blood-stained hands"

ANONYMOUS

Frank Moore writes: "A Rebel soldier, after burying a Federal who had been killed during one of those sanguinary engagements which terminated in the retreat of the Union army from before Richmond, fixed a shingle over the grave, bearing this inscription":

The Yankee hosts with blood-stained hands
Came southward to divide our lands.
This narrow and contracted spot
Is all that this poor Yankee got!

★ ★ ★

L-E-G on My Leg

ANONYMOUS

This rueful and comic poem was attributed to a soldier in a New Haven hospital who had lost his leg at the battle of Fair Oaks (May 31, 1862).

Good leg, thou wast a faithful friend,
 And truly hast thy duty done;
I thank thee most that to the end
 Thou didst not let this body run.

Strange paradox! that in the fight
　　Where I of thee was thus bereft,
I lost my left leg for "the Right,"
　　And yet the right's the one that's left!

But while the sturdy stump remains,
　　I may be able yet to patch it,
For even now I've taken pains
　　To make an L-E-G to match it.

★　★　★

Hopeful Tackett—His Mark

RICHMOND WOLCOTT

Wolcott (1840–1908) served in the Tenth Illinois regiment from Sangamon County. The young man's comically narrated story was published in September 1862 in The Continental Monthly.

"*An' the Star-Spangle' Banger in triump' shall wave O! the lan dov the free-e-e, an' the ho mov the brave.*" Thus sang Hopeful Tackett, as he sat on his little bench in the little shop of Herr Kordwaner, the village shoemaker. Thus he sang, not artistically, but with much fervor and unction, keeping time with his hammer, as he hammered away at an immense "stoga." And as he sang, the prophetic words rose upon the air, and were wafted, together with an odor of new leather and pastepot, out of the window, and fell upon the ear of a ragged urchin with an armful of handbills.

"Would you lose a leg for it, Hope?" he asked, bringing to bear upon Hopeful a pair of crossed eyes, a full complement of white teeth, and a face promiscuously spotted with its kindred dust.

"For the Banger?" replied Hopeful; "guess I would. Both on 'em—an' a head, too."

"Well, here's a chance for you." And he tossed him a hand-bill.

Hopeful laid aside his hammer and his work, and picked up the hand-bill; and while he is reading it, let us briefly describe him. Hopeful is not a beauty, and he knows it; and though some of the rustic wits call him "Beaut," he is well aware that they intend it for irony. His countenance runs too much to nose—rude, amorphous nose at that—to be classic, and is withal rugged in general outline and pimply in spots. His hair is decidedly too dingy a red to be called, even by the utmost stretch of courtesy, auburn; dry, coarse, and pertinaciously obstinate in its resistance to the civilizing efforts of comb and brush. But there is a great deal of big bone and muscle in him, and he may yet work out a noble destiny. Let us see.

By the time he had spelled out the hand-bill, and found that Lieutenant was in town and wished to enlist recruits for Company —, — Regiment, it was nearly sunset; and he took off his apron, washed his hands, looked at himself in the piece of looking-glass that stuck in the window—a defiant look, that said that he was not afraid of all that nose—took his hat down from its peg behind the door, and in spite of the bristling resistance of his hair, crowded it down over his head, and started for his supper. And as he walked he mused aloud, as was his custom, addressing himself in the second person. "Hopeful, what do you think of it? They want more soldiers, eh? Guess them fights at Donelson and Pittsburg Lannen 'bout used up some o' them ridgiments. By Jing!" (Hopeful had been piously brought up, and his emphatic exclamations took a mild form.) "Hopeful, 'xpect you'll have to go an' stan' in some poor feller's shoes. 'Twon't do for them there blasted Seceshers to be killin' off our boys, an' no one there to pay 'em back. It's time this here thing was busted! Hopeful, you an't pretty, an' you an't smart; but you used to be a mighty nasty hand with a shot-gun. Guess you'll have to try your hand on old Borey's (Beauregard's) chaps; an' if you ever git a bead on one, he'll enter his land mighty shortly. What do you say to goin'? You wanted to go last year, but mother was sick, an' you couldn't; and now mother's gone to glory, why, show your grit an' go. Think about it, anyhow."

And Hopeful did think about it—thought till late at night of the insulted flag, of the fierce fights and glorious victories, of the dead and the dying lying out in the pitiless storm, of the dastardly outrages of rebel fiends—thought of all this, with his great warm heart overflowing with love for the dear old "Banger," and resolved to go. The next morning, he notified his "boss" of his intention to quit his service for that of Uncle Sam. The old fellow only opened his eyes very wide, grunted, brought out the stocking, (a striped relic of the departed Frau Kordwaner,) and from it counted out and paid Hopeful every cent that was due him. But there was one thing that sat heavily upon Hopeful's mind. He was in a predicament that all of us are liable to fall into—he was in love, and with Christina, Herr Kordwaner's daughter. Christina was a plump maiden, with a round, rosy face, an extensive latitude of shoulders, and a general plentitude and solidity of figure. All these she had; but what had captivated Hopeful's eye was her trim ankle, as it had appeared to him one morning, encased in a warm white yarn stocking of her own knitting. From this small beginning, his great heart had taken in the whole of her, and now he was desperately in love. Two or three times he had essayed to tell her of his proposed departure; but every time that the words were coming to his lips, something rushed up into his throat ahead of them, and he couldn't speak. At last, after walking home from church with her on Sunday evening, he held out his hand and blurted out:

"Well, goodbye. We're off tomorrow."

"Off! Where?"

"I've enlisted."

Christina didn't faint. She didn't take out her delicate and daintily perfumed *mouchoir* to hide the tears that were not there. She looked at him for a moment, while two great real tears rolled down her cheeks, and then—precipitated all her charms right into his arms. Hopeful stood it manfully—rather liked it, in fact. But this is a tableau that we've no right to be looking at; so let us pass by how they parted—with what tears and embraces, and extravagant protestations of undying affection, and wild promises of eternal remembrance; there is no need of telling, for we all know how foolish young people will be under such circumstances. We older heads know all about such little matters, and what they amount to. Oh! yes, certainly we do.

The next morning found Hopeful, with a dozen others, in charge of the lieutenant, and on their way to join the regiment. Hopeful's first experience of camp-life was not a singular one. He, like the rest of us, at first exhibited the most energetic awkwardness in drilling. Like the rest of us, he had occasional attacks of home-sickness; and as he stood at his post on picket in the silent night-watches, while the camps lay quietly sleeping in the moonlight, his thoughts would go back to his far-away home, and the little shop, and the plentiful charms of the fair-haired Christina. So he went on, dreaming sweet dreams of home, but ever active and alert, eager to learn and earnest to do his duty, silencing all selfish suggestions of his heart with the simple logic of a pure patriotism.

"Hopeful," he would say, "the Banger's took care o' you all your life, an' now you're here to take care of it. See that you do it the best you know how."

It would be more thrilling and interesting, and would read better, if we could take our hero to glory amid the roar of cannon and muskets, through a storm of shot and shell, over a serried line of glistening bayonets. But strict truth—a matter of which newspaper correspondents, and sensational writers, generally seem to have a very misty conception—forbids it.

It was only a skirmish—a bushwhacking fight for the possession of a swamp. A few companies were deployed as skirmishers, to drive out the rebels.

"Now, boys," shouted the captain, "after 'em! Shoot to kill, not to scare 'em!"

"Ping! ping!" rang the rifles.

"Z-z-z-z-vit!" sang the bullets.

On they went, crouching among the bushes, creeping along under the banks of the brook, cautiously peering from behind trees in search of "butternuts."

Hopeful was in the advance; his hat was lost, and his hair more defiantly bristling than ever. Firmly grasping his rifle, he pushed on, carefully watching every tree and bush. A rebel sharpshooter started to run from one tree to another, when, quick as thought, Hopeful's rifle was at his shoulder, a puff of blue smoke rose from its mouth, and the rebel sprang into the air and fell back—dead. Almost at the same instant, as Hopeful leaned forward to see the effect of his shot, he felt a sudden shock, a sharp, burning pain, grasped at a bush, reeled, and sank to the ground.

"Are you hurt much, Hope?" asked one of his comrades, kneeling beside him and staunching the blood that flowed from his wounded leg.

"Yes, I expect I am; but that red wamus over yonder's redder 'n ever now. That feller won't need a pension."

They carried him back to the hospital, and the old surgeon looked at the wound, shook his head, and briefly made his prognosis.

"Bone shattered—vessels injured—bad leg—have to come off. Good constitution, though; he'll stand it."

And he did stand it; always cheerful, never complaining, only regretting that he must be discharged—that he was no longer able to serve his country.

And now Hopeful is again sitting on his little bench in Mynheer Kordwaner's little shop, pegging away at the coarse boots, singing the same glorious prophecy that we first heard him singing. He has had but two troubles since his return. One is the lingering regret and restlessness that attends a civil life after an experience of the rough, independent life in camp. The other trouble was when he first saw Christina after his return. The loving warmth with which she greeted him pained him; and when the worthy Herr considerately went out of the room, leaving them alone, he relapsed into gloomy silence. At length, speaking rapidly, and with choked utterance, he began:

"Christie, you know I love you now, as I always have, better 'n all the world. But I'm a cripple now—no account to nobody—just a dead weight—an' I don't want you, 'cause o' your promise before I went away, to tie yourself to a load that'll be a drag on you all your life. That contract—ah—promises—an't—is—is hereby repealed! There!" And he leaned his head upon his hands and wept bitter tears, wrung by a great agony from his loving heart.

Christie gently laid her hand upon his shoulder, and spoke, slowly and calmly: "Hopeful, your soul was not in that leg, was it?"

It would seem as if Hopeful had always thought that such was the case, and was just receiving new light upon the subject, he started up so suddenly.

"By jing! Christie!" And he grasped her hand, and—but that is another of those scenes that don't concern us at all. And Christie has promised next Christmas to take the name, as she already has the heart, of Tackett. Herr Kordwaner, too, has come to the conclusion that he wants a partner, and on the day of the wedding a new sign is to be put up over a new and larger shop, on which "Co." will mean Hopeful Tackett. In the mean time, Hopeful hammers away lustily, merrily whistling, and singing the praises of the "Banger." Occasionally, when he is resting, he will tenderly embrace his stump of a leg, gently patting and stroking it, and talking to it as to a pet. If a stranger is in the shop, he will hold it out admiringly, and ask:

"Do you know what I call that? I call *that 'Hopeful Tackett—his mark.'*"

And it is a mark—a mark of distinction—a badge of honor, worn by many a brave fellow who has gone forth, borne and upheld by a love for the dear old flag, to fight, to suffer, to die if need be, for it; won in the fierce contest, amid the clashing strokes of the steel and the wild whistling of bullets; won by unflinching nerve and unyielding muscle; worn as a badge of the proudest distinction an American can reach. If these lines come to one of those that have thus fought and suffered—though his scars were received in some unnoticed, unpublished skirmish, though official bulletins spoke not of him, "though fame shall never know his story"—let them come as a tribute to him; as a token that he is not forgotten; that those that have been with him through the trials and the triumphs of the field, remember him and the heroic courage that won for him those honorable scars; and that while life is left to them they will work and fight in the same cause, cheerfully making the same sacrifices, seeking no higher reward than to take him by the hand and call him "comrade," and to share with him the proud consciousness of duty done. Shoulder-straps and stars may bring renown; but he is no less a real hero who, with rifle and bayonet, throws himself into the breach, and, uninspired by hope of official notice, battles manfully for the right.

Hopeful Tackett, humble yet illustrious, a hero for all time, we salute you.

★ ★ ★

Three Hundred Thousand More

James Sloan Gibbons

"An abolitionist, Gibbons's poem was written in response to Lincoln's call in July 1862 for 300,000 volunteers to enlist in the Union Army. The poem was quickly set to music by several composers, the most famous version being by L. O. Emerson," writes Paul Negri.

We are coming, Father Abraham, three hundred thousand more.
From Mississippi's winding stream and from New England's shore;
We leave our ploughs and workshops, our wives and children dear.
With hearts too full for utterance, with but a silent tear;
We dare not look behind us, but steadfastly before:
We are coming, Father Abraham, three hundred thousand more!

If you look across the hill-tops that meet the northern sky,
Long moving lines of rising dust your vision may descry;
And now the wind, an instant, tears the cloudy veil aside,
And floats aloft our spangled flag in glory and in pride,
And bayonets in the sunlight gleam, and bands brave music pour:
We are coming, Father Abraham, three hundred thousand more!

If you look all up our valleys where the growing harvests shine,
You may see our sturdy farmer boys fast forming into line;
And children from their mother's knees are pulling at the weeds,
And learning how to reap and sow against their country's needs;
And a farewell group stands weeping at every cottage door:
We are coming, Father Abraham, three hundred thousand more!

You have called us, and we're coming, by Richmond's bloody tide
To lay us down, for Freedom's sake, our brothers' bones beside,

Or from foul treason's savage grasp to wrench the murderous blade,
And in the face of foreign foes its fragments to parade.
Six hundred thousand loyal men and true have gone before:
We are coming, Father Abraham, three hundred thousand more!

★ ★ ★

A Bundle of Socks

S. E. B.

The editor Frank Moore says this poem was "found in a bundle of socks, sent by a 'Lively Old Lady,' in Amherst, N. H., to the U. S. Hospital, corner of Broad and Cherry streets, Philadelphia."

By the fireside, cosily seated,
   With spectacles riding her nose,
The lively old lady is knitting
   A wonderful pair of hose.
She pities the shivering soldier,
   Who is out in the pelting storm;
And busily plies her needles,
   To keep him hearty and warm.

Her eyes are reading the embers,
   But her heart is off to the war,
For she knows what those brave fellows
   Are gallantly fighting for.
Her fingers as well as her fancy
   Are cheering them on their way,
Who, under the good old banner,
   Are saving their Country today.

She ponders, how in her childhood,
   Her grandmother used to tell—
The story of barefoot soldiers,
   Who fought so long and well.
And the men of the Revolution
   Are nearer to her than us;
And that perhaps is the reason
   Why she is toiling thus.

She cannot shoulder a musket,
    Nor ride with cavalry crew,
But nevertheless she is ready
    To work for the boys who do.
And yet in "official despatches,"
    That come from the army or fleet,
Her feats may have never a notice,
    Though ever so mighty the *feet!*

So prithee, proud owner of muscle,
    Or purse-proud owner of stocks,
Don't sneer at the labors of woman,
    Or smile at her bundle of socks.
Her heart may be larger and braver
    Than his who is tallest of all,
The work of her hands as important
    As cash that buys powder and ball.

And thus while her quiet performance
    Is being recorded in rhyme,
The tools in her tremulous fingers
    Are running a race with Time.
Strange that four needles can form
    A perfect triangular bound;
And equally strange that their antics
    Result in perfecting "the round."

And now, while beginning "to narrow,"
    She thinks of the Maryland mud,
And wonders if ever the stocking
    Will wade to the ankle in blood.
And now she is "shaping the heel,"
    And now she ready is "to bind,"
And hopes if the soldier is wounded,
    It never will be from behind.

And now she is "raising the instep,"
    Now "narrowing off at the toe,"
And prays that this end of the worsted
    May ever be turned to the foe.
She "gathers" the last of the stitches,
    As if a new laurel were won,
And placing the ball in the basket,
    Announces the stocking as "done."

Ye men who are fighting our battles,
  Away from the comforts of life,
Who thoughtfully muse by your camp-fires,
  On sweetheart, or sister, or wife;
Just think of their elders a little,
  And pray for the grandmothers too,
Who, patiently sitting in corners,
  Are knitting the stockings for you.

★ ★ ★

Dirge for a Soldier:
In Memory of General Philip Kearny

George Henry Boker

Union General Kearny was killed after Second Bull Run at the Battle of Chantilly on September 1, 1862.

Close his eyes; his work is done!
  What to him is friend or foeman,
Rise of moon, or set of sun,
  Hand of man, or kiss of woman?
    Lay him low, lay him low,
    In the clover or the snow!
    What cares he? he cannot know:
    Lay him low!

As man may, he fought his fight,
  Proved his truth by his endeavor;
Let him sleep in solemn night,
  Sleep forever and forever.
    Lay him low, lay him low,
    In the clover or the snow!
    What cares he? he cannot know:
    Lay him low!

Fold him in his country's stars,
  Roll the drum and fire the volley!
What to him are all our wars,
  What but death bemocking folly?

Lay him low, lay him low,
  In the clover or the snow!
What cares he? he cannot know:
  Lay him low!

Leave him to God's watching eye,
  Trust him to the hand that made him.
Mortal love weeps idly by:
  God alone has power to aid him.
    Lay him low, lay him low,
    In the clover or the snow!
    What cares he? he cannot know:
    Lay him low!

★ ★ ★

"Ein Feste Burg Ist Unser Gott" (Luther's Hymn)

JOHN GREENLEAF WHITTIER

We wait beneath the furnace-blast
  The pangs of transformation;
Not painlessly doth God recast
  And mould anew the nation.
    Hot burns the fire
    Where wrongs expire;
    Nor spares the hand
    That from the land
  Uproots the ancient evil.

The hand-breadth cloud the sages feared
  Its bloody rain is dropping;
The poison plant the fathers spared
  All else is overtopping.
    East, West, South, North,
    It curses the earth;
    All justice dies,
    And fraud and lies
  Live only in its shadow.

What gives the wheat-field blades of steel?
  What points the rebel cannon?

What sets the roaring rabble's heel
  On the old star-spangled pennon?
    What breaks the oath
    Of the men o' the South?
    What whets the knife
    For the Union's life?—
Hark to the answer: Slavery!

Then waste no blows on lesser foes
  In strife unworthy freemen.
God lifts today the vail, and shows
  The features of the demon!
    O North and South,
    Its victims both,
    Can ye not cry,
    "Let slavery die!"
And union find in freedom?

What though the cast-out spirit tear
  The nation in his going?
We who have shared the guilt must share
  The pang of his o'erthrowing!
    Whate'er the loss,
    Whate'er the cross,
    Shall they complain
    Of present pain
Who trust in God's hereafter?

For who that leans on His right arm
  Was ever yet forsaken?
What righteous cause can suffer harm
  If He its part has taken?
    Though wild and loud
    And dark the cloud
    Behind its folds
    His hand upholds
The calm sky of tomorrow!

Above the maddening cry for blood,
  Above the wild war-drumming,
Let Freedom's voice be heard, with good
  The evil overcoming.
    Give prayer and purse

To stay the Curse
Whose wrong we share,
Whose shame we bear,
Whose end shall gladden Heaven!

In vain the bells of war shall ring
Of triumphs and revenges,
While still is spared the evil thing
That severs and estranges.
But blest the ear
That yet shall hear
The jubilant bell
That rings the knell
Of Slavery forever!

Then let the selfish lip be dumb,
And hushed the breath of sighing;
Before the joy of peace must come
The pains of purifying.
God give us grace
Each in his place
To bear his lot,
And, murmuring not,
Endure and wait and labor!

★   ★   ★

The Empty Sleeve

J. R. BAGBY

The author was a doctor in Virginia. The last of the Seven Days Battles, the Battle of Malvern Hill, where "Tom" lost his arm, took place on July 1, 1862.

Tom, old fellow, I grieve to see
The sleeve hanging loose at your side;
The arm you lost was worth to me
Every Yankee that ever died,
But you don't mind it at all,
You swear you've a beautiful stump,
And laugh at that damnable ball—
Tom, I knew you were always a trump.

A good right arm, a nervy hand,
 A wrist as strong as a sapling oak,
Buried deep in the Malvern sand—
 To laugh at that is a sorry joke.
Never again your iron grip
 Shall I feel in my shrinking palm—
Tom, Tom, I see your trembling lip;
 All within is not calm.

Well! the arm is gone, it is true;
 But the one that is nearest the heart
Is left—and that's as good as two;
 Tom, old fellow, what makes you start?
Why, man, she thinks that empty sleeve
 A badge of honor; so do I,
And all of us—I do believe
 The fellow is going to cry!

"She deserves a perfect man," you say;
 "You were not worth her in your prime;"
Tom! the arm that has turned to clay,
 Your whole body has made sublime;
For you have placed in the Malvern earth
 The proof and pledge of a noble life—
And the rest, henceforward of higher worth
 Will be dearer than all to your wife,

I see the people in the street
 Look at your sleeve with kindling eyes;
And you know, Tom, there's naught so sweet
 As homage shown in mute surmise.
Bravely your arm in battle strove,
 Freely for Freedom's sake you gave it;
It has perished—but a nation's love
 In proud remembrance will save it.

Go to your sweetheart, then, forthwith—
 You're a fool for staying so long—
Woman's love you'll find no myth,
 But a truth—living, tender, strong.
And when around her slender belt
 Your left is clasped in fond embrace,
Your right will thrill, as if it felt,
 In its grave, the usurper's place.

As I look through the coming years,
   I see a one-armed married man;
A little woman, with smiles and tears,
   Is helping as hard as she can
To put on his coat, to pin his sleeve,
   Tie his cravat, and cut his food;
And I say, as these fancies I weave,
   "That is Tom, and the woman he wooed."

The years roll on, and then I see
   A wedding picture, bright and fair;
I look closer, and it's plain to me
   That is Tom with the silver hair.
He gives away the lovely bride,
   And the guests linger, loth to leave
The house of him in whom they pride—
   "Brave old Tom with the empty sleeve."

★ ★ ★

Joe Parsons, a Maryland Brave

ANONYMOUS

In his Rebellion Record, *Frank Moore published this very short heroic story from "a correspondent, writing from the hospitals of Alexandria, Va." The very bloody battle of Antietam Creek, at Sharpsburg, Maryland, took place on September 17, 1862.*

Joe enlisted in the First Maryland regiment, and was plainly a "rough" originally. As we passed along the hall we first saw him crouched near an open window, lustily singing, *"I'm a bold soldier boy,"* and observing the broad bandage over his eyes, I said: "What's your name, my good fellow?"

"Joe, sir," he answered, "Joe Parsons."

"And what is the matter with you?"

"Blind, sir, blind as a bat."

"In battle?"

"Yes, at Antietam; both eyes shot out at one clip."

Poor Joe was in the front, at Antietam Creek, and a Minie ball had passed directly through his eyes, across his face, destroying his sight forever. He was but twenty years old, but he was as happy as a lark! "It is dreadful," I said.

"I'm very thankful I'm alive, sir. It might ha' been worse, yer see," he continued.

And then he told us his story.

"I was hit," he said, "and it knocked me down. I lay there all night, and the next day the fight was renewed. I could stand the pain, yer see, but the balls was flyin' all round, and I wanted to get away. I couldn't see nothin',, though. So I waited and listened; and at last I heard a feller groanin' beyond me.

"'Hello!' says I.

"'Hello yourself,' says he.

"'Who be yer?' says I—'a rebel?'

"'You're a Yankee,' says he.

"'So I am,' says I; 'what's the matter with yer?'

"'My leg's smashed,' says he.

"'Can't yer walk?'

"'No.'

"'Can yer see?'

"'Yes.'

"'Well,' says I, 'you're a rebel, but will you do me a little favor?'

"'I will,' says he, 'ef I ken.'

"Then I says: 'Well, ole butternut, I can't see nothin.' My eyes is knocked out; but I ken walk. Come over yere. Let's git out o' this. You p'int the way, an' I'll tote yer off the field on my back.'

"'Bully for you,' says he.

"And so we managed to git together. We shook hands on it. I took a wink out o' his canteen, and he got on to my shoulders.

"I did the walkin' for both, an' he did the navigatin'. An' ef he didn't make me carry him straight into a rebel colonel's tent, a mile away, I'm a liar! Hows'ever, the colonel came up, an' says he, 'Whar d'yer come from? who be yer?' I told him. He said I was done for, and couldn't do no more shoot'n; an' he sent me over to our lines. So, after three days, I came down here with the wounded boys, where we're doin' pretty well, all things considered."

"But you will never see the light again, my poor fellow," I suggested, sympathetically.

"That's so," he answered, glibly, "but I can't help it, you notice. I did my dooty—got shot, pop in the eye—an' that's my misfort'n, not my fault—as the old man said of his blind hoss. But—'*I'm a bold soldier boy,*'" he continued, cheerily renewing his song; and we left him in his singular merriment.

Poor, sightless, unlucky, but stouthearted Joe Parsons!

The Sergeant's Little Story

William H. Kemper

Kemper, a Confederate veteran, published his story in October 1873 in Southern
Magazine.

To our great surprise and commensurate gratification, the Sergeant
was less reticent than usual, and seemed to be growing even auto-
biological. He was not a painfully handsome man: that odd-looking
cavern, or sunken scar, in his leathery cheek was plainly not a dimple,
nor could it in a spirit of the most elastic courtesy be regarded as a
beauty-spot. The Sergeant sat next the decanter.

"Well, 'twas touch and go—a snap for him, a snap-shot for me; but
the luck was mine. After catching the horse—a troublesome busi-
ness—I went up to the man and inquired how he felt. He was lying
on his face and made no answer. I turned him over. He seemed to be a
fine-looking fellow, as well as I could judge in the deepening twilight,
and about my own age. My ball had struck plumb-center, a little above
the line of his eyebrows; but as he'd fallen and bled face downward,
he was not much disfigured. No time was lost in going through his
pockets and haversack; the ford being not more than half a mile away,
I was afraid they might have a double picket there, in which case
they'd like enough be sending presently to see what the shot meant.
Finding nothing about his person worth conveying, save his official
dispatches, I hurriedly crammed them into my haversack along with a
lot of late Washington and New York papers that I had got for General
Lee's amusement from a lady friend near Frederick, then mounted
the horse—a fine tight-built trotter, apparently of Morgan blood—
and moved slowly and warily down toward the river. Two hundred
yards from the ford I drew rein and listened. Everything seemed quiet.
A solitary light shone in an upper window of the house at the canal
bridge—you ought to remember the house, Captain S——The roar-
ing of the water among the rocks ahead was the only sound that broke
the silence of the night, until presently a big owl began his melancholy
laughter in the wood behind me. Having been born in the woods, I
didn't allow the solemn old cuss to frighten me, though I did wish he'd
shut up, that's a fact. Dismounting, I pulled the horse up a steep bank
into the dense shadows of the woods skirting the roadside, hitched him
securely to a swinging limb, and limped along as best I might afoot to
reconnoitre the ford. The coast was clear. This important discovery I
effected by a simple little stratagem which had served my purpose on

a previous occasion: without going dangerously near, or even crossing the canal, I merely brought my school-boy skill at yerking into play, and dropped a stone, like a shell from a miniature mortar, just where the vidette would be standing if about there at all. Having repeated the experiment without eliciting so much as a cuss-word in response, I advanced with confidence. The river was considerably lower than I had expected to find it. Groping along the water's edge I found a place where the mud was stiff enough to sit upon, then shucked my boots and peeled off my socks, bringing several square inches of blistered skin with them, and paddled my feet in the cool water. Dead beat as I was, the delightful sensation of relief from long agony almost sent me to sleep in spite of myself; but I thought of Uncle Bob's impatience, my own great danger, the importance of the dispatch I bore, the rest and refreshment and well-earned praise that awaited me at headquarters; in truth, I was thinking of too many things, and was nodding once more, but with a sudden exertion of will I straightened up like a Jack-in-the-box and drew on my boots, without socks, despite the pain, and limped back toward where I'd left the horse, resolved to get across the river at once. I found him all right; but that ominous old owl had taken advantage of my absence to come and perch himself in a tree right over him, where he was tohoo-hooing at a great rate. Before mounting I thought of a good plan to secure the dispatch; for you must understand I didn't more than half like the outlook: things were a little *too* quiet. Somehow I began to fear that a rough road and danger still lay between me and camp. I took a little air-tight India-rubber bag in which I carried 'fine-cut' (when I had any) and put the dispatch, neatly folded, inside of that; then I poked the bag down the neck of my canteen, blew it up with my breath as tight as I could, and tied a string around the neck so as to keep the air in and the water out, or whiskey, as the case might be. You will observe now that by keeping the canteen about half-full of water, or whiskey, as I said before, the bag would float always out of sight, keeping always on top, no matter which way the canteen might be held, while it would make no noise if shaken.

"When mounted, I felt better, and struck into a brisk trot for the river. My feet stopped paining me for one thing, and on reaching the ford I was so gay and imprudent as to let off a rousing war-whoop which reverberated for a mile around. I instantly sobered down, regretting the senseless act on finding that I got no answer from the Virginia shore save the startling echo of my own voice; for I had hoped to find there a picket of Fitz Lee's or Hampton's men. If there, they were afraid to answer my challenge. I didn't comprehend the situation; in fact, I hardly had sense enough left to comprehend anything: I was emphatically a used-up man, so weary and sleepy that I swayed in the saddle like a drunken man as I forced the horse down the bank and into the river. Owing to my stupid condition, or the darkness of the night, for the clouds hung low and heavy, I missed the proper line of ford and struck too low down stream. Before getting forty feet from the bank the horse stumbled and scrambled over a large slippery rock, nearly pitching me out of the saddle, then plunged head down into almost swimming water, soaking the little round button on top of my Scotch cap and waking me up. Three or four plunges and desperate struggles brought us out to a little island—I reckon some of you recollect it?—about thirty-five or forty yards from the Maryland shore. It was covered with willow trees and thick undergrowth quite down to the water's edge, except on the Maryland side and around the lower end, where there was a strip of clean sandy beach some ten or fifteen feet in width. 'Humph!' says I,' here's a nice berth for a fox-nap! Buck me! but I'll risk forty winks anyhow!'

"The fact is, gentlemen, human endurance has limits. I had now been on the trot for over two days and nights, and not even a sense of danger would make me hold up longer. So I rolled off the horse—leaving the saddle on him, but removing the bit from his mouth—fastened him to a willow-branch, crept round under cover of the thickest foliage at the lower point of the little island, and lay down to rest, using my well-stuffed haversack for a pillow. It was a dangerous chance I was taking. I knew it; but the night was so still, and everything seemed inviting me to snatch an hour's rest before continuing a perilous journey, the worst of which, for all I knew, might be still before me. Not a sound was to be heard betokening approach of danger—nothing save the rush and gurgle of the inky waters, the crunching of my horse's teeth leisurely chewing the willow leaves, and the far-off whistle of the whippoor-will away up the river. Just before losing all sense in heavy slumber I noticed dreamily that the clouds broke away in the east, and I caught a glimpse of the crescent moon hanging by one horn in the top of a tall dead pine tree high up on the Maryland bluff. It swung to and fro like a binnacle-light, and I remember thinking in a drowsy sort of way that if it wasn't careful it would drop off the limb and get broken. Just then the old owl opened again; only it seemed to me he had changed his base, and was now perched upon a leafless limb overhanging the roadside on the hill, and was talking to the poor fellow stretched out beneath, lying there so still and ghastly, the white face upturned to the moonlight, the wide-staring eyes, the purple spot in the pale forehead where the bullet went in and life came out. I seemed to be standing over him again, it was all so plain. Well, well, such is war—as the scout must wage it. There's no denying the fact though, it does make a man feel worse—more like a wild beast, like our elder brother Cain—to be obliged to slay his foe under such circumstances: alone, with no witness but his own conscience and the All-seeing Eye that pierces through the gathering gloom of night on the lonely forest road. But why it should be really worse than to do the same thing with the roar and crash and rattle of wholesale murder around you, I confess is not so plain to my mind. To single out your men—men not even aiming at you, neither—and pick 'em off one at a time, as some of us here have done, for an hour or two, that now appears to me—I beg pardon; where was I? Let's licker."

Having "lickered," the Sergeant proceeded.

"I must have slept like a Mississippi sawyer for I don't know how long, two or three hours perhaps, when *spi-yow! zweep!*—a shot from the Virginia shore, then three or four more in quick succession, answered by a rattling fusillade from the Maryland side. I was on my feet of course ere the second shot was fired and about to spring to saddle, but too late. The ford was crowded with Federal cavalry, cursing, yelling, stumbling and spurring furiously across the river, where our boys (a small picket from Hampton's command, as I afterwards learned) didn't stay to swop horses, as indeed there would have been no sense in doing; though why in thunder they didn't answer my challenge I never could discover. Now indeed I found myself entrapped and entangled in the meshes woven by my own folly. Although, as you remember, the island is not exactly in the line of ford, being some twenty-five or thirty yards down stream, it was impossible for my horse to long escape notice, standing, or rather plunging impatiently, in the full light of the moon, now high in the heavens. Luckily for me I was in deep shadow cast by overhanging willows, and had time to beat the assembly, so to speak, to collect my startled faculties and make them fall in line. My first thought was for the dispatch. Having gone through purgatory to get it and fetch it so far, you may safely bet I hadn't any notion of lightly losing it. Raising the canteen to my lips, I drained it of the last swallow of "blue ruin," somewhat improved by the flavor of India-rubber; then stooping down, I cautiously refilled it about half-way with Potomac water and corked it tightly. By this time they had seen the horse; and some had stopped and were pointing toward him, but seemed rather shy about coming down. An officer ordered 'three or four' of them to 'ride down there and see what it meant.' While they hesitated I took advantage of their timidity and delay to cast about for a chance of escape, and make a few little arrangements, such as strapping my belt outside of my haversack and canteen cords, so's to keep 'em down to my side in case I took water. And that same I meant to do too; for I had already discovered from their talk that they'd found the dead courier, and I knew mighty well what to expect if they found me too. I have been in and got out of some pretty rasping scrapes, but this was the only occasion save one during the entire war when I remember to have made up my mind deliberately to die rather than be caught. Bitterly I cursed my stupidity in not concealing the courier's body; and then, by way of change, I believe I tried my hand at praying, but couldn't get any further than 'now I lay me down to sleep,' when I remembered what a blamed fool I'd been to do that very thing, and that set me to cussin' again. Fact is, it was a little too late for either cussin' or prayin', and I soon came to that conclusion. Dropping silently on my hands and knees, I crept along under the willow-branches close to the water's edge and listened. Noticing just ahead of where I was, on the western side of the island, a long drooping branch of willow hung out almost touching the surface of what looked like pretty deep water, on the instant a vague undefined plan or hope of escape began to shape itself in my mind.

"By this time two or three of 'em had got round the horse on the other side of the bushes, talking. 'Why, how is this? What's this here on the saddle now?' 'Feels sorter wet and sticky, don't—' 'Blood, by jingo!' cries another. 'Can't you smell it, corp'ral?' Then the corporal yells out, 'Ride down here, Kurnel! Dang me if this here ain't the courier's horse!' 'What the should the horse be doing thar without a rider?' growled back a deep hoarse voice like the mate's of a three-master. 'Look alive there, blast yer blockheads, and ye'll mebby find the chap that rode him!'

"The devils now commenced shooting into the willow thicket, one of the balls grazing my right elbow: must get out of that some way. Sliding down into the water like a skilpot off a log, I found to my great joy that it was deep enough for my purpose; and so I lay low right under the overhanging limb, just keeping eyes, nose and ears out of water. Had hardly got settled comfortably (our ideas of comfort, you know, as of all else, are entirely relative) before the big Colonel himself was there, knocking, ripping and snorting around, poking his five-foot sabre into the bushes wherever he thought he spied something, and popping away every now and then with his revolver. Twice or three times the blamed officious old blunderbore came nigh hitting me, and I was getting right mad, when what should he do but come and stand on the limb, so's it pushed my head clean under water. Being taken unawares (I thought of course he was going to step over the limb, as anybody but a cussed old fool like him would have done), I couldn't help spluttering a little as my mouth went under. 'Aha!' says he, 'what's that?' I had worked my mouth and nose out, and was trying to draw my breath easy, but the strain on my lungs was terrible. He wasn't at all sure he had heard anything, but just out of downright deviltry and officiousness he gave point in tierce right down through the willow. Instinctively I ducked; but for all that I got the point of his confounded sabre through my cheek here, and have been trying ever since to digest a couple of big jaw-teeth. In making the thrust he lost his balance and came within an ace of piling in atop of me. That was all that saved me: by the time he had gathered himself up I also had recovered in some degree my desperate composure, and was breathing as softly and steadily as a sleeping bull-frog. The limb knocked my cap off when he stumbled, and it was nearly floating out from under the willow; but I caught it in time and drew it down beneath me. I could feel that I was bleeding like a stuck pig, but it was no time for squealing. By this time a dozen or so, mostly officers, were crowding down to the island to see what the row was about; but the Colonel—God bless the old pudding-head!—ordered 'em all back, and away they went and he with them. Just as the last man was turning the corner, almost out of sight, he stopped, faced about, and I caught the click-click as he cocked his revolver. Says he, 'Thar's a big fish under that limb, and I knows it.' Down went my devoted head deep as I could get it. I heard no report; but the peculiar metallic ripping sound of the ball as it cut the water just above my ear I shall not soon forget. It sounded like tearing sheet-iron.

"That appeared to satisfy them. When I ventured to raise my head and look about me, they had taken my horse and were hurrying on to overtake their command. The long line of horsemen, riding by twos, still stumbled and splashed and clattered across the moonlit river, and plunging up the steep bank, disappeared in the silent shadows beyond. How long I remained in the water I cannot tell; it seemed to me many hours. I was growing sensibly weaker from the loss of blood, while the water chilled me to the very marrow; yet still I kept my position, kneeling in the water beneath the sheltering willow. At length, as the moon forged slowly down the western skies, fleecy clouds began to gather and obscure her light once more. At length too the cavalry had all passed by; some ambulances and a light wagon or two followed, and I was just crawling out from my hiding-place, bracing my resolution for a bold push toward the old Virginia shore, when the head of a column of light artillery appeared. Here was a go! I had seen some crossing of artillery at this ford before: easy enough going in, but the very old Tommy to get out if it should chance to be a large battalion, at all commensurate with the force of cavalry which had preceded it, there was very great probability that they wouldn't get over till long after daylight, in which event, you will understand, it was likely to be quite interesting for me. Pass the decanter, if you please.

"Still I felt quite confident of getting out of the trap in some way, particularly since the moon now shed so feeble a light that I could venture to stand up and shake myself—a very primitive, Newfoundland mode of making the toilette, but quite refreshing and satisfactory under some circumstances. Well, just as I feared, the leading carriage stalled at the steep and slippery bank on the Virginia side. No use to hitch in more horses: only a certain number—not more than four— had room to pull to advantage. Hearing the word passed back for picks and shovels and axes, I knew well what was to be done: while some were grading the ascent, others would be set to work cutting branches to throw under the horses' feet. To leave the island at the lower end and attempt to make the Virginia shore by wading and swimming in the rapids among the big boulders below the ford, I felt would be sheer madness in my exhausted condition. I was so wrapped in thought, striving to strike out some plan of escape from the perils thickening around me, that I failed to notice two men who had left the column near the Maryland side and were riding down toward the island, till the foremost one was nearly upon me. I drew back farther behind the willows, crouched, watched, listened. Never dog with hydrophobia dreaded water more than I did then; but I slowly edged off toward my former hiding-place, ready to take another plunge if it should prove necessary. The leading man was plainly drunk in the first degree, and when the other joined him there was a pair of 'em. From their thick-tongued talk about wagons, chests and such matters, it seemed they belonged to the bomb-proof departments. There was a rattling of canteens; the first comer handed his companion a key which he swore 'was the one t' th' blue ch-chist, 'n' the d-dimijohn was the one in th' lef'-han' corner.' He enjoined upon him to 'fill both canteens ch-chuck-fulli 'n' not to g-guzzle it 'fore he g-got back, neither'; meantime he (the speaker) would 'knock it off' there. While giving his directions he had managed to roll off the saddle and fasten his horse to the very limb which I had used for the same purpose. The other chap rode off toward the rear, declaring he 'wouldn't be gone more'n half an hour.' My man then staggered to the lower end of the island, worked himself out of his overcoat, bundled it up awkwardly for a pillow, and laid himself out to 'knock it off.' Here was my chance: I was saved! Stealthily and slowly I grasped the handle of my trusty bowie-knife—the only friend I could depend on now, and the better for being a silent one, not given to noisy demonstrations—and drew him gently from the modest retirement and obscurity of my dexter boot-leg, where be had so long lain *perdu,* biding his time. Stand by me now, if ever, old 'Buck-Horn,' friend and mess-mate! Let but this one stroke be straight, sure and deadly, and never again shall thy glittering blade be condemned and degraded to the ignominious office of slicing mess-pork! A sword, a battle-axe, and perchance a razor shalt thou be all the days of thy—life I was going to say, but changed my mind and substituted existence, as being more correct."

"You did, did you?" here broke in Sammy G——, a pert young nephew of the Sergeant, who believed in "turning things around and looking at 'em both ways," as he said. Then I put in. "Sergeant," said I, "you should remember that you are not telling this story for publication in the *Scribblers Scrap-Book.* Do you mean to assert that you really were going to murder that person in cold blood, and that you really did apostrophise your bowie-knife in those terrible, awe-inspiring words, or words to that effect?"

"Sir," said he, with dignity slightly marred by a manifestation of temper, "I don't wish to be criticized in this way. If I didn't use precisely those words, 'those words,' as you style them, would have admirably expressed my sentiments, and would have been appropriate to the occasion. That should suffice. As to murdering people in cold blood, you should consider that I was about as cold and bloody as a man can well be, and laboring under heavy provocation besides; but if any of you gentlemen think you can tell the story, that is to say if you imagine that you can narrate the circumstances better than I can, why just push ahead and do it."

Here Sammy thought it high time for him to say something again, and he cried out: "That's all in my eye! Them cavalry was Hampton's men, an' I heard Kurnel Toliver say 'at he ketched Uncle Tom (that's the Sergeant) on a island, and all wet, and give him a drink, *I* did!"

"O you be durned!" said the Sergeant, and immediately proposed a game of euchre.

Fredericksburgh

W. F. W.

The poem was published in New York, December 17, 1862, immediately after the Battle of Fredericksburg, in Virginia, when Union General Burnside unsuccessfully attempted to break through Confederate General Robert E. Lee's army to attack Richmond.

Eighteen hundred and sixty-two—
　　That is the number of wounded men
Who, if the telegraph's tale be true,
　　Reached Washington City but yester e'en,

And it is but a handful, the telegrams add,
　　To those who are coming by boats and by cars;
Weary and wounded, dying and sad;
　　Covered—but only in front—with scars.

Some are wounded by Minie shot,
　　Others are torn by the hissing shell,
As it burst upon them as fierce and as hot
　　As a demon spawned in a traitor's hell.

Some are pierced by the sharp bayonet,
　　Others are crushed by the horses' hoof;
Or fell 'neath the shower of iron which met
　　Them as hail beats down on an open roof.

Shall I tell what they did to meet this fate?
　　Why was this living death their doom—
Why did they fall to this piteous state
　　'Neath the rifle's crack and the cannon's boom?

Orders arrived, and the river they crossed—
　　Built the bridge in the enemy's face—
No matter how many were shot and lost,
　　And floated—sad corpses—away from the place.

Orders they heard, and they scaled the height,
　　Climbing right "into the jaws of death;"
Each man grasping his rifle-piece tight—
　　Scarcely pausing to draw his breath.

Sudden flashed on them a sheet of flame
　　From hidden fence and from ambuscade;

A moment more—(they say this is fame)—
 A thousand dead men on the grass were laid.

Fifteen thousand in wounded and killed,
 At least, is "our loss," the newspapers say.
This loss to our army must surely be filled
 Against another great battle-day.

"Our loss!" Whose loss? Let demagogues say
 That the Cabinet, President, all are in wrong.
What do the orphans and widows pray?
 What is the burden of their sad song?

'Tis *their* loss! But the tears in their weeping eyes
 Hide Cabinet, President, Generals—all;
And they only can see a cold form that lies
 On the hillside slope, by that fatal wall.

They cannot discriminate men or means—
 They only demand that this blundering cease.
In their frenzied grief they would end such scenes,
 Though that end be—even with traitors—peace.

Is thy face from thy people turned, O God?
 Is thy arm for the Nation no longer strong?
We cry from our homes—the dead cry from the sod—
 How long, O our righteous God! how long?

★ ★ ★

A Day

Louisa May Alcott

This is one of the several stories Alcott (1832–1888) wrote and published in 1863 based on her personal experiences as a nurse in Washington. The future author of Little Women *arrived in the capital at the end of December 1862, in time to aid the wounded soldiers from Fredericksburg.*

"They've come! they've come! hurry up, ladies—you're wanted."

"Who have come? the rebels?"

This sudden summons in the gray dawn was somewhat startling to a three days' nurse like myself, and, as the thundering knock came at our door, I sprang up in my bed, prepared

> *"To gird my woman's form,*
> *And on the ramparts die,"*

if necessary; but my roommate took it more coolly, and, as she began a rapid toilet, answered my bewildered question,—

"Bless you, no child; it's the wounded from Fredericksburg; forty ambulances are at the door, and we shall have our hands full in fifteen minutes."

"What shall we have to do?"

"Wash, dress, feed, warm and nurse them for the next three months, I dare say. Eighty beds are ready, and we were getting impatient for the men to come. Now you will begin to see hospital life in earnest, for you won't probably find time to sit down all day, and may think yourself fortunate if you get to bed by midnight. Come to me in the ballroom when you are ready; the worst cases are always carried there, and I shall need your help."

So saying, the energetic little woman twirled her hair into a button at the back of her head, in a "cleared for action" sort of style, and vanished, wrestling her way into a feminine kind of pea-jacket as she went.

I am free to confess that I had a realizing sense of the fact that my hospital bed was not a bed of roses just then, or the prospect before me one of unmingled rapture. My three days' experiences had begun with a death, and, owing to the defalcation of another nurse, a somewhat abrupt plunge into the superintendence of a ward containing forty beds, where I spent my shining hours washing faces, serving rations, giving medicine, and sitting in a very hard chair, with pneumonia on one side, diptheria on the other, two typhoids opposite, and a dozen dilapidated patriots, hopping, lying, and lounging about, all staring more or less at the new "nuss," who suffered untold agonies, but concealed them under as matronly an aspect as a spinster could assume, and blundered through her trying labors with a Spartan firmness, which I hope they appreciated, but am afraid they didn't. (Having a taste for "ghastliness," I had rather longed for the wounded to arrive, for rheumatism wasn't heroic, neither was liver complaint, or measles; even fever had lost its charms since "bathing burning brows" had been used up in romances, real and ideal. But when I peeped into the dusky street lined with what I at first had innocently called market carts, now unloading their sad freight at our door, I recalled sundry reminiscences I had heard from nurses of longer standing, my ardor experienced a sadden chill, and I indulged in a most unpatriotic wish that I was safe at home again, with a quiet day before me, and no necessity for being hustled up, as if I were a hen and had only to hop off my roost, give my plumage a peck, and be ready for action. A second bang at the door sent this recreant desire to the right about, as a little woolly head popped in, and Joey, (a six years' old contraband,) announced—

"Miss Blank is jes' wild fer ye, and says fly round right away. They's comin' in, I tell yer, heaps on 'em—one was took out dead, and I see him,—hi! warn't he a goner!"

With which cheerful intelligence the imp scuttled away, singing like a blackbird, and I followed, feeling that Richard was *not* himself again, and wouldn't be for a long time to come.

The first thing I met was a regiment of the vilest odors that ever assaulted the human nose, and took it by storm. Cologne, with its seven and seventy evil savors, was a posy-bed to it; and the worst of this affliction was, everyone had assured me that it was a chronic weakness of all hospitals, and I must bear it. I did, armed with lavender water, with which I so besprinkled myself and premises, that I was soon known among my patients as "the nurse with the bottle." Having been run over by three excited surgeons, bumped against by migratory coal-hods, water-pails, and small boys, nearly scalded by an avalanche of newly filled tea-pots, and hopelessly entangled in a knot of colored sisters coming to wash, I progressed by slow stages up stairs and down, till the main hall was reached, and I paused to take breath and a survey. There they were! "our brave boys," as the papers justly call them, for cowards could hardly have been so riddled with shot and shell, so torn and shattered, nor have borne suffering for which we have no name, with an uncomplaining fortitude, which made one glad to cherish each like a brother. In they came, some on stretchers, some in men's arms, some feebly staggering along propped on rude crutches, and one lay stark and still with covered face, as a comrade gave his name to be recorded before they carried him away to the dead house. All was hurry and confusion; the hall was full of these wrecks of humanity, for the most exhausted could not reach a bed till duly ticketed and registered; the walls were lined with rows of such as could sit, the floor covered with the more disabled, the steps and doorways filled with helpers and lookers on; the sound of many feet and voices made that usually quiet hour as noisy as noon; and, in the midst of it all, the matron's motherly face brought more comfort to many a poor soul, than the cordial draughts she administered, or the cheery words that welcomed all, making of the hospital a home.

The sight of several stretchers, each with its legless, armless, or desperately wounded occupant, entering my ward, admonished me that I was there to work, not to wonder or weep; so I corked up my feelings, and returned to the path of duty, which was rather "a hard road to travel" just then. The house had been a hotel before hospitals were needed, and many of the doors still bore their old names; some not so inappropriate as might be imagined, for that ward was in truth a ballroom, if gunshot wounds could christen it. Forty beds were prepared, many already tenanted by tired men who fell down anywhere, and drowsed till the smell of food roused them. Round the great stove was gathered the dreariest group I ever saw—ragged, gaunt and pale, mud to the knees, with bloody bandages untouched since put on days before; many bundled up in blankets, coats being lost or useless; and all wearing that disheartened look which proclaimed defeat, more plainly than any telegram of the Burnside blunder. I pitied them so much, I dared not speak to them, though, remembering all they had been through since the fight at Fredericksburg, I yearned to serve the dreariest of them all. Presently, Miss Blank tore me from my refuge behind piles of one-sleeved shirts, odd socks, bandages and lint; put basin, sponge, towels, and a block of brown soap into my hands, with these appalling directions:

"Come, my dear, begin to wash as fast as you can. Tell them to take off socks, coats and shirts, scrub them well, put on clean shirts, and the attendants will finish them off, and lay them in bed."

If she had requested me to shave them all, or dance a hornpipe on the stove funnel, I should have been less staggered; but to scrub some dozen lords of creation at a moment's notice, was really——really——. However, there was no time for nonsense, and, having resolved when I came to do everything I was bid, I drowned my scruples in my washbowl, clutched my soap manfully, and, assuming a businesslike air, made a dab at the first dirty specimen I saw, bent on performing my task *vi et armis* if necessary. I chanced to light on a withered old Irishman, wounded in the head, which caused that portion of his frame to be tastefully laid out like a garden, the bandages being the walks, his hair the shrubbery. He was so overpowered by the honor of having a lady wash him, as he expressed it, that he did nothing but roll up his eyes, and bless me, in an irresistible style which was too much for my sense of the ludicrous; so we laughed together, and when I knelt down to take off his shoes, he "flopped" also, and wouldn't hear of my touching "them dirty craters. May your bed above be aisy darlin', for the day's work ye are doon!—Whoosh I there ye are, and bedad, it's hard tellin' which is the dirtiest, the fat or the shoe." It was; and if he hadn't been to the fore, I should have gone on pulling, under the impression that the "fut" was a boot, for trousers, socks, shoes and legs were a mass of mud. This comical tableau produced a general grin, at which propitious beginning I took heart and scrubbed away like any tidy parent on a Saturday night. Some of them took the performance like sleepy children, leaning their tired heads against me as I worked, others looked grimly scandalized, and several of the roughest colored like bashful girls. One wore a soiled little bag about his neck, and, as I moved it, to bathe his wounded breast, I said,

"Your talisman didn't save you, did it?"

"Well, I reckon it did, marm, for that shot would a gone a couple a inches deeper but for my old mammy's camphor bag," answered the cheerful philosopher.

Another, with a gunshot wound through the cheek, asked for a looking-glass, and when I brought one, regarded his swollen face with a dolorous expression, as he muttered—

"I vow to gosh, that's too bad! I warn't a bad looking chap before, and now I'm done for; won't there be a thunderin' scar? and what on earth will Josephine Skinner say?"

He looked up at me with his one eye so appealingly, that I controlled my risibles, and assured him that if Josephine was a girl of sense, she would admire the honorable scar, as a lasting proof that he had faced the enemy, for all women thought a wound the best decoration a brave soldier could wear. I hope Miss Skinner verified the good opinion I so rashly expressed of her, but I shall never know.

The next scrubbee was a nice-looking lad, with a curly brown mane, honest blue eyes, and a merry mouth. He lay on a bed, with one leg gone, and the right arm so shattered that it must evidently follow: yet the little sergeant was as merry as if his afflictions were not worth lamenting over; and when a drop or two of salt water mingled with my suds at the sight of this strong young body, so marred and maimed, the boy looked up, with a brave smile, though there was a little quiver of the lips, as he said,

"Now don't you fret yourself about me, miss; I'm first rate here, for it's nuts to lie still on this bed, after knocking about in those confounded ambulances, that shake what there is left of a fellow to jelly. I never was in one of these places before, and think this cleaning up a jolly thing for us, though I'm afraid it isn't for you ladies."

"Is this your first battle, Sergeant?"

"No, miss; I've been in six scrimmages, and never got a scratch till this last one; but it's done the business pretty thoroughly for me, I should say. Lord! what a scramble there'll be for arms and legs, when we old boys come out of our graves, on the Judgtnent Day: wonder if we shall get our own again? If we do, my leg will have to tramp from Fredericksburg, my arm from here, I suppose, and meet my body, wherever it may be."

The fancy seemed to tickle him mightily, for he laughed blithely, and so did I; which, no doubt, caused the new nurse to be regarded as a light-minded sinner by the Chaplain, who roamed vaguely about, with his hands in his pockets, preaching resignation to cold, hungry, wounded men, and evidently feeling himself, what he certainly was, the wrong man in the wrong place.

"I say, Mrs.!" called a voice behind me; and, turning, I saw a rough Michigander, with an arm blown off at the shoulder, and two or three bullets still in him—as he afterwards mentioned, as carelessly as if gentlemen were in the habit of carrying such trifles about with them. I went to him, and, while administering a dose of soap and water, he whispered, irefully:

"That red-headed devil, over yonder, is a reb, hang him! He's got shet of a foot, or he'd a cut like the rest of the lot. Don't you wash him, nor feed him, but jest let him holler till he's tired. It's a blasted shame to fetch them fellers in here, along side of us; and so I'll tell the chap that bosses this concern; cuss me if I don't."

I regret to say that I did not deliver a moral sermon upon the duty of forgiving our enemies, and the sin of profanity, then and there; but, being a red-hot Abolitionist, stared fixedly at the tall rebel, who was a copperhead, in every sense of the word, and privately resolved to put soap in his eyes, rub his nose the wrong way, and exoriate his cuticle generally, if I had the washing of him.

My amiable intentions, however, were frustrated; for, when I approached, with as Christian an expression as my principles would allow, and asked the question—"Shall I try to make you more comfortable, sir?" all I got for my pains was a gruff—

"No; I'll do it myself."

"Here's your Southern chivalry, with a witness," thought I, dumping the basin down before him, thereby quenching a strong desire to give him a summary baptism, in return for his ungraciousness; for my angry passions rose, at this rebuff, in a way that would have scandalized good Dr. Watts. He was a disappointment in all respects, (the rebel, not the blessed Doctor,) for he was neither fiendish, romantic, pathetic, or anything interesting; but a long, fat man, with a head like a burning bush, and a perfectly expressionless face: so I could dislike him without the slightest drawback, and ignored his existence from that day forth. One redeeming trait he certainly did possess, as the floor speedily testified; for his ablutions were so vigorously performed, that his bed soon stood like an isolated island, in a sea of soap-suds, and he resembled a dripping merman, suffering from the loss of a fin. If cleanliness is a near neighbor to godliness, then was the big rebel the godliest man in my ward that day.

Having done up our human wash, and laid it out to dry, the second syllable of our version of the word War-fare was enacted with much success. Great trays of bread, meat, soup and coffee appeared; and both nurses and attendants turned waiters, serving bountiful rations to all who could eat. I can call my pinafore to testify to my good will in the work, for in ten minutes it was reduced to a perambulating bill of fare, presenting samples of all the refreshments going or gone. It was a lively scene; the long room lined with rows of beds, each filled by an occupant, whom water, shears, and clean raiment had transformed from a dismal ragamuffin into a recumbent hero, with a cropped head. To and fro rushed matrons, maids, and convalescent "boys," skirmishing with knives and forks; retreating with empty plates; marching and countermarching, with unvaried success, while the clash of busy spoons made most inspiring music for the charge of our Light Brigade:

> *Beds to the front of them,*
> *Beds to the right of them,*
> *Beds to the left of them,*
>   *Nobody blundered.*
> *Beamed at by hungry souls,*
> *Screamed at with brimming bowls,*
> *Steamed at by army rolls,*
>   *Buttered and sundered.*
> *With coffee not cannon plied,*
>   *Each must be satisfied,*
>   *Whether they lived or died;*
>   *All the men wondered.*

Very welcome seemed the generous meal, after a week of suffering, exposure, and short commons; soon the brown faces began to smile, as food, warmth, and rest, did their pleasant work; and the grateful "Thankee's" were followed by more graphic accounts of the battle and retreat, than any paid reporter could have given us. Curious contrasts of the tragic and comic met one everywhere; and some touching as well as ludicrous episodes, might have been recorded that day. A six-foot New Hampshire man, with a leg broken and perforated by a piece of shell, so large that, had I not seen the wound, I should have regarded the story as a Munchausenism, beckoned me to come and help him,

as he could not sit up, and both his bed and beard were getting plenti-
fully anointed with soup. As I fed my big nestling with corresponding
mouthfuls, I asked him how he felt during the battle.

"Well, 'twas my fust, you see, so I aint ashamed to say I was a trifle
flustered in the beginnin', there was such an all-fired racket; for ef
there's anything I do spleen agin, it's noise. But when my mate, Eph
Sylvester, fell, with a bullet through his head, I got mad, and pitched
in, licketty cut. Our part of the fight didn't last long; so a lot of us
larked round Fredericksburg, and give some of them houses a pretty
consid'able of a rummage, till we was ordered out of the mess. Some
of our fellows cut like time; but I warn't a-goin to run for nobody;
and, fust thing I knew, a shell bust, right in front of us, and I keeled
over, feelin' as if I was blowed higher'n a kite. I sung out, and the boys
come back for me, double quick; but the way they chucked me over
them fences was a caution, I tell you. Next day I was most as black as
that darkey yonder, lickin' plates on the sly. This is bully coffee, ain't it?
Give us another pull at it, and I'll be obleeged to you."

I did; and, as the last gulp subsided, he said, with a rub of his old
handkerchief over eyes as well as mouth:

"Look a here; I've got a pair a earbobs and a handkercher pin I'm a
goin' to give you, if you'll have them; for you're the very moral o' Lizy
Sylvester, poor Eph's wife: that's why I signalled you to come over here.
They aint much, I guess, but they'll do to memorize the rebs by."

Burrowing under his pillow, he produced a little bundle of what
he called "truck," and gallantly presented me with a pair of earrings,
each representing a cluster of corpulent grapes, and the pin a basket
of astonishing fruit, the whole large and coppery enough for a small
warming-pan. Feeling delicate about depriving him of such valuable
relics, I accepted the earrings alone, and was obliged to depart, some-
what abruptly, when my friend stuck the warming-pan in the bosom
of his night-gown, viewing it with much complacency, and, perhaps,
some tender memory, in that rough heart of his, for the comrade he
had lost.

Observing that the man next him had left his meal untouched, I of-
fered the same service I had performed for his neighbor, but he shook
his head.

"Thank you, ma'am; I don't think I'll ever eat again, for I'm shot in
the stomach. But I'd like a drink of water, if you aint too busy."

I rushed away, but the water-pails were gone to be refilled, and it
was some time before they reappeared. I did not forget my patient
patient, meanwhile, and, with the first mugful, hurried back to him.
He seemed asleep; but something in the tired white face caused me

to listen at his lips for a breath. None came. I touched his forehead; it was cold: and then I knew that, while he waited, a better nurse than I had given him a cooler draught, and healed him with a touch. I laid the sheet over the quiet sleeper, whom no noise could now disturb; and, half an hour later, the bed was empty. It seemed a poor requital for all he had sacrificed and suffered,—that hospital bed, lonely even in a crowd; for there was no familiar face for him to look his last upon; no friendly voice to say, Goodbye; no hand to lead him gently down into the Valley of the Shadow; and he vanished, like a drop in that red sea upon whose shores so many women stand lamenting. For a moment I felt bitterly indignant at this seeming carelessness of the value of life, the sanctity of death; then consoled myself with the thought that, when the great muster roll was called, these nameless men might be promoted above many whose tall monuments record the barren honors they have won.

All having eaten, drank, and rested, the surgeons began their rounds; and I took my first lesson in the art of dressing wounds. It wasn't a festive scene, by any means; for Dr. P., whose aide I constituted myself, fell to work with a vigor which soon convinced me that I was a weaker vessel, though nothing would have induced me to confess it then. He had served in the Crimea, and seemed to regard a dilapidated body very much as I should have regarded a damaged garment; and, turning up his cuffs, whipped out a very unpleasant looking housewife, cutting, sawing, patching and piecing, with the enthusiasm of an accomplished surgical seamstress; explaining the process, in scientific terms, to the patient, meantime; which, of course, was immensely cheering and comfortable. There was an uncanny sort of fascination in watching him, as he peered and probed into the mechanism of those wonderful bodies, whose mysteries he understood so well. The more intricate the wound, the better he liked it. A poor private, with both legs off, and shot through the lungs, possessed more attractions for him than a dozen generals, slightly scratched in some "masterly retreat"; and had anyone appeared in small pieces, requesting to be put together again, he would have considered it a special dispensation.

The amputations were reserved till the morrow, and the merciful magic of ether was not thought necessary that day, so the poor souls had to bear their pains as best they might. It is all very well to talk of the patience of woman; and far be it from me to pluck that feather from her cap, for, heaven knows, she isn't allowed to wear many; but the patient endurance of these men, under trials of the flesh, was truly wonderful. Their fortitude seemed contagious, and scarcely a cry escaped them, though I often longed to groan for them, when pride kept their white lips shut, while great drops stood upon their foreheads, and the bed shook with the irrepressible tremor of their tortured bodies. One or two Irishmen anathematized the doctors with the frankness of their nation, and ordered the Virgin to stand by them, as if she had been the wedded Biddy to whom they could administer the poker, if she didn't; but, as a general thing, the work went on in silence, broken only by some quiet request for roller, instruments, or plaster, a sigh from the patient, or a sympathizing murmur from the nurse.

It was long past noon before these repairs were even partially made; and, having got the bodies of my boys into something like order, the next task was to minister to their minds, by writing letters to the anxious souls at home; answering questions, reading papers, taking possession of money and valuables; for the eighth commandment was reduced to a very fragmentary condition, both by the blacks and whites, who ornamented our hospital with their presence. Pocket books, purses, miniatures, and watches, were sealed up, labelled, and handed over to the matron, till such times as the owners thereof were ready to depart homeward or campward again. The letters dictated to me, and revised by me, that afternoon, would have made an excellent chapter for some future history of the war; for, like that which Thackeray's "Ensign Spooney" wrote his mother just before Waterloo, they were "full of affection, pluck, and bad spelling"; nearly all giving lively accounts of the battle, and ending with a somewhat sudden plunge from patriotism to provender, desiring "Marm," "Mary Ann," or "Aunt Peters," to send along some pies, pickles, sweet stuff, and apples, "to yourn in haste," Joe, Sam, or Ned, as the case might be.

My little Sergeant insisted on trying to scribble something with his left hand, and patiently accomplished some half dozen lines of hieroglyphics, which he gave me to fold and direct, with a boyish blush, that rendered a glimpse of "My Dearest Jane," unnecessary, to assure me that the heroic lad had been more successful in the service of Commander-in-Chief Cupid than that of Gen. Mars; and a charming little romance blossomed instanter in Nurse Periwinkle's romantic fancy, though no further confidences were made that day, for Sergeant fell asleep, and, judging from his tranquil face, visited his absent sweetheart in the pleasant land of dreams.

At five o'clock a great bell rang, and the attendants flew, not to arms, but to their trays, to bring up supper, when a second uproar announced that it was ready. The newcomers woke at the sound; and I presently discovered that it took a very bad wound to incapacitate the defenders of the faith for the consumption of their rations; the amount that some of them sequestered was amazing; but when I suggested the probability of a famine hereafter, to the matron, that motherly lady cried out: "Bless their hearts, why shouldn't they eat? It's their only amusement; so fill everyone, and, if there's not enough ready tonight, I'll lend my share to the Lord by giving it to the boys." And, whipping up her coffee-pot and plate of toast, she gladdened the eyes and stomachs of two or three dissatisfied heroes, by serving them with a liberal hand; and I haven't the slightest doubt that, having cast her bread upon the waters, it came back buttered, as another large-hearted old lady was wont to say.

Then came the doctor's evening visit; the administration of medicines; washing feverish faces; smoothing tumbled beds; wetting wounds; singing lullabies; and preparations for the night. By twelve, the last labor of love was done; the last "goodnight" spoken; and, if any needed a reward for that day's work, they surely received it, in the silent eloquence of those long lines of faces, showing pale and peaceful in the shaded rooms, as we quitted them, followed by grateful glances that lighted us to bed, where rest, the sweetest, made our pillows soft, while Night and Nature took our places, filling that great house of pain with the healing miracles of Sleep, and his diviner brother, Death.

★   ★   ★

Oremus

GEORGE HENRY BOKER

An "oreumus" is an invitation to pray.

> We will not raise, O God! the formal prayer
>   Of broken heart and shattered nerve;
> Thou know'st our griefs, our wants, and whatsoe'er
>   Is best for those who serve.
>
> Before thy feet, in silence and in awe,
>   We open lay our cause and need;
> As brave men may, the patriot sword we draw,
>   But thine must be the deed.
>
> We have no pageantry to please thy eye,
>   Save marshaled men, who marching come
> Beneath thy gaze in armed panoply;
>   No music save the drum.

We have no altar builded in thy sight,
    From which the fragrant offerings rise,
Save this wild field of hot and bloody fight;
    These dead our sacrifice.

To this great cause the force of prayer is given,
    The wordless prayer of righteous will,
Before whose strength the ivory gates of heaven
    Fall open, and are still.

For we believe, within our inmost souls,
    That what men do with spirit sad,
To thee in one vast cloud of worship rolls—
    Rolls up, and makes thee glad.

O God! if reason may presume so far,
    We say our cause is also thine;
We read its truth in every flashing star,
    In every sacred line.

By thy commission freedom first was sent,
    To hold the tyrant's force at bay;
The chain that broke in Egypt was not meant
    To bind our shining day.

Freedom to all! in Thy great name we cry,
    And lift to heaven thy bloody sword;
Too long have we been blind in heart and eye
    To thy outspoken word.

Before the terrors of that battle-call,
    As flax before the gusty flame,
Down, down, the vanquished enemy shall fall,
    Stricken with endless shame!

Here let division cease. Join hand with hand,
    Join voice with voice; a general shout
Shall, like a whirlwind, sweep our native land,
    And purge the traitors out!

Fear not or faint not. God, who ruleth men,
    Marks where his noble martyrs lie;
They shall all rise beneath his smile again;
    His foes alone shall die.

1863

Mosby at Hamilton

MADISON CAWEIN

John S. Mosby was one of the Confederate guerillas who repeatedly vexed the Union
with his raids; this one occurred in March 1863.

Down Loudon Lanes, with swinging reins
    And clash of spur and sabre,
And bugling of the battle horn,
Six score and eight we rode at morn,
Six score and eight of Southern born,
    All tried in love and labor.

Full in the sun at Hamilton,
    We met the South's invaders;
Who, over fifteen hundred strong,
'Mid blazing homes had marched along
All night, with Northern shout and song
    To crush the rebel raiders.

Down Loudon Lanes, with streaming manes,
    We spurred in wild March weather;
And all along our war-scarred way
The graves of Southern heroes lay,
Our guide-posts to revenge that day,
    As we rode grim together.

Old tales still tell some miracle
    Of saints in holy writing—
But who shall say while hundreds fled
Before the few that Mosby led.

Unless the noblest of our dead
    Charged with us then when fighting?

While Yankee cheers still stunned our ears,
    Of troops at Harper's Ferry,
While Sheridan led on his Huns,
And Richmond rocked to roaring guns,
We felt the South still had some sons
    She would not scorn to bury.

★ ★ ★

Stonewall Jackson

HERMAN MELVILLE

Mortally wounded at Chancellorsville (May, 1863)

The Man who fiercest charged in fight,
    Whose sword and prayer were long—
        Stonewall!
    Even him who stoutly stood for Wrong,
How can we praise? Yet coming days
    Shall not forget him with this song.

Dead is the Man whose Cause is dead,
    Vainly he died and set his seal—
        Stonewall!
    Earnest in error, as we feel;
True to the thing he deemed was due,
    True as John Brown or steel.

Relentlessly he routed us;
    But we relent, for he is low—
        Stonewall!
    Justly his fame we outlaw; so
We drop a tear on the bold Virginian's bier,
    Because no wreath we owe.

"Let Us Cross Over the River": Jackson's Last Words

ANONYMOUS

"A few moments before his death, Stonewall Jackson called out in his delirium: 'Order A. P. Hill to prepare for action. Pass the infantry rapidly to the front. Tell Major Hawks . . .' Here the sentence was left unfinished. But, soon after, a sweet smile overspread his face, and he murmured quietly, with an air of relief: 'Let us cross over the river and rest under the shade of the trees.' These were his last words; and, without any expression of pain, or sign of struggle, his spirit passed away," writes the editor and Confederate veteran Henry M. Wharton.

Come, let us cross the river, and rest beneath the trees,
And list the merry leaflets at sport with every breeze;
Our rest is won by fighting, and Peace awaits us there.
Strange that a cause so blighting produces fruit so fair!

Come, let us cross the river, those that have gone before,
Crushed in the strife for freedom, await on yonder shore;
So bright the sunshine sparkles, so merry hums the breeze,
Come, let us cross the river, and rest beneath the trees.

Come, let us cross the river, the stream that runs so dark;
'Tis none but cowards quiver, so let us all embark.
Come, men with hearts undaunted, we'll stem the tide with ease,
We'll cross the flowing river, and rest beneath the trees.

Come, let us cross the river, the dying hero cried,
And God, of life the giver, then bore him o'er the tide.
Life's wars for him are over, the warrior takes his ease,
There, by the flowing river, at rest beneath the trees.

The Scout's Narration

ANONYMOUS

The story was published in Harper's Weekly *on January 9, 1864.*

It was in the bleak mountain country of East Tennessee; the evening was growing late, and the camp-fire was smouldering lower and lower, but we still sat round it, for the spell of the scout's marvellous gift of story-telling we were none of us willing to dissolve. Captain Charlie Leighton had been a lieutenant in a Michigan Battery at the commencement of the war, but a natural love of excitement and restlessness of soul had early prompted him to seek employment as a scout, in which he soon rose to unusual eminence. He is a man of much refinement, well educated, and of a "quick inventive brain." The tale I am about to relate is my best recollection of it as it fell from his lips, and if there is aught of elegance in its diction, as here presented, it is all his own. He had been delighting us with incidents of the war, most of which were derived from his own experience, when I expressed a desire to know something of his first attempt at scouting. He willingly assented, took a long pull at my brandy flask, and commenced his yarn; and I thought that I had never seen a handsomer man than Charlie Leighton the scout, as he carelessly lounged there, with the ruddy gleams of the dying camp-fire occasionally flickering over his strongly marked intelligent face, and his curling black hair waving fitfully in the night wind, which now came down from the mountain fresher and chillier.

★ ★ ★

It happened in Western Virginia, said he. I had been personally acquainted with our commander, General R., before the war commenced, and having intimated, a short time previous to the date of my story, that I desired to try my luck in the scouting service—of which a vast deal was required to counteract the guerrillas with which the Blue Ridge fairly teemed at that time—one night, late in the fall of the year, I was delighted to receive orders to report at his head-quarters. The general was a man of few words, and my instructions were brief.

"Listen," said he. "My only reliable scout (Mackworth) was killed last night at the lower ford; and General F. (the rebel commander) has his head-quarters at the Sedley Mansion on the Romney road."

"Very well," said I, beginning to feel a little queer.

"I want you to go to the Sedley Mansion," was the cool rejoinder.

"To go there! Why, it's in the heart of the enemy's position!" was my amazed ejaculation.

"Just the reason I want it done," resumed the general. "Listen: I attack tomorrow at daybreak. F. knows it, or half suspects it, and will mass either on the center or the left wing. I must know which. The task is thick with danger—regular life and death. Two miles from here, midway to the enemy's outposts, and six paces beyond the second mile-stone, are two rockets propped on the inside of a hollow stump. Mackworth placed them there yesterday. You are to slip to F.'s quarters tonight, learn what I want, and hurry back to the hollow stump. If he masses on the center, let off one rocket; if on the left, let off both. This duty, I repeat, abounds with danger. You must start immediately, and alone. Will you go?"

Everything considered, I think I voted in the affirmative pretty readily, but it required a slight struggle. Nevertheless, consent I did, and immediately left the tent to make ready.

It was near ten o'clock when, having received a few additional words of advice from the chief, I set forth on my perilous ride. The country was quite familiar to me, so I had little fear of losing my way, which was no inconsiderable advantage, I can tell you. Riding slowly at first, as soon as I had passed our last outpost, I put spurs to my horse (a glorious gray thoroughbred which the general had lent me for the occasion) and fled down the mountain at a breakneck pace. It was a cool, misty, uncertain night—almost frosty, and the country was wild and desolate. Mountains and ravines were the ruling features, with now and then that diversification of the broomy, irregular plateau, with which our mountain scenery is occasionally softened. I continued my rapid pace with but little caution until I arrived at the further extremity of one of these plateaux. Here I brought up sharply beside a block of granite, which I recognized as the second milestone. Dismounting, I proceeded to the hollow stump which the general had intimated, and finding the rockets there, examined them well to make sure of their efficiency—remounted, and was away again. But now I exercised much more caution in my movements. I rode more slowly, kept my horse on the turf at the edge of the road, in order to deaden the hoof-beats, and also shortened the chain of my sabre, binding the scabbard with my knee to prevent its jingling. Still I was not satisfied, but tore my handkerchief in two, and made fast to either heel the rowel of my spurs, which otherwise had a little tinkle of their own. Then I kept wide awake, with my eyes everywhere at once, in the hope of catching a glimpse of some clew or landmark—the glimmer of a camp-fire—a tent-top in the moonlight, which now began to shine faintly—or to hear the snort of a steed, the signal of a picket— anything to guide me or to give warning of the lurking foe. But no: if there had been any campfires they were dead; if there had been any tents they were struck. Not a sign—not a sound. Everything was quiet as the tomb.

The great mountains rose around me in their mantles of pine and hoods of mist, cheerless and repelling, as if their solitude had never been broken. The moon was driving through a weird and ragged sky, with something desolate and solemn in her haggard face that seemed like an omen of ill. And in spite of my efforts to be cheerful, I felt the iron loneliness and sense of danger creep through my flesh and touch the bones.

None but those who have actually experienced it can properly conceive of the apprehensions which throng the breast of him, howsoever brave, who knows himself to be alone in the midst of enemies who are *invisible*. The lion hunter of Abyssinia is encompassed with peril when he makes a pillow of his gun in the desert; and our own pioneer slumbers but lightly in his new cabin when he knows that the savage, whose monomania is vengeance, is prowling the forest that skirts his clearing. But the lion is not always hungry; and even the Indian may be conciliated. The hunter confronts his terrible antagonist with something deadlier than ferocity. The hand that levels and the eye that directs the rifled tube are nerved and fired by "the mind, the spirit, the Promethean spark," which, in this case, is indeed a "tower of strength." And the settler, with promises and alcohol, may have won the savage to himself. But to the solitary scout, at midnight, every turn of the road may conceal a finger on a hair trigger; every stump or bush may hold a foe in waiting. If he rides through a forest, it is only in the deepest shadow that he dares ride upright; and should he cross an open glade, where the starlight or moonshine drops freely, he crouches low on the saddle and hurries across, for every second he feels he may be a target. His senses are painfully alive, his faculties strained to their utmost tension.

By way of a little episode, I knew a very successful scout, who met his death, however, on the Peninsula, who would always require a long sleep immediately after an expedition of peril, if it had lasted but a few hours, and had apparently called forth no more muscular exertion than was necessary to sit the saddle. But, strange as it may seem, he would complain of overpowering fatigue, and immediately drop into the most profound slumber. And I have been informed that this is very frequently the case. I can only attribute it to the fact that, owing to the extreme and almost abnormal vivacity—I think of no better word—

of the faculties and senses, a man on these momentous occasions lives *twice or thrice as fast* as ordinarily; and the usual nerve-play and wakefulness of a day and night may thus be concentrated in the brief period of a few hours.

But to resume: I felt to the full this apprehension, this anxiety, this exhaustion, but the knowledge of my position and the issues at stake kept my blood flowing. I had come to the termination of the last plateau or plain, when the road led me down the side of a ravine, with a prospect ahead of nothing but darkness. Here, too, I was compelled to make more noise, as there was no sod for my horse to tread on, and the road was flinty and rough in the extreme. But I kept on as cautiously as possible, when suddenly, just at the bottom of the ravine, where the road began to ascend the opposite declivity, I came to a dead halt, confronted by a group of several horsemen, so suddenly that they seemed to have sprung from the earth like phantoms.

"Why do you return so slowly?" said one of them, impatiently. "What have you seen? Did you meet Colonel Craig?"

For a moment—a brief one—I gave myself up for lost; but, with the rapid reflection and keen invention which a desperate strait will sometimes superinduce, I grasped the language of the speaker, and formed my plan accordingly.

"Why do you return so slowly?" I had been sent somewhere, then.

"What have you seen?" I had been sent as a spy, then.

"Did you meet Colonel Craig?"

Oho! I thought, *I* will be Colonel Craig. No, I won't; I will be Colonel Craig's orderly. So I spoke out boldly:

"Colonel Craig met your messenger, who had seen nothing, and advised him to scout down the edge of the creek for half a mile. But he dispatched me, his orderly, to say that the enemy appear to be retreating in heavy masses. I am also to convey this intelligence to General F."

The troopers had started at the tones of a strange voice, but seemed to listen with interest and without suspicion.

"Did the colonel think the movement a real retreat, or only a feint?" asked the leader.

"He was uncertain," I replied, beginning to feel secure and roguish at the same time; "but he bade me to say that he would ascertain; and in an hour or two, if you should see one rocket up to the north there, you might conclude that the Yankees were retreating; if you should see two, then you might guess that they were not retreating, but stationary, with likelihood of remaining inert for another day."

"Good!" cried the rebel. "Do you know the way to the general's quarters?"

"I think I can find it," said I; "although I am not familiar with this side of the mountain."

"It's a mile this side of the Sedley Mansion," said the trooper. "You will find some pickets at the head of the road. You must there leave your horse, and climb the steep, when you will see a farmhouse, and fifteen minutes' walk toward it will bring you to the general's tent. I will go with you to the top of the road." And setting off at a gallop, the speaker left me to follow, which I hesitated not to do. Now, owing to their mistake, the countersign had not been thought of; but the next picket would not be likely to swallow the same dose of silence, and it was a lucky thing that the trooper led the way, for he would reach them first, and I would have a chance to catch the password from his lips. But he passed the picket so quickly, and dropped the precious syllables so indistinctly, that I only caught the first of them—"*Tally*"—while the remainder might as well have been Greek. *Tally, tally, tally* what? Good God! thought I, what can it be? *Tally, tally*—here I am almost up to the pickets—what can it be? Tallyho? No, that's English. Talleyrand? No, that's French. God help me! *Tally, tally*—

"Tallahassee!" I yelled with the inspiration of despair, as I dashed through the picket, and their levelled carbines sank toothless before that wonderful spell—the Countersign.

Blessing my stars, and without further mishap, I reached the place indicated by the trooper, which was high up on the side of the mountain—so high that clouds were forming in the deep valley below. Making my bridle fast, I clambered with some difficulty the still ascending slope on my left. Extraordinary caution was required. I almost crept towards the farmhouse, and soon perceived the tent of the rebel chief. A solitary guard was pacing between it and me—probably a hundred yards from the tent. Perceiving that boldness was my only plan, I sauntered up to him with as free-and-easy an air as I could muster.

"Who goes there?"

"A friend."

"Advance and give the countersign."

I advanced as near as was safe, and whispered "Tallahassee," with some fears as to the result.

"It's a d—d lie!" said the sentry, bringing his piece to the shoulder in the twinkle of an eye. "That answers the pickets, but not me." Click, click, went the rising hammer of the musket.

I am a dead man, thought I to myself; I am a dead man unless the cap fails. Wonderful, marvelous to relate, the cap *did* fail. The hammer dropped with a dull, harmless thug on the nipple. With the rapidity of thought and the stealth of a panther I glided forward and clutched his windpipe, forcing him to his knees, while the gun slipped to the ground. There was a fierce but silent struggle. The fellow could not speak, for my hand on his throat; but he was a powerful man, with a bowie-knife in his belt, if he could only get at it. But I got it first, hesitated a moment, and then drove it in his midriff to the hilt; and just at that instant his grinders closed on my arm and bit to the bone. Restraining a cry with the utmost difficulty, I got in another blow, this time home, and the jaws of the rebel flew apart with a start, for my blade had pressed the spring of the casket. Breathless from the struggle, I lay still to collect my thoughts, and listened to know if the inmates of the tent had been disturbed. But no; a light was shining through the canvas, and I could hear the low murmur of voices from within, which I had before noticed, and which seemed to be those of a number of men in earnest consultation. I looked at the corpse of the rebel remorsefully. The slouched hat had fallen off in the scuffle, and the pale face of the dead man was upturned to the scant moonlight. It was a young, noble, and exceedingly handsome face, and I noticed that the hands and feet were small and beautifully shaped; while everything about the body denoted it to have been the mansion of a gallant, gentle soul.

Was it a fair fight? did I attack him justly? thought I; and in the sudden contrition of my heart, I almost knelt to the ground. But the sense of my great peril recurred to me, stifling everything else, however worthy. I took off the dead man's overcoat and put it on, threw my cap away and replaced it with the fallen sombrero, and then dragged the corpse behind an outhouse of the farm that stood close by. Returning, I picked up the gun, and began to saunter up and down in a very commendable way indeed; but a sharp observer might have noticed a furtiveness and anxiety in the frequent glances I threw at the tent, which would not have augured well for my safety. I drew nearer and nearer to the tent at every turn, until I could almost distinguish the voices within; and presently after taking a most minute survey of the premises, I crept up to the tent, crouched down to the bottom of the trench, and listened with all my might. I could also see under the canvas. There were half a dozen rebel chieftains within, and a map was spread on a table in the center of the apartment. At length the consultation was at an end, and the company rose to depart. I ran back to my place, and resumed the watchful saunter of the guard with as indifferent an air as possible, drawing the hat well over my eyes.

The generals came outside of the tent and looked about a little
before they disappeared. Two of them came close to me and passed
almost within a yard of the sentry's body. But they passed on, and I
drew a deep breath of relief. A light still glimmered through the tent,
but presently that, too, vanished, and all was still. But occasionally I
would hear the voice of a fellow sentry, or perhaps the rattle of a halter
in some distant manger.

I looked at my watch. It was two o'clock—would be five before I
could fire the signal, and the attack was to be at daybreak.

Cautiously as before, I started on my return, reaching my horse
without accident. Here I abandoned the gun and overcoat, remounted
and started down the mountain. "Tallahassee" let me through the first
picket again, but something was wrong when I cantered down the ra-
vine to the troopers to whom I had been so confidentially dispatched
by Colonel Craig. Probably the genuine messenger, or perhaps the
gallant Colonel himself, had paid them a visit during my absence. At
any rate, I saw that something unpleasant was up, but resolved to make
the best of it.

"Tallahassee!" I cried, as I began to descend the ravine.

"Halt, or you're a dead man!" roared the leading trooper. "He's a
Yank!"

"Cut him down!" chimed in the others.

"Tallahassee! Tallahassee!" I yelled. And committing my soul to God,
I plunged down the gulley with sabre and revolver in either hand.

Click—bang! something grazed my cheek like a hot iron. *Click—
bang* again! something whistled by my ear with an ugly intonation.
And then I was in their midst, shooting, stabbing, slashing, and swear-
ing like a fiend. The rim of my hat flapped over my face from a sabre
cut, and I felt blood trickling down my neck. But I burst away from
them, up the banks of the ravine, and along the bare plateau, all the
time yelling "Tallahassee! Tallahassee!" without knowing why. I could
hear the alarm spread back over the mountain by halloos and drums,
and presently the clatter of pursuing steeds. But I fled onward like a
whirlwind, almost fainting from excitement and loss of blood, until I
reeled off at the hollow stump.

Fiz, fiz! one, two! and my heart leaped with exultation as the rush-
ing rockets followed each other in quick succession to the zenith, and
burst on the gloom in glittering showers. Emptying the remaining
tubes of my pistol at the nearest pursuer, now but fifty yards off, I was
in the saddle and away again without waiting to see the result of my
aim. It was a ride for life for a few moments; but I pressed as noble a
steed as ever spurned the footstool, and as we neared the Union lines

the pursuit dropped off. When I attained the summit of the first ridge of our position, and saw the day break faintly and rosily beyond the pine-tops and along the crags, the air fluttered violently in my face, the solid earth quivered beneath my feet, as a hundred cannon opened simultaneously above, below, and around me. Serried columns of men were swinging irresistibly down the mountain toward the opposite slope; flying field-pieces were dashing off into position; long lines of cavalry were haunting the gullies, or hovering like vultures on the steep; and the blare of bugles rose above the roar of the artillery with a wild, victorious peal. The two rockets had been answered, and the veterans of the Union were bearing down upon the enemy's weakened center like an avalanche of fire.

★ ★ ★

"So that is all," said the scout, rising and yawning. "The battle had begun in earnest. And maybe I didn't dine with General R. when it was over and the victory gained. Let's go to bed."

★ ★ ★

The Northern Invasion of Lee

ANONYMOUS

Confederate General Robert E. Lee's Army of Northern Virginia began its second "invasion" of the North, into Pennsylvania, in the beginning of June (the invasion would end on July 4, when Lee's troops began retreating to Virginia after the Battle of Gettysburg).

What means this invasion of Lee?
This Northern invasion by Lee?
Can anyone tell the extent of his lines ?
And why he cuts up such impertinent shines?
And where it is going? Has any one guessed?
On a frolic up North, or a raid in the West,
　　This great rebel army of Lee?

Some say that this army of Lee,
　　This half famished army of Lee,
Has invaded the North to secure the relief
Of old Pennsylvania's bread, butter, and beef,
And horses and blankets, and shirts, boots and shoes

And that her choice whisky they will not refuse,
    These tatterdemalions of Lee.

    Some guess that this army of Lee,
    This penniless army of Lee,
Is destined to play us some ruinous pranks,
To surprise Philadelphia, and clean out her banks
And Uncle Sam's mint, and their treasures untold
In "greenbacks" and nickel, and silver and gold,
    This vagabond army of Lee.

    And others will have it that Lee,
    Or a part of this army of Lee
Is moving North-West, and to Pittsburgh is bound,
To sack it, and blow up, or burn to the ground
Its factories of great guns, and gunboats—that all
Its warlike establishments surely must fall
    To the wrath of this army of Lee.

    And others are certain that Lee,
    And the savage battalions of Lee,
Are moving for Baltimore, there, in the name
Of pious Jeff Davis, to kindle the flame
Of a roaring rebellion—that this is the game,
The grand calculation and object and aim,
    Of these terrible Tartars of Lee.

    Some think that these movements of Lee,
    And these raids from the army of Lee,
Are only deceptions, the tricks and the show
Of a Northern invasion, to cheat "Fighting Joe,"
And then to push on, without pausing to rest.
To a junction with Bragg to recover the West,
    By these bold Carthaginians of Lee.

    Some think that abandoning Lee,
    The Cotton State Legions of Lee,
Care little for Richmond—that Davis & Co.
Have packed up their traps and are ready to go
To some safer refuge down South—that, in fine,
In Georgia they next will establish their shrine,
    And leave old Virginia to Lee.

But it is our impression that Lee,
　　And this wonderful army of Lee,
Are moving with Washington still in their eyes.
Looming up as the grand and desirable prize
Which will gain the alliance of England and France,
And bring in John Bull to assist in the dance,
　　Hand in hand with the army of Lee.

'Tis the last chance remaining to Lee,
　　And the last to this army of Lee,
And the last to Jeff Davis; for, sure as they fail
In this desperate game, nothing else will avail
To keep their frail craft and its masters adrift,
Or to rescue from ruin, disastrous and swift,
　　This grand rebel army of Lee.

All these Border State movements of Lee
　　Are but the diversions of Lee
To divide our main army which holds him at bay,
To divide it, and crush it, and open the way
To "Old Abe's" headquarters; for, these once possessed,
King Jeff will retrieve his misfortunes out West,
　　As he thinks, by this triumph of Lee.

But this Northern invasion of Lee,
　　With the loss of this army of Lee,
To Richmond so strongly invites us that way.
That we are expecting the tidings some day
That Dix has gone in, and that Davis has saddled
His steed, and has over the river skedaddled
　　To hunt up the army of Lee.

And we think in these movements of Lee,
　　With this hide-and-seek army of Lee,
The occasion has come when his game may be foiled,
And we hope that his schemes will be thoroughly spoiled
By our war-chiefs at Washington waiting the day
To bring our whole army en masse into play
　　On the broken battalions of Lee.

The Battle of Gettysburg

HOWARD GLYNDON

The days of June were nearly done;
The fields, with plenty overrun,
Were ripening 'neath the harvest sun,
    In fruitful Pennsylvania!

Sang buds and children—"All is well!"
When, sudden, over hill and dell,
The gloom of coming battle fell
    On peaceful Pennsylvania!

Through Maryland's historic land,
With boastful tongue and spoiling hand.
They burst—a fierce and famished band—
    Right into Pennsylvania!

In Cumberland's romantic vale
Was heard the plundered farmer's wail;
And every mother's cheek was pale.
    In blooming Pennsylvania!

With taunt and jeer, and shout and song.
Through rustic towns, they passed along—
A confident and braggart throng—
    Through frightened Pennsylvania!

The tidings startled hill and glen;
Up sprang our hardy Northern men,
And there was speedy travel then
    All into Pennsylvania!

The foe laughed out in open scorn;
For Union men were coward-born,
And then—they wanted all the corn
    That grew in Pennsylvania!

It was the languid hour of noon,
When all the birds were out of tune,
And Nature in a sultry swoon,
    In pleasant Pennsylvania!

When—sudden o'er the slumbering plain,
Red flashed the battle's fiery rain—

The volleying cannon shook again
    The hills of Pennsylvania!

Beneath that curse of iron hail,
That threshed the plain with flashing flail,
Well might the stoutest soldier quail,
    In echoing Pennsylvania!

Then, like a sudden, summer rain,
Storm-driven o'er the darkened plain,
They burst upon our ranks and main,
    In startled Pennsylvania!

"We felt the old, ancestral thrill,
From sire to son, transmitted still;
And fought for Freedom with a will,
    In pleasant Pennsylvania!

The breathless shock—the maddened toil—
The sudden clinch—the sharp recoil—
And we were masters of the soil,
    In bloody Pennsylvania!

To westward fell the beaten foe—
The growl of battle hoarse and low
Was heard anon, but dying slow,
    In ransomed Pennsylvania!

Sou' westward, with the sinking sun,
The cloud of battle, dense and dun,
Flashed into fire—and all was won
    In joyful Pennsylvania.

But ah! the heaps of loyal slain!
The bloody toil! the bitter pain!
For those who shall not stand again
    In pleasant Pennsylvania!

Back through the verdant valley lands,
East fled the foe, in frightened bands;
With broken swords and empty hands,
    Out of Pennsylvania!

How Are You, General Lee?

ANONYMOUS

Of General Lee, the Rebel chief, you all perhaps do know
How he came North a short time since to spend a month or so;
But soon he found the climate warm, although a Southern man,
And quickly hurried up his cakes, and toddled home again.

Chorus—How are you, General Lee? it is; why don't you longer stay?
          How are your friends in Maryland and Pennsylvania?

Jeff Davis met him coming back; "Why, General Lee," he said,
"What makes you look and stagger so? There's whiskey in
     your head."
"Not much, I think," says General Lee. "No whiskey's there, indeed;
What makes me feel so giddy is, I've taken too much Meade!"

Chorus—How are you, General Lee? it is; why don't you longer stay?
          How are your friends in Maryland and Pennsylvania?

"But you seem ill, yourself, dear Jeff. You look quite sad enough;
I think, while I've been gone, Old Abe has used you rather rough."
"Well, yes, he has, and that's a fact; it makes me feel downcast,
For they've bothered us at Vicksburg, so 'tis *Granted* them at last."

Chorus—Then, how are you, Jeff Davis? What is it makes you sigh?
          How are your friends at Vicksburg and in Mississippi—i?

"Yes, Vicksburg they have got quite sure, and Richmond soon
     they'll take;
At Port Hudson, too, they have some *Banks* I fear we cannot break:
While Rosecrans, in Tennessee, swears he'll our army flog,
And prove if Bragg's a terrier good, Holdfast's a better dog."

Chorus—How are you, Jeff Davis? Would you not like to be
          A long way out of Richmond and the Confederacy?

For with "Porter" on the river, and "Meade" upon the land,
I guess you'll find that these mixed drinks are more than you can
     stand.

A Midnight Scene at Vicksburg

Horace B. Durant

The author was serving in Union General U. S. Grant's Company A, One Hundredth Regiment P.V., First Division Ninth Army Corps, besieging Vicksburg, the Southern stronghold on the Mississippi. The poem was composed or published June 21, 1863; Vicksburg was taken on July 4.

By Mississippi's mighty tide, our camp-fires flick'ring glow,
O'er weary, tented, slumb'ring men, are burning dim and low;
Calm be their rest beneath the shade of bending forest bough,
And soft the night-wind as it creeps across the dreamer's brow;
The hot glare that tomorrow shines within this Southern land
May drink its draught of crimson life that stains the burning sand;
And some, alas! of this brave band their mortal course shall run,
And be but ghastly, mould'ring clay ere sets another sun.
'Tis midnight lone. The moon has climbed high up the eastern
    steeps.
While in her holy, pensive gaze the trembling dewdrop weeps;
Across the river's moaning flow, the bold, gray bluffs arise,
Like banks of rugged, slumb'ring clouds against the sapphire skies;
There Vicksburg stands upon the slope and on the frowning height,
While spire and dome gleam strangely out upon the fearful night.
Ay, there is fear within the gloom, such fear as guilt may know,
When it has drawn upon its crimes the swift, avenging blow.
There comes no slumber to the eyes that gaze with horror dread
Upon the upturned, frightful face of all the mangled dead.
There is no peace to those who list the shriek of woe and pain
That, never ceasing, rises from the weeping and the slain.
Proud one, thy hour of doom is traced upon the burning wall,
And leaguered round with armed hosts, thy boasted might shall fall.
See, where the smoke of battle hangs, above the water's breast!
See how it wreathes the trodden height and winds along their crest!
Around, above, both friend and foe, the dead, the dying—all,
It floats and wraps the dreadful scene in one vast funeral pall!
Look there, that lightning flash, close by the lurid, winding shore!
See how the flaming shell mounts up! Hark to the awful roar!
The shell, up higher, higher still; the zenith reached at last,
Down, down it goes, with fiery curve, in thunder bursts, 'tis past;
Another—there, and there, with vengeful scream, and orb of fire,
They circle through the skies! Look there! it bursts above the spire!

List! list! Do ye not hear that cry, that shrieking comes away
Where fell that dreadful, burning bolt, to mangle and to slay?
Did you not hear that horrid crash of shivered timbers then,
As bursting down through roof and house, 'mongst women,
    children, men.
Upon the cowering throng it fell, and with sulphurous breath,
Spread fiery ruin all around within that house of death?
The ramparts answer. Flash on flash run all along their line,
And many a gleaming, hissing track athwart the heavens shine;
'Tis all in vain; their shot and shell fall short of every mark;
Or, wildly erring, sullen plunge beneath the waters dark.
'Tis all in vain; our marksmen true, with an unerring aim,
Behind their very ramparts lie, and bathe them red in flame;
No foeman bold above those works may show his daring form;
Down sentry, gunner, soldier, go beneath that leaden storm!
Thou frowning battlement, Rebellion's only, fondest trust,
With all their hopes, thy stubborn strength must topple to the dust;
These waters, mingling from afar, as they sweep to the sea,
Proclaim that they must still unite, that they must still be free!
The time shall come when these proud hills no more shall quake
    with dread;
Beneath their peaceful breast shall lie the heaps of gory dead;
Redeemed from slavery's blighting curse, the battle's war shall cease,
And all Columbia's broad domain shall smile in golden peace.

★ ★ ★

Opening of the Mississippi

R. H. CHITTENDEN

The author, who composed the celebratory poem on July 7, 1863, after Vicksburg's fall before Union forces, was a captain in the First Wisconsin Cavalry.

Hail, Father of Waters! again thou art free!
And miscreant treason hath vainly enchained thee;
Roll on, mighty river, and bear to the sea
The praises of those who so gallantly gained thee!
    From fountain to ocean, from source to the sea,
    The west is exulting: "Our River is free."

Fit emblem of Freedom! thy home is the North!
And thou wert not forgot by the mother that bore thee;
From snows everlasting thou chainless burst forth,
And chainless we solemnly swore to restore thee!
  O'er river and prairie, o'er mountain and lea,
   The North is exulting: "Our River is free!"

'Twas midnight—in secret the traitor conclave
Had sworn: "We will throw off the bonds that unite us:
Our king shall be cotton, our watchword be slave!"
What ghostly intruder hath come to affright us!
  "I'm the god of the river, from source to the sea,
   I bear proudly onward the flag of the free!"

"Accursed is your treason—no power can break
The bond with which God hath united the nation,
And, thrice perjured ingrates, well may ye quake
At the certain approach of your dark condemnation!
  So long as my waters flow south to the sea
   Shall the flag of the Union float over the free!"

Glad River, thy bosom doth gratefully swell
Toward the heroes who bravely have fought to regain thee,
And proudly thou bearest them onward where dwell
Their comrades, who, crescent crowned, fight to retain thee!
  But hark! what echo comes over the sea?
   'Tis the Nation exulting: "Our River is free!"

★ ★ ★

The Swamp Angel

T. N. J.

The Union Army's Parrott Rifle sent 150-pound bombs into Charleston, South Carolina, on August 12, 1863.

> "The large Parrott used in bombarding Charleston from
> the marshes of James Island is called the Swamp Angel."
> —A Soldier's Letter

Down in the land of rebel Dixie,
Near to the hot-bed of treason,

Five miles away from Charleston,
Amid the sands of James Island,
Swept by the tides of the ocean,
Is the Swamp Angel.
                              Can parrot,
With plumage as black as a raven,
And scream unlike her tropical sisters'—
A hundred-pounder, with terrible voice!—
Be called bird or angel?
                              She's for Freedom,
And Uncle Sam! synonymous terms;
An angel of vengeance and not of mercy,
Come to execute wrath upon the city
Whence sprang secession.

At night this angel raiseth her voice,
And her cry is "woe," and not "rejoice."
She sendeth far her meteor shell,
And it soareth up as if to dwell
With the twinkling stars in the fadeless blue;
There poiseth itself for the mighty blow,
Then downward shoots like a bolt from God:
Crushes the dwelling and crimsons the sod!
Fire leaps out from its iron heart,
Rives the defences of treason apart,
Till ruin spreads her sulphur pall
O'er shattered tower and crumbling wall;
And fearful crowds from the city fly,
Seeing the day of her doom is nigh!

O ye who herd with traitors!—say,
Is this the dawn of that promised day
Your poets sung and your prophets told?
Is this age of iron your age of gold?
For tins did ye rouse the Southern hate,
To rend the Union strong and great?
And build on the low Palmetto's shore
An empire proud for evermore—
And shut in the face of the North your door?

Hear ye in the Angel the Northern call,
Thundered on Sumter's broken wall,

Echoed in Charleston's silent street,
Shouted in Treason's proud retreat:

"Freemen must share with you the land!
Choose olive leaf—or blazing brand;
Choose peaceful Commerce's flag of stars,
Or rifled guns and monitors!

"By you were words of treason spoken,
By you the nation's peace was broken;
The first gun fired whose startling jar
Sent through the land the shock of war!

Hear truth by Gospel trumpet blown—
Shall ye not reap as ye have sown?
Thistles for thistles, tares for tares,
The whirlwind's breath—a rain of snares!

"The avenging Angel rides the blast—
You fired the first gun—we'll fire the last!"

★ ★ ★

"I am monarch of all I survey"

ANONYMOUS

The editor Frank Moore writes that the poem pretends to be in the voice of the Confederate raider John Morgan "on surveying his solitary abode in his cell in the Ohio Penitentiary at Columbus." General Morgan and his men raided Ohio in the summer of 1863 before Morgan was captured in late July and imprisoned. He escaped in November.

I am monarch of all I survey,
    My right there is none to dispute;
Naked walls, a stone floor, a tin tray.
    Iron spoon, checkered pants and clean suit.

I am out of Jeff Davis's reach,
    I must finish my journey in stone,
Never hear a big secession speech—
    I start at the sound of my own.

O solitude! strange are the fancies
    Of those who see charms in thy face;
Better dwell in the midst of the Yankees,
    Than reign in this horrible place.

Ye steeds that have made me your sport,
    Convey to this desolate cell
Some cordial, endearing report
    Of the thefts I have practiced so well.

Horse-stealing, bridge-burning, and fight,
    Divinely bestowed upon man;
Oh! had I the wings of a kite,
    How soon would I taste you again!

My sorrows I then might assuage
    In the work of destruction and raiding;
Might laugh at the wisdom of age,
    Nor feel the least pang of upbraiding.

Rebellion! what music untold
    Resides in that heavenly word!
It helps me to silver and gold,
    And all that the earth can afford.

But the sweet sound of burning and plunder
    These prison-walls never yet heard,
Never echoed the chivalry's thunder,
    Nor mocked at the Union's grand bird.

How fleet is a glance of the mind
    Compared with the speed of my flight;
But Shackelford came up behind,
    So I found 'twas no use to fight.

The Buckeyes that gave me a race,
    My form with indifference see;
They are so light of foot on the chase,
    Their coolness is shocking to me.

When I think of my dear native land,
    I confess that I wish I was there;
Confound these hard stone walls at hand,
    And my bald pate, all shaven of hair.

My friends, do they now and then send
    A wish or a thought after me?

Like Burbeck, that quick-coming friend?
    For a friend in need truly was he.

But the sea-fowl is gone to her rest,
    The beast is laid down in his lair;
Yet not like John Morgan unblest,
    As I to my straw bed repair.

★ ★ ★

The Guerillas

S. Teackle Wallis

Wallis was a lawyer from Baltimore. "It may add something to the interest with which these stirring lines will be read," writes the editor Frank Moore, "to know that they were composed within the walls of a Yankee Bastille. They reach us in manuscript, through the courtesy of a returned prisoner."

Awake and to horse, my brothers!
    For the dawn is glimmering gray,
And hark! in the crackling brushwood
    There are feet that tread this way.

"Who cometh?" "A friend." "What tidings?"
    "O God! I sicken to tell;
For the earth seems earth no longer,
    And its sights are sights of hell!

"From the far-off conquered cities
    Comes a voice of stifled wail,
And the shrieks and moans of the houseless
    Ring out, like a dirge on the gale.

"I've seen from the smoking village
    Our mothers and daughters fly;
I've seen where the little children
    Sank down in the furrows to die.

"On the banks of the battle-stained river
    I stood as the moonlight shone,
And it glared on the face of my brother,
    As the sad wave swept him on.

"Where my home was glad, are ashes,
    And horrors and shame had been there,
For I found on the fallen lintel
    This tress of my wife's torn hair!

"They are turning the slaves upon us,
    And with more than the fiend's worst art,
Have uncovered the fire of the savage,
    That slept in his untaught heart!

"The ties to our hearths that bound him,
    They have rent with curses away,
And maddened him, with their madness,
    To be almost as brutal as they.

"With halter, and torch, and Bible,
    And hymns to the sound of the drum,
They preach the gospel of murder,
    And pray for lust's kingdom to come.

"To saddle! to saddle! my brothers!
    Look up to the rising sun,
And ask of the God who shines there,
    Whether deeds like these shall be done!

"Wherever the vandal cometh,
    Press home to his heart with your steel,
And when at his bosom you can not,
    Like the serpent, go strike at his heel.

"Through thicket and wood, go hunt him,
    Creep up to his camp-fire side,
And let ten of his corpses blacken
    Where one of our brothers hath died.

"In his fainting, foot-sore marches,
    In his flight from the stricken fray,
In the snare of the lonely ambush,
    The debts we owe him, pay.

"In God's hand alone is vengeance,
    But he strikes with the hands of men,
And his blight would wither our manhood,
    If we smite not the smiter again.

"By the graves where our fathers slumber,
　　By the shrines where our mothers prayed,
By our homes, and hopes, and freedom,
　　Let every man swear on his blade,

"That he will not sheathe nor stay it,
　　Till from point to hilt it glow
With the flush of Almighty vengeance,
　　In the blood of the felon foe."

They swore—and the answering sunlight
　　Leaped red from their lifted swords,
And the hate in their hearts made echo
　　To the wrath in their burning words.

There's weeping in all New England,
　　And by Schuylkill's banks a knell,
And the widows there and the orphans,
　　How the oath was kept, can tell.

★　★　★

Barbara Frietchie

JOHN GREENLEAF WHITTIER

Up from the meadows rich with corn,
Clear in the cool September morn,

The clustered spires of Frederick stand
Green-walled by the hills of Maryland.

Round about them orchards sweep,
Apple and peach tree fruited deep,

Fair as the garden of the Lord
To the eyes of the famished rebel horde,

On that pleasant morn of the early fall
When Lee marched over the mountain wall,—

Over the mountains winding down,
Horse and foot, into Frederick town.

Forty flags with their silver stars,
Forty flags with their crimson bars,

Flapped in the morning wind: the sun
Of noon looked down, and saw not one.

Up rose old Barbara Frietchie then,
Bowed with her fourscore years and ten;

Bravest of all in Frederick town,
She took up the flag the men hauled down;

In her attic window the staff she set,
To show that one heart was loyal yet.

Up the street came the rebel tread,
Stonewall Jackson riding ahead.

Under his slouched hat left and right
He glanced: the old flag met his sight.

"Halt!"—the dust-brown ranks stood fast.
"Fire!"—out blazed the rifle-blast.

It shivered the window, pane and sash;
It rent the banner with seam and gash.

Quick, as it fell, from the broken staff
Dame Barbara snatched the silken scarf;

She leaned far out on the window sill,
And shook it forth with a royal will.

"Shoot, if you must, this old gray head,
But spare your country's flag," she said.

A shade of sadness, a blush of shame,
Over the face of the leader came;

The nobler nature within him stirred
To life at that woman's deed and word:

"Who touches a hair of yon gray head
Dies like a dog! March on!" he said.

All day long through Frederick street
Sounded the tread of marching feet:

All day long that free flag tost
Over the heads of the rebel host.

Ever its torn folds rose and fell
On the loyal winds that loved it well;

And through the hill-gaps sunset light
Shone over it with a warm goodnight.

Barbara Frietchie's work is o'er,
And the Rebel rides on his raids no more.

Honor to her! and let a tear
Fall, for her sake, on Stonewall's bier.

Over Barbara Frietchie's grave
Flag of Freedom and Union, wave!

Peace and order and beauty draw
Round thy symbol of light and law;

And ever the stars above look down
On thy stars below in Frederick town!

★ ★ ★

A Negro-Volunteer Song

ANONYMOUS

According to its editor, Frank Moore, this song was written by a private in Company A,
Fifty-Fourth (colored) Regiment, Massachusetts Volunteers.

(Air— "Hoist up the Flag")

Fremont told them when the war it first begun,
How to save the Union, and the way it should be done;
But Kentucky swore so hard, and old Abe he had his fears,
Till every hope was lost but the colored volunteers;

Chorus—O, give us a flag, all free without a slave;
　　　　　We'll fight to defend it as our fathers did so brave;
　　　　　The gallant Comp'ny "A" will make the Rebels dance,
　　　　　And we'll stand by the Union if we only have a chance.

McClellan went to Richmond with two hundred thousand brave;
He said "keep back the niggers," and the Union he would save.
Little Mac he had his way, still the Union is in tears,
Now they call for the help of the colored volunteers.

Chorus—O, give us a flag, all free without a slave; &c.

Old Jeff, says he'll hang us if we dare to meet him armed,—
A very big thing, but we are not at all alarmed,—
For he first has got to catch us, before the way is clear,
And "that is what's the matter" with the colored volunteer.

Chorus—O, give us a flag, all free without a slave; &c.

So rally, boys, rally, let us never mind the past.
We had a hard road to travel, but our day is coming fast;
For God is for the Right, and we have no need to fear;
The Union must be saved by the colored volunteer.

Chorus—O, give us a flag, all free without a slave; &c.

★ ★ ★

Charge of the Mule Brigade

Anonymous

"On the night of October 28, 1863, when [Union] General Geary's division of the Twelfth Corps repulsed the attacking forces of Longstreet at Wautuchie, Tenn., a number of mules, affrighted by the noise of battle, dashed into the ranks of Hampton's Legion, causing much dismay among the rebels, and compelling many of them to fall back under a supposed charge of cavalry. Captain Thomas H. Elliott, of General Geary's staff, gives the following rendition of the incident, which he gleaned from an interior contemporary. Its authorship is not known," writes the editor Frank Moore.

I.
Half a mile, half a mile,
    Half a mile onward,
Right toward the Georgia troops,
    Broke the two hundred.
"Forward the Mule Brigade,"
"Charge for the Rebs!" they neighed;
Straight for the Georgia troops
    Broke the two hundred.

II.
"Forward, the Mule Brigade!"
Was there a mule dismayed?
Not when the long ears felt
    All their ropes sundered;

Theirs not to make reply;
Theirs not to reason why;
Theirs but to make them fly.
On! to the Georgia troops,
 Broke the two hundred.

III.

Mules to the right of them,
Mules to the left of them,
Mules behind them,
 Pawed, neighed, and thundered
Breaking their own confines,
Breaking through Longstreet's lines,
Into the Georgia troops
 Stormed the two hundred.

IV.

Wild all their eyes did glare,
Whisked all their tails in air,
Scatt'ring the chivalry there,
 While all the world wondered.
Not a mule back bestraddled,
Yet how they all skeddadled;
 Fled every Georgian,
Unsabred, unsaddled,
 Scattered and sundered,
How they were routed there
 By the two hundred.

V.

Mules to the right of them,
Mules to the lea of them,
Mules behind them
 Pawed, neighed, and thundered;
Followed by hoof and head,
Full many a hero fled,
Fain in the last ditch dead,
Back from an "ass's jaw,"
All that was left of them,
 Left by the two hundred.

VI.

When can their glory fade?
O! the wild charge they made!

All the world wondered.
Honor the charge they made,
Honor the Mule Brigade,
    Long-eared two hundred.

★   ★   ★

My Dream: To Thomas Carlyle

WILLIAM C. BENNETT

Bennett was a London poet who mocked the British historian Thomas Carlyle for equating slavery and work.

Peter of the North to Paul of the South—"Paul, you
unaccountable scoundrel, I find you hire your servants
for life, not by the month or year, as I do."
—Thomas Carlyle's "American Iliad in a Nutshell,"
    Macmillan's Magazine, August 1863

O Thomas of Chelsea! I've dreamed such a dream!
    I've been reading that dialogue, more smart than grave,
In which you've so settled the case, as you deem,
    Of North against South, and of Whip versus Slave.
Excuse me—I wandered—I nodded—I dozed,
    And straight to your Eden of fetters I flew,
And scenes I saw stranger than you'd have supposed;
    Bless your stars, brother Thomas, those scenes were not true!

Yes, 'twas South-Carolina—'twas Charleston, no doubt—
    But changed—why has quite from my memory slipped—
For the whites now were "hired," as it straightway turned out,
    "For life," by the blacks, to be labored and whipped.
I've never been given, like you, to regard
    Men treated as beasts as a comical sight;
In the case, as it had been, of blacks, it seemed hard,
    And as hard it seemed now that the niggers were white.

But a negro, your namesake, was luckily by,
    And this sablest of sages, oh! how he did grin,
As I uttered my doublings. "They men like us! why
    The chattels! had they any black in their skin?

Were they not white all over? What, had I no eyes?
  They fitted for freedom!—why, where was their wool?"
He couldn't help sneering out lofty surprise
  That my brain could of such silly nonsense be full.

"To be worked, to be walloped for nothing," he said,
  "The eternities sent forth all whites—'twas their doom."
Just then an old graybeard was livelily led
  To the block—for an auction went on in the room;
And think how I stared! why, the chattel, alack!
  Yes, 'twas you—no mistake!—you put up there to sell!
You grumbled—whack! down came the thong on your back;
  Good lord! how you, Thomas, did wriggle and yell!

My black sage looked on with a sneering disdain,
  Stepped up to the block and examined your mouth;
Poked your ribs with his stick; you objected in vain—
  "Whites were made to be served so by blacks in the South."
A lively discussion around you arose,
  On the strength of your legs—on your age; thump on thump.
Tried to straighten you upright; one would tweak your nose;
  One hustled you down, just to see how you'd jump.

'Twas fun to their blackships, but Thomas, I've fears
  Your temper that moment was none of the best;
There was rage in your scowl; in your old eyes were tears;
  For it seems Mrs. Carlyle had just been sold West;
And what might, too, put some hard words in your mouth—
  Though it did not affect your black namesake the least—
Master Carlyle was "hired for life," right down South—
  Miss Carlyle had been ditto right away East.

So you didn't jump lively, and laugh as you ought.
  Though, cursed in a whisper, you tried to look gay,
But at last for a rice-swamp you, Thomas, were bought,
  Or "hired for life," as your sageship would say;
Rather "hired for death"—so I dared to suggest;
  But then, that's all right, as the world must have rice,
If lives of old whites raise the whitest and best,
  Why, we must have our crop, and we must pay the price.

You were handcuffed, and off to twelve hours a day
  In a sweltering swamp, with a smart overseer,

Sure, if you do any thing—speak, think, or pray,
    But as master allows, for that crime to pay dear:
A beast—every right of a man set at naught—
    Every power chained down—every feeling defied—
To exist for the labor for which you were bought,
    Till the memory of manhood has out of you died.

And as you went off, looking rueful enough,
    I couldn't help thinking, my sage, in my dream,
You perhaps might be taught in a school rather rough,
    On "hirings for life" to have views less extreme,
That when you've tried slavery's hell for awhile,
    The misery of millions won't seem a good joke,
A grin from the dullness of fools to beguile—
    And thinking this, Thomas, thank heaven! I awoke.

★ ★ ★

Music in Camp

JOHN R. THOMPSON

*Thompson (1823–1873) was an editor from Virginia who during the war promoted
in London the Southern cause.*

Two armies covered hill and plain,
    Where Rappahannock's waters
Ran deeply crimsoned with the stain
    Of battle's recent slaughters.

The summer clouds lay pitched like tents
    In meads of heavenly azure;
And each dread gun of the elements
    Slept in its hid embrasure.

The breeze so softly blew, it made
    No forest leaf to quiver;
And the smoke of the random cannonade
    Rolled slowly from the river.

And now, where circling hills looked down
    With cannon grimly planted,

O'er listless camp and silent town
　　The golden sunset slanted.

When on the fervid air there came
　　A strain—now rich, now tender;
The music seemed itself aflame
　　With day's departing splendor.

A Federal band, which, eve and morn,
　　Played measures brave and nimble,
Had just struck up, with flute and horn
　　And lively clash of cymbal.

Down flocked the soldiers to the banks,
　　Till, margined by its pebbles,
One wooded shore was blue with "Yanks,"
　　And one was gray with "Rebels."

Then all was still, and then the band,
　　With movement light and tricksy,
Made stream and forest, hill and strand,
　　Reverberate with "Dixie."

The conscious stream with burnished glow
　　Went proudly o'er its pebbles,
But thrilled throughout its deepest flow
　　With yelling of the Rebels.

Again a pause, and then again
　　The trumpets pealed sonorous,
And "Yankee Doodle" was the strain
　　To which the shore gave chorus.

The laughing ripple shoreward flew,
　　To kiss the shining pebbles;
Loud shrieked the swarming Boys in Blue
　　Defiance to the Rebels.

And yet once more the bugles sang
　　Above the stormy riot;
No shout upon the evening rang—
　　There reigned a holy quiet.

The sad, slow stream its noiseless flood
　　Poured o'er the glistening pebbles;

All silent now the Yankees stood,
    And silent stood the Rebels.

No unresponsive soul had heard
    That plaintive note's appealing,
So deeply "Home, Sweet Home" had stirred
    The hidden founts of feeling.

Or Blue or Gray, the soldier sees,
    As by the wand of fairy,
The cottage 'neath the live-oak trees,
    The cabin by the prairie.

Or cold or warm, his native skies
    Bend in their beauty o'er him;
Seen through the tear-mist in his eyes,
    His loved ones stand before him.

As fades the iris after rain,
    In April's tearful weather,
The vision vanished, as the strain
    And daylight died together.

But memory, waked by music's art
    Exprest in simplest numbers,
Subdued the sternest Yankee's heart,
    Made light the Rebel's slumbers.

And fair the form of Music shines,
    That bright, celestial creature,
Who still, 'mid War's embattled lines,
    Gave this one touch of Nature.

★ ★ ★

The War-Christian's Thanksgiving

GEORGE H. MILES

The author of this bitter satire, unmatched by anything even Mark Twain would later write, was from Baltimore.

Oh, God of battles! once again,
    With banner, trump, and drum,

And garments in the wine-press dyed,
　To give Thee thanks we come.

No goats or bullocks garlanded,
　Unto Thine altars go;
With brothers' blood, by brothers shed,
　Our glad libations flow,

From pest-house and from dungeon foul,
　Where, maimed and torn, they die,
From gory trench and charnel-house,
　Where, heap on heap, they lie.

In every groan that yields a soul,
　Each shriek a heart that rends,
With every breath of tainted air,
　Our homage, Lord, ascends.

We thank Thee for the sabre's gash,
　The cannon's havoc wild;
We bless Thee for the widow's tears,
　The want that starves her child!

We give Thee praise that Thou hast lit
　The torch, and fanned the flame;
That lust and rapine hunt their prey,
　Kind Father, in Thy name!

That, for the songs of idle joy
　False angels sang of yore,
Thou sendest War on earth—ill-will
　To men for evermore!

We know that wisdom, truth and right
　To us and ours are given;
That Thou hast clothed us with the wrath,
　To do the work of Heaven.

We know that plains and cities waste
　Are pleasant in Thine eyes—
Thou lov'st a hearthstone desolate,
　Thou lov'st a mourner's cries.

Let not our weakness fall below
　The measure of Thy will,
And while the press hath wine to bleed,
　Oh, tread it with us still!

Teach us to hate—as Jesus taught
   Fond fools, of yore, to love;
Give us Thy vengeance as our own—
   Thy pity, hide above!

Teach us to turn, with reeking hands,
   The pages of Thy Word,
And learn the blessed curses there,
   On them that sheathe the sword.

Where'er we tread may deserts spring,
   'Till none are left to slay;
And when the last red drop is shed,
   We'll kneel again—and pray!

★ ★ ★

The Color Sergeant

A. D. F. RANDOLPH

Poems of grieving by mothers, wives, and families were a genre in themselves, published in the thousands. This and the following four poems, published from 1863 to 1866, are particularly touching.

You say that in every battle
   No soldier was braver than he,
As, aloft in the roar and the rattle,
   He carried the flag of the free:
I knew, ah! I knew he'd ne'er falter,
   I could trust him, the dutiful boy.
My Robert was wilful—but Walter,
   Dear Walter, was ever a joy.

And if he was true to his mother,
   Do you think he his trust would betray,
And give up his place to another,
   Or turn from the danger away?
He knew while afar he was straying,
   He felt in the thick of the fight,
That at home his poor mother was praying
   For him and the cause of the right!

Tell me, comrade, who saw him when dying,
   What he said, what he did, if you can;
On the field in his agony lying,
   Did he suffer and die like a man?
Do you think he once wished he had never
Borne arms for the right and the true?
Nay, he shouted Our Country forever!
   When he died he was praying for you!

O my darling! my youngest and fairest,
   Whom I gathered so close to my breast;
I called thee my dearest and rarest,
   And thou wert my purest and best!
I tell you, O friend! as a mother,
   Whose full heart is breaking today,
The Infinite Father—none other—
   Can know what he's taken away!

I thank you once more for your kindness,
   For this lock of his auburn hair:
Perhaps 'tis the one I in blindness
   Last touched, as we parted just there!
When he asked, through his tears, should he linger
   From duty, I answered him, Nay:
And he smiled, as he placed on my finger
   The ring I am wearing today.

I watched him leap into that meadow;
   There, a child, he with others had played;
I saw him pass slowly the shadow
   Of the trees where his father was laid;
And there, where the road meets two others,
   Without turning he went on his way:
Once his face toward the foe—not his mother's
   Should unman him, or cause him delay.

It may be that some day your duty
   Will carry you that way again;
When the field shall be riper in beauty,
   Enriched by the blood of the slain;
Would you see if the grasses are growing
   On the grave of my boy? Will you see
If a flower, e'en the smallest, is blowing,
   And pluck it, and send it to me?

Don't think, in my grief, I'm complaining;
  I gave him, God took him, 'tis right;
And the cry of his mother remaining
  Shall strengthen his comrades in fight.
Not for vengeance, today, in my weeping,
  Goes my prayer to the Infinite Throne.
God pity the foe when he's reaping
  The harvest of what he has sown!

Tell his comrades these words of his mother:
  All over the wide land today,
The Rachels who weep with each other,
  Together in agony pray.
They know in their great tribulation,
  By the blood of their children outpoured.
We shall smite down the foes of the Nation,
  In the terrible day of the Lord.

★   ★   ★

A Mother's Story

Anonymous

Amid the throng that gathers where
The mail dispenses joy and care,
I saw a woeful woman stand,
A letter falling from her hand:

She spoke no word, she breathed no sigh;
Her bloodless cheek, her sad, fixed eye,
And pallid, quivering lips apart,
Showed hopeless grief had seized her heart.

I spoke—a word of kindness cheers
The heavy heart, and heaven-sent tears
Refresh the eye dry sorrow sears.

  "Ah! sir, my boy! my brave, bright boy!"
    In broken voice, she said;
  "My only son! my only joy!
    My brave, bright boy is dead!"

"Sorrow is sacred!" and the eye
That looks on grief is seldom dry:
I listened to her piteous moan,
Then followed to her dwelling lone,
Where sheltered from the biting cold,
She thus her simple story told:

"My gran'father, sir, for freedom died,
    On Eutaw's bloody plain;
My father left his youthful bride,
    And fell at Lundy's Lane.

"And when my boy, with burning brow,
    Told of the nation's shame—
How Sumter fell!—oh! how, sir, how
    Could blood like mine be tame!

"I blessed him; and I bade him go—
    Bade him our honor keep:
He proudly went to meet the foe;
    Left me to pray and weep.

"In camp—on march—of picket round—
    He did his equal share;
And still the call to battle found
    My brave boy always there.

"And when the fleet was all prepared
    To sail upon the main,
He all his comrades' feelings shared—
    But *fever scorched his brain!*

"He told the general: 'He would ne'er
    From toil or danger shrink,
But, though the waves he did not fear,
    It chilled his heart to think

"How drear the flowerless grave must be,
    Beneath the ocean's foam,
And that he knew 'twould comfort me
    To have him die at home.'

"They tell me that the general's eye
    With tears did overflow:
GOD BLESS THE BRAVE MAN!—with a sigh,
    He gave him leave to go.

"Quick down the vessel's side came he;
    Joy seemed to kill his pain;
'Comrades!' he cried, 'I yet shall see
    My mother's face again!'

"The boat came bounding o'er the tide;
    He sprang upon the strand:
God's will be done !—*my bright boy died,*
    His furlough in his hand!"

Ye, who this artless story read,
If Pity in your bosoms plead,
    And "Heaven has blessed your store"—
If broken-hearted woman, meek,
Can win your sympathy—go, seek
    That childless widow's door!

★ ★ ★

Driving Home the Cows

KATE PUTNAM OSGOOD

Out of the clover and blue-eyed grass
    He turned them into the river-lane;
One after another he let them pass,
    Then fastened the meadow-bars again.

Under the willows, and over the hill,
    He patiently followed their sober pace;
The merry whistle for once was still,
    And something shadowed the sunny face.

Only a boy! and his father had said
    He never could let his youngest go:
Two already were lying dead
    Under the feet of the trampling foe.

But after the evening work was done,
    And the frogs were loud in the meadow-swamp,
Over his shoulder he slung his gun
    And stealthily followed the foot-path damp.

Across the clover, and through the wheat,
　With resolute heart and purpose grim,
Though cold was the dew on his hurrying feet
　And the blind bat's flitting startled him.

Thrice since then had the lanes been white,
　And the orchards sweet with apple-bloom;
And now, when the cows came back at night,
　The feeble father drove them home.

For news had come to the lonely farm
　That three were lying where two had lain;
And the old man's tremulous, palsied arm
　Could never lean on a son's again.

The summer day grew cool and late.
　He went for the cows when the work was done;
But down the lane, as he opened the gate,
　He saw them coming one by one:

Brindle, Ebony, Speckle, and Bess,
　Shaking their horns in the evening wind;
Cropping the buttercups out of the grass —
　But who was it following close behind?

Loosely swung in the idle air
　The empty sleeve of army blue;
And worn and pale, from the crisping hair
　Looked out a face that the father knew.

For war's grim prisons will sometimes yawn,
　And yield their dead unto life again;
And the day that comes with a cloudy dawn
　In golden glory at last may wane.

The great tears sprang to their meeting eyes,
　For the heart must speak when the lips are dumb;
And under the silent evening skies,
　Together they followed the cattle home.

Killed at the Ford

HENRY WADSWORTH LONGFELLOW

This poem was first published in The Atlantic Monthly *in 1866; Longfellow said it was not based on an actual event.*

He is dead, the beautiful youth,
The heart of honor, the tongue of truth,
He, the life and light of us all,
Whose voice was blithe as a bugle-call,
Whom all eyes followed with one consent,
The cheer of whose laugh, and whose pleasant word,
Hashed all murmurs of discontent.

Only last night, as we rode along,
Down the dark of the mountain gap,
To visit the picket-guard at the ford,
Little dreaming of any mishap,
He was humming the words of some old song:
"Two red roses he had on his cap
And another he bore at the point of his sword."

Sudden and swift a whistling ball
Came out of a wood, and the voice was still;
Something I heard in the darkness fall,
And for a moment my blood grew chill;
I spake in a whisper, as he who speaks
In a room where some one is lying dead;
But he made no answer to what I said.

We lifted him up to his saddle again,
And through the mire and the mist and the rain
Carried him back to the silent camp,
And laid him as if asleep on his bed;
And I saw by the light of the surgeon's lamp
Two white roses upon his cheeks,
And one, just over his heart, blood-red!

And I saw in a vision how far and fleet
That fatal bullet went speeding forth,
Till it reached a town in the distant North,
Till it reached a house in a sunny street,

Till it reached a heart that ceased to beat
Without a murmur, without a cry;
And a bell was tolled, in that far-off town,
For one who had passed from cross to crown,
And the neighbors wondered that she should die.

1864

Cavalry Crossing a Ford

WALT WHITMAN

Whitman, the most renown poet of the war, who seemingly was able to catch more of its feelings and details in his long tumbling lines than all the other war-era poets together, not only described his experiences as a nurse in various Washington, D.C. hospitals, but traveled in his imagination to the soldiers on the battlegrounds and on the march.

A line in long array, where they wind betwixt green islands;
They take a serpentine course—their arms flash in the sun—
    hark to the musical clank;
Behold the silvery river—in it the splashing horses, loitering,
    stop to drink;
Behold the brown-faced men—each group, each person,
    a picture—the negligent rest on the saddles;
Some emerge on the opposite bank—others are just entering
    the ford—while,
Scarlet, and blue, and snowy white,
The guidon flags flutter gaily in the wind.

★ ★ ★

An Army Corps on the March

WALT WHITMAN

With its cloud of skirmishers in advance,
    With now the sound of a single shot, snapping like a whip,
        and now an irregular volley,

The swarming ranks press on and on, the dense brigades
   press on;
Glittering dimly, toiling under the sun—the dust-cover'd men,
In columns rise and fall to the undulations of the ground,
With artillery interspers'd—the wheels rumble, the horses sweat,
As the army corps advances.

★ ★ ★

A March in the Ranks Hard-Prest, and the Road Unknown

WALT WHITMAN

A march in the ranks hard-prest, and the road unknown;
A route through a heavy wood, with muffled steps in the
   darkness;
Our army foil'd with loss severe, and the sullen remnant
   retreating;
Till after midnight glimmer upon us, the lights of a dim-lighted
   building;
We come to an open space in the woods, and halt by the
   dim-lighted building;
'Tis a large old church at the crossing roads—'tis now an
   impromptu hospital;
Entering but for a minute, I see a sight beyond all the pictures
   and poems ever made:
Shadows of deepest, deepest black, just lit by moving candles
   and lamps,
And by one great pitchy torch, stationary, with wild red flame
   and clouds of smoke;
By these, crowds, groups of forms, vaguely I see, on the floor,
   some in the pews laid down;
At my feet more distinctly, a soldier, a mere lad, in danger of
   bleeding to death, (he is shot in the abdomen;)
I staunch the blood temporarily, (the youngster's face is white
   as a lily;)
Then before I depart I sweep my eyes o'er the scene, fain to
   absorb it all;
Faces, varieties, postures beyond description, most in obscurity,
      some of them dead; Surgeons operating, attendants holding
      lights, the smell of ether, the odor of blood;

The crowd, O the crowd of the bloody forms of soldiers—the
  yard outside also fill'd; Some on the bare ground, some on
  planks or stretchers, some in the death-spasm sweating;
An occasional scream or cry, the doctor's shouted orders or
  calls;
The glisten of the little steel instruments catching the glint of
  the torches;
These I resume as I chant—I see again the forms, I smell the
  odor;
Then hear outside the orders given, *Fall in, my men, Fall in;*
But first I bend to the dying lad—his eyes open—a half-smile
  gives he me;
Then the eyes close, calmly close, and I speed forth to the
  darkness,
Resuming, marching, ever in darkness marching, on in the
  ranks,
The unknown road still marching.

★ ★ ★

The Unknown Dead

Henry Timrod

*Timrod (1828–1867) was sometimes referred to as the "Poet Laureate of the
Confederacy."*

> The rain is plashing on my sill,
> But all the winds of heaven are still;
> And so, it falls with that dull sound
> Which thrills us in the churchyard ground,
> When the first spadeful drops like lead
> Upon the coffin of the dead.
> Beyond my streaming window-pane,
> I cannot see the neighboring vane,
> Yet from its old familiar tower
> The bell comes, muffled, through the shower.
> What strange and unsuspected link
> Of feeling touched has made me think—
> While with a vacant soul and eye
> I watch that gray and stony sky—
> Of nameless graves on battle plains,

Washed by a single winter's rains,
Where, some beneath Virginian hills,
And some by green Atlantic rills,
Some by the waters of the West,
A myriad unknown heroes rest.
Ah! not the chiefs who, dying, see
Their flags in front of victory,
Or, at their life-blood's noblest cost
Pay for a battle nobly lost,
Claim from their monumental beds
The bitterest tears a nation sheds.
Beneath yon lonely mound—the spot,
By all save some fond few forgot—
Lie the true martyrs of the fight,
Which strikes for freedom and for right.
Of them, their patriot zeal and pride,
The lofty faith that with them died,
No grateful page shall further tell
Than that so many bravely fell;
And we can only dimly guess
What worlds of all this world's distress,
What utter woe, despair, and dearth,
Their fate has brought to many a hearth.
Just such a sky as this should weep
Above them, always, where they sleep;
Yet, haply, at this very hour,
Their graves are like a lover's bower;
And Nature's self, with eyes unwet
Oblivious of the crimson debt
To which she owes her April grace,
Laughs gayly o'er their burial place.

★ ★ ★

A Sight in Camp in the Daybreak Gray and Dim

Walt Whitman

A sight in camp in the day-break grey and dim,
As from my tent I emerge so early, sleepless,
As slow I walk in the cool fresh air, the path near by the
   hospital tent,

Three forms I see on stretchers lying, brought out there,
    untended lying,
Over each the blanket spread, ample brownish woollen blanket,
Grey and heavy blanket, folding, covering all.

Curious, I halt, and silent stand;
Then with light fingers I from the face of the nearest, the first,
    just lift the blanket:
Who are you, elderly man so gaunt and grim, with well-grey'd
    hair, and flesh all sunken about the eyes?
Who are you, my dear comrade?
Then to the second I step—And who are you, my child and
    darling?
Who are you, sweet boy, with cheeks yet blooming?

Then to the third—a face nor child, nor old, very calm, as of
    beautiful yellow-white ivory;
Young man, I think I know you—I think this face of yours is the
    face of the Christ himself;
Dead and divine, and brother of all, and here again he lies.

★   ★   ★

An Occurrence at Owl Creek Bridge

AMBROSE BIERCE

This, the most anthologized short story about the war, was not published until 1890. It may remind some present-day readers of the fantastical tales of the Argentine Jorge Luis Borges.

I.

A man stood upon a railroad bridge in Northern Alabama, looking down into the swift waters twenty feet below. The man's hands were behind his back, the wrists bound with a cord. A rope loosely encircled his neck. It was attached to a stout cross-timber above his head, and the slack fell to the level of his knees. Some loose boards laid upon the sleepers supporting the metals of the railway supplied a footing for him, and his executioners—two private soldiers of the Federal army, directed by a sergeant, who in civil life may have been a deputy sheriff. At a short remove upon the same temporary platform was an officer in the uniform of his rank, armed. He was a captain. A sentinel at each end of the bridge stood with his rifle in the position known as "support," that is to say, vertical in front of the left shoulder, the hammer resting on the forearm thrown straight across the chest—a formal and unnatural position, enforcing an erect carriage of the body. It did not appear to be the duty of these two men to know what was occurring at the center of the bridge; they merely blockaded the two ends of the foot plank which traversed it.

Beyond one of the sentinels nobody was in sight; the railroad ran straight away into a forest for a hundred yards, then, curving, was lost to view. Doubtless there was an outpost further along. The other bank of the stream was open ground—a gentle acclivity crowned with a stockade of vertical tree trunks, loop-holed for rifles, with a single embrasure through which protruded the muzzle of a brass cannon commanding the bridge. Midway of the slope between bridge and fort were the spectators—a single company of infantry in line, at "parade rest," the butts of the rifles on the ground, the barrels inclining slightly backward against the right shoulder, the hands crossed upon the stock. A lieutenant stood at the right of the line, the point of his sword upon the ground, his left hand resting upon his right. Excepting the group of four at the center of the bridge not a man moved. The company faced the bridge, staring stonily, motionless. The sentinels, facing the banks of the stream, might have been statues to adorn the bridge. The captain stood with folded arms, silent, observing the work of his subordinates but making no sign. Death is a dignitary who, when he comes announced, is to be received with formal manifestations of respect, even by those most familiar with him. In the code of military etiquette silence and fixity are forms of deference.

The man who was engaged in being hanged was apparently about thirty-five years of age. He was a civilian, if one might judge from his dress, which was that of a planter. His features were good—a straight nose, firm mouth, broad forehead, from which his long, dark hair was combed straight back, falling behind his ears to the collar of his well-fitting frock coat. He wore a mustache and pointed beard but no whiskers; his eyes were large and dark gray and had a kindly expression which one would hardly have expected in one whose neck was in the hemp. Evidently this was no vulgar assassin. The liberal military code makes provision for hanging many kinds of people, and gentlemen are not excluded.

The preparations being complete, the two private soldiers stepped aside and each drew away the plank upon which he had been standing. The sergeant turned to the captain, saluted and placed himself immediately behind that officer, who in turn moved apart one pace.

These movements left the condemned man and the sergeant standing on the two ends of the same plank, which spanned three of the cross-ties of the bridge. The end upon which the civilian stood almost, but not quite, reached a fourth. This plank had been held in place by the weight of the captain; it was now held by that of the sergeant. At a signal from the former, the latter would step aside, the plank would tilt and the condemned man go down between two ties. The arrangement commended itself to his judgment as simple and effective. His face had not been covered nor his eyes bandaged. He looked a moment at his "unsteadfast footing," then let his gaze wander to the swirling water of the stream racing madly beneath his feet. A piece of dancing driftwood caught his attention and his eyes followed it down the current. How slowly it appeared to move! What a sluggish stream!

He closed his eyes in order to fix his last thoughts upon his wife and children. The water, touched to gold by the early sun, the brooding mists under the banks at some distance down the stream, the fort, the soldiers, the piece of drift—all had distracted him. And now he became conscious of a new disturbance. Striking through the thought of his dear ones was a sound which he could neither ignore nor understand, a sharp, distinct, metallic percussion like the stroke of a blacksmith's hammer upon the anvil; it had the same ringing quality. He wondered what it was, and whether immeasurably distant or near by—it seemed both. Its recurrence was regular, but as slow as the tolling of a death knell. He awaited each stroke with impatience and—he knew not why—apprehension. The intervals of silence grew progressively longer; the delays became maddening. With their greater infrequency the sounds increased in strength and sharpness. They hurt his ear like the thrust of a knife; he feared he would shriek. What he heard was the ticking of his watch.

He unclosed his eyes and saw again the water below him. "If I could free my hands," he thought, "I might throw off the noose and spring into the stream. By diving I could evade the bullets, and, swimming vigorously, reach the bank, take to the woods, and get away home. My home, thank God, is as yet outside their lines; my wife and little ones are still beyond the invader's farthest advance."

As these thoughts, which have here to be set down in words, were flashed into the doomed man's brain rather than evolved from it, the captain nodded to the sergeant. The sergeant stepped aside.

II.

Peyton Farquhar was a well-to-do planter, of an old and highly-respected Alabama family. Being a slave owner, and, like other slave

owners, a politician, he was naturally an original secessionist and ar-
dently devoted to the Southern cause. Circumstances of an imperious
nature which it is unnecessary to relate here, had prevented him from
taking service with the gallant army which had fought the disastrous
campaigns ending with the fall of Corinth, and he chafed under the
inglorious restraint, longing for the release of his energies, the larger
life of the soldier, the opportunity for distinction. That opportunity,
he felt, would come, as it comes to all in war time. Meanwhile he did
what he could. No service was too humble for him to perform in
aid of the South, no adventure too perilous for him to undertake if
consistent with the character of a civilian who was at heart a soldier,
and who in good faith and without too much qualification assented
to at least a part of the frankly villainous dictum that all is fair in love
and war.

One evening while Farquhar and his wife were sitting on a rustic
bench near the entrance to his grounds, a gray-clad soldier rode up to
the gate and asked for a drink of water. Mrs. Farquhar was only too
happy to serve him with her own white hands. While she was gone
to fetch the water, her husband approached the dusty horseman and
inquired eagerly for news from the front.

"The Yanks are repairing the railroads," said the man, "and are get-
ting ready for another advance. They have reached the Owl Creek
bridge, put it in order, and built a stockade on the other bank. The
commandant has issued an order, which is posted everywhere, declar-
ing that any civilian caught interfering with the railroad, its bridges,
tunnels, or trains, will be summarily hanged. I saw the order."

"How far is it to the Owl Creek bridge?" Farquhar asked.

"About thirty miles?"

"Is there no force on this side the creek?"

"Only a picket post half a mile out, on the railroad, and a single
sentinel at this end of the bridge."

"Suppose a man—a civilian and student of hanging—should elude
the picket post and perhaps get the better of the sentinel," said Farquhar,
smiling, "what could he accomplish?"

The soldier reflected. "I was there a month ago," he replied. "I ob-
served that the flood of last winter had lodged a great quantity of
driftwood against the wooden pier at this end of the bridge. It is now
dry and would burn like tow."

The lady had now brought the water, which the soldier drank. He
thanked her ceremoniously, bowed to her husband, and rode away. An
hour later, after nightfall, he repassed the plantation, going northward
in the direction from which he had come. He was a Federal scout.

III.

As Peyton Farquhar fell straight downward through the bridge, he lost consciousness and was as one already dead. From this state he was awakened—ages later, it seemed to him—by the pain of a sharp pressure upon his throat, followed by a sense of suffocation. Keen, poignant agonies seemed to shoot from his neck downward through every fiber of his body and limbs. These pains appeared to flash along well-defined lines of ramification and to beat with an inconceivably rapid periodicity. They seemed like streams of pulsating fire heating him to an intolerable temperature. As to his head, he was conscious of nothing but a feeling of fullness—of congestion. These sensations were unaccompanied by thought. The intellectual part of his nature was already effaced; he had power only to feel, and feeling was torment. He was conscious of motion. Encompassed in a luminous cloud, of which he was now merely the fiery heart, without material substance, he swung through unthinkable arcs of oscillation, like a vast pendulum. Then all at once, with terrible suddenness, the light about him shot upward with the noise of a loud plash; a frightful roaring was in his ears, and all was cold and dark. The power of thought was restored; he knew that the rope had broken and he had fallen into the stream. There was no additional strangulation; the noose about his neck was already suffocating him and kept the water from his lungs. To die of hanging at the bottom of a river!—the idea seemed to him ludicrous. He opened his eyes in the blackness and saw above him a gleam of light, but how distant, how inaccessible! He was still sinking, for the light became fainter and fainter until it was a mere glimmer. Then it began to grow and brighten, and he knew that he was rising toward the surface—knew it with reluctance, for he was now very comfortable. "To be hanged and drowned," he thought, "that is not so bad; but I do not wish to be shot. No; I will not be shot; that is not fair."

He was not conscious of an effort, but a sharp pain in his wrists apprised him that he was trying to free his hands. He gave the struggle his attention, as an idler might observe the feat of a juggler, without interest in the outcome. What splendid effort!—what magnificent, what superhuman strength! Ah, that was a fine endeavor! Bravo! The cord fell away; his arms parted and floated upward, the hands dimly seen on each side in the growing light. He watched them with a new interest as first one and then the other pounced upon the noose at his neck. They tore it away and thrust it fiercely aside, its undulations resembling those of a water snake. "Put it back, put it back!" He thought he shouted these words to his hands, for the undoing of the noose had been succeeded by the direst pang which he had yet experienced.

His neck ached horribly; his brain was on fire; his heart, which had been fluttering faintly, gave a great leap, trying to force itself out at his mouth. His whole body was racked and wrenched with an insupportable anguish! But his disobedient hands gave no heed to the command. They beat the water vigorously with quick, downward strokes, forcing him to the surface. He felt his head emerge; his eyes were blinded by the sunlight; his chest expanded convulsively, and with a supreme and crowning agony his lungs engulfed a great draught of air, which instantly he expelled in a shriek!

He was now in full possession of his physical senses. They were, indeed, preternaturally keen and alert. Something in the awful disturbance of his organic system had so exalted and refined them that they made record of things never before perceived. He felt the ripples upon his face and heard their separate sounds as they struck. He looked at the forest on the bank of the stream, saw the individual trees, the leaves and the veining of each leaf—saw the very insects upon them, the locusts, the brilliant-bodied flies, the gray spiders stretching their webs from twig to twig. He noted the prismatic colors in all the dewdrops upon a million blades of grass. The humming of the gnats that danced above the eddies of the stream, the beating of the dragon flies' wings, the strokes of the water spiders' legs, like oars which had lifted their boat—all these made audible music. A fish slid along beneath his eyes and he heard the rush of its body parting the water.

He had come to the surface facing down the stream; in a moment the visible world seemed to wheel slowly round, himself the pivotal point, and he saw the bridge, the fort, the soldiers upon the bridge, the captain, the sergeant, the two privates, his executioners. They were in silhouette against the blue sky. They shouted and gesticulated, pointing at him; the captain had drawn his pistol, but did not fire; the others were unarmed. Their movements were grotesque and horrible, their forms gigantic.

Suddenly he heard a sharp report and something struck the water smartly within a few inches of his head, spattering his face with spray. He heard a second report, and saw one of the sentinels with his rifle at his shoulder, a light cloud of blue smoke rising from the muzzle. The man in the water saw the eye of the man on the bridge gazing into his own through the sights of the rifle. He observed that it was a gray eye, and remembered having read that gray eyes were keenest and that all famous marksmen had them. Nevertheless, this one had missed.

A counter swirl had caught Farquhar and turned him half round; he was again looking into the forest on the bank opposite the fort. The sound of a clear, high voice in a monotonous singsong now rang out behind him and came across the water with a distinctness that pierced and subdued all other sounds, even the beating of the ripples in his ears. Although no soldier, he had frequented camps enough to know the dread significance of that deliberate, drawling, aspirated chant; the lieutenant on shore was taking a part in the morning's work. How coldly and pitilessly—with what an even, calm intonation, presaging and enforcing tranquillity in the men—with what accurately measured intervals fell those cruel words:

"Attention, company.... Shoulder arms.... Ready.... Aim.... Fire."

Farquhar dived—dived as deeply as he could. The water roared in his ears like the voice of Niagara, yet he heard the dulled thunder of the volley, and, rising again toward the surface, met shining bits of metal, singularly flattened, oscillating slowly downward. Some of them touched him on the face and hands, then fell away, continuing their descent. One lodged between his collar and neck; it was uncomfortably warm, and he snatched it out.

As he rose to the surface, gasping for breath, he saw that he had been a long time under water; he was perceptibly farther down stream—nearer to safety. The soldiers had almost finished reloading; the metal ramrods flashed all at once in the sunshine as they were drawn from the barrels, turned in the air, and thrust into their sockets. The two sentinels fired again, independently and ineffectually.

The hunted man saw all this over his shoulder; he was now swimming vigorously with the current. His brain was as energetic as his arms and legs; he thought with the rapidity of lightning.

"The officer," he reasoned, "will not make that martinet's error a second time. It is as easy to dodge a volley as a single shot. He has probably already given the command to fire at will. God help me, I cannot dodge them all!"

An appalling plash within two yards of him, followed by a loud rushing sound, diminuendo, which seemed to travel back through the air to the fort and died in an explosion which stirred the very river to its deeps! A rising sheet of water, which curved over him, fell down upon him, blinded him, strangled him! The cannon had taken a hand in the game. As he shook his head free from the commotion of the smitten water, he heard the deflected shot humming through the air ahead, and in an instant it was cracking and smashing the branches in the forest beyond.

"They will not do that again," he thought; "the next time they will use a charge of grape. I must keep my eye upon the gun; the smoke will apprise me—the report arrives too late; it lags behind the missile. It is a good gun."

Suddenly he felt himself whirled round and round—spinning like a top. The water, the banks, the forest, the now distant bridge, fort and men—all were commingled and blurred. Objects were represented by their colors only; circular horizontal streaks of color—that was all he saw. He had been caught in a vortex and was being whirled on with a velocity of advance and gyration which made him giddy and sick. In a few moments he was flung upon the gravel at the foot of the left bank of the stream—the southern bank—and behind a projecting point which concealed him from his enemies. The sudden arrest of his motion, the abrasion of one of his hands on the gravel, restored him and he wept with delight. He dug his fingers into the sand, threw it over himself in handfuls and audibly blessed it. It looked like gold, like diamonds, rubies, emeralds; he could think of nothing beautiful which it did not resemble. The trees upon the bank were giant garden plants; he noted a definite order in their arrangement, inhaled the fragrance of their blooms. A strange, roseate light shone through the spaces among their trunks, and the wind made in their branches the music of aeolian harps. He had no wish to perfect his escape, was content to remain in that enchanting spot until retaken.

A whizz and rattle of grapeshot among the branches high above his head roused him from his dream. The baffled cannoneer had fired him a random farewell. He sprang to his feet, rushed up the sloping bank, and plunged into the forest.

All that day he traveled, laying his course by the rounding sun. The forest seemed interminable; nowhere did he discover a break in it, not even a woodman's road. He had not known that he lived in so wild a region. There was something uncanny in the revelation.

By nightfall he was fatigued, footsore, famishing. The thought of his wife and children urged him on. At last he found a road which led him in what he knew to be the right direction. It was as wide and straight as a city street, yet it seemed untraveled. No fields bordered it, no dwelling anywhere. Not so much as the barking of a dog suggested human habitation. The black bodies of the great trees formed a straight wall on both sides, terminating on the horizon in a point, like a diagram in a lesson in perspective. Overhead, as he looked up through this rift in the wood, shone great golden stars looking unfamiliar and grouped in strange constellations. He was sure they were arranged in some order which had a secret and malign significance. The wood on either side was full of singular noises, among which—once, twice, and again—he distinctly heard whispers in an unknown tongue.

His neck was in pain, and, lifting his hand to it, he found it horribly swollen. He knew that it had a circle of black where the rope had bruised it. His eyes felt congested; he could no longer close them. His tongue was swollen with thirst; he relieved its fever by thrusting it forward from between his teeth into the cool air. How softly the turf had carpeted the untraveled avenue! He could no longer feel the roadway beneath his feet!

Doubtless, despite his suffering, he fell asleep while walking, for now he sees another scene—perhaps he has merely recovered from a delirium. He stands at the gate of his own home. All is as he left it, and all bright and beautiful in the morning sunshine. He must have traveled the entire night. As he pushes open the gate and passes up the wide white walk, he sees a flutter of female garments; his wife, looking fresh and cool and sweet, steps down from the veranda to meet him. At the bottom of the steps she stands waiting, with a smile of ineffable joy, an attitude of matchless grace and dignity. Ah, how beautiful she is! He springs forward with extended arms. As he is about to clasp her, he feels a stunning blow upon the back of the neck; a blinding white light blazes all about him, with a sound like the shock of a cannon— then all is darkness and silence!

Peyton Farquhar was dead; his body, with a broken neck, swung gently from side to side beneath the timbers of the Owl Creek bridge.

★ ★ ★

The Wound-Dresser

Walt Whitman

Whitman's famous poem describes the activities of a wound-dresser, a job which he himself did not have. He did, however, spend much time in the hospitals "among new faces," ministering to the wounded soldiers' hearts and souls.

1.

An old man bending, I come, among new faces,
Years looking backward, resuming, in answer to children,
Come tell us, old man, as from young men and maidens that love me;
Years hence of these scenes, of these furious passions, these chances,
Of unsurpass'd heroes, (was one side so brave? the other was
    equally brave;)
Now be witness again—paint the mightiest armies of earth;
Of those armies so rapid, so wondrous, what saw you to tell us?'

What stays with you latest and deepest? of curious panics,
Of hard-fought engagements, or sieges tremendous, what deepest
    remains?

2.

O maidens and young men I love, and that love me,
What you ask of my days, those the strangest and sudden your talking
    recalls;
Soldier alert I arrive, after a long march, cover'd with sweat and dust;
In the nick of time I come, plunge in the fight, loudly shout in the
    rush of successful charge;
Enter the captur'd works . . . yet lo! like a swift-running river, they
    fade;
Pass and are gone, they fade—I dwell not on soldiers' perils or
    soldiers' joys;
(Both I remember well—many the hardships, few the joys, yet I was
    content.)

But in silence, in dreams' projections,
While the world of gain and appearance and mirth goes on,
So soon what is over forgotten, and waves wash the imprints off
    the sand,
In nature's reverie sad, with hinged knees returning, I enter the
    doors—(while for you up there,
Whoever you are, follow me without noise, and be of strong heart.)

3.

Bearing the bandages, water and sponge,
Straight and swift to my wounded I go,
Where they lie on the ground, after the battle brought in;
Where their priceless blood reddens the grass, the ground;
Or to the rows of the hospital tent, or under the roof'd hospital;
To the long rows of cots, up and down, each side, I return;
To each and all, one after another, I draw near—not one do I miss;
An attendant follows, holding a tray—he carries a refuse pail,
Soon to be fill'd with clotted rags and blood, emptied and fill'd again.

I onward go, I stop,
With hinged knees and steady hand, to dress wounds; I am firm with
    each—the pangs are sharp, yet unavoidable;
One turns to me his appealing eyes—(poor boy! I never knew you,
Yet I think I could not refuse this moment to die for you, if that
    would save you.)

4.

On, on I go !—(open doors of time! open hospital doors!)
The crush'd head I dress, (poor crazed hand, tear not the bandage
    away;)
The neck of the cavalry-man, with the bullet through and through,
    I examine;
Hard the breathing rattles, quite glazed already the eye, yet life
    struggles hard;
(Come, sweet death! be persuaded, O beautiful death!
In mercy come quickly.)

From the stump of the arm, the amputated hand,
I undo the clotted lint, remove the slough, wash off the matter and
    blood;
Back on his pillow the soldier bends, with curv'd neck, and
    side-falling head;
His eyes are closed, his face is pale, (he dares not look on the bloody
    stump,
And has not yet look'd on it.)

I dress a wound in the side, deep, deep;
But a day or two more—for see, the frame all wasted already, and
    sinking,
And the yellow-blue countenance see.

I dress the perforated shoulder, the foot with the bullet wound,
Cleanse the one with a gnawing and putrid gangrene, so sickening,
    so offensive,
While the attendant stands behind aside me, holding the tray and pail.

I am faithful, I do not give out;
The fractur'd thigh, the knee, the wound in the abdomen,
These and more I dress with impassive hand—(yet deep in my breast
    a fire, a burning flame.)

5.

Thus in silence, in dreams' projections,
Returning, resuming, I thread my way through the hospitals;
The hurt and wounded I pacify with soothing hand,
I sit by the restless all the dark night—some are so young;
Some suffer so much—I recall the experience sweet and sad;
(Many a soldier's loving arms about this neck have cross'd and rested,
Many a soldier's kiss dwells on these bearded lips.)

"I Fights Mit Sigel!"

Grant P. Robinson

General Franz Sigel, a native German who was instrumental in bringing Germans and German-Americans into the Union Army, was the commander of the Department of West Virginia when he brought that army into the Shenandoah Valley, where it was defeated at the Battle of New Market on May 15.

I met him again, he was trudging along,
　　His knapsack with chickens was swelling;
He 'd "Blenkered" these dainties, and thought it no wrong,
　　From some secessionist's dwelling.
"What regiment's yours? and under whose flag
　　Do you fight?" said I, touching his shoulder;
Turning slowly around, he smilingly said,
　　For the thought made him stronger and bolder,
　　　　"I fights mit Sigel!"

The next time I saw him his knapsack was gone,
　　His cap and canteen were missing,
Shell, shrapnel, and grape, and the swift rifle-ball,
　　Around him, and o'er him were hissing.
"How are you, my friend, and where have you been,
　　And for what, and for whom are you fighting?"
He said, as a shell from the enemy's gun
　　Sent his arm and his musket a "kiting":
　　　　"I fights mit Sigel!"

And once more I saw him and knelt by his side;
　　His life-blood was rapidly flowing;
I whispered of home, wife, children, and friends,
　　The bright land to which he was going;
"And have you no word for the dear ones at home,
　　The 'wee one,' the father or mother?"
"Yaw! yaw!" said he, "tell them! oh! tell them I fights"—
　　Poor fellow! he thought of no other—
　　　　"I fights mit Sigel!"

We scraped out a grave, and he dreamlessly sleeps
　　On the banks of the Shenandoah River;
His home or his kindred alike are unknown,
　　His reward in the hands of the Giver.

We placed a rough board at the head of his grave,
  "And we left him alone in his glory,"
But on it we marked, ere we turned from the spot,
  The little we knew of his story—
    "I fights mit Sigel!"

★   ★   ★

Buried Alive

ANONYMOUS

This fictional account of the real horrors that Nathan Bedford Forrest carried out on the black soldiers at Fort Pillow, Tennessee, on April 12, 1864, can be closely compared to the eyewitness testimony provided to the Joint Committee on the Conduct and Expenditures of the War by the survivors of the massacre. (See, for example, Document 1 in Frank Moore's Rebellion Record, *Volume 8.) The story was first published in* Harper's Weekly *on May 7, 1864.*

My name is Daniel Tyler, and my skin is dark, as my mother's was before me. I have heard that my father had a white face, but I think his heart and life were blacker than my mother's skin. I was born a slave, and remained a slave until last April, when I found deliverance and shelter under the flag that my master was fighting to dishonor.

I shall never forget the day when freedom came to me. I was working in the fields down in Alabama, my heart full of bitterness and unutterable longings. I had dreamed for two long years of escape from my bondage; the thought sung to me through the dark nights, and filled all the days with a weird sort of nervous expectation. But my dreams had proved nothing more than dreams; the opportunity I yearned for did not come. But that day, working in the fields, suddenly along the dusty road there flashed a long column of loyal cavalry, the old flag flying at its head. How my heart leaped at the sight; how, like revelation, came the thought: "This, Daniel Tyler, is your opportunity!" Need I tell you how I acted upon that thought; how, in one second of time, I leaped out of slavery into freedom, and from a slave became a man?

Well, joining the flashing column, I rode with them for days, coming at last into Baton Rouge, and thence, having joined a regiment of my own people, came to Memphis. Thence four hundred of us came to Fort Pillow. But there are not four hundred of us today, for three hundred and odd were murdered in cold blood only a week ago by Forrest's rough-riders.

It was a day of horrors—that 12th of April. There were seven hundred of us in all in the fort—three hundred whites of the Thirteenth Tennessee Cavalry, and four hundred blacks, as I have said, all under command of brave Major Booth. The fort consisted simply of earthworks, on which we had mounted half a dozen guns. We knew that Forrest had been pillaging the country all about us, and imagined that perhaps he would pay us a visit; but the thought did not alarm us, though we knew, those of us who were black, that we had little to expect at the hands of the rebels. At last, about sunrise on the morning of the 12th, Forrest, with some 6,000 men, appeared and at once commenced an attack. We met the assault bravely, and for two hours the fight went on briskly. Then a flag of truce came in from Forrest, asking an unconditional surrender, but Major Bradford—Major Booth having been wounded—declined to surrender unless the enemy would treat those of us who were black as prisoners of war, which, of course, they refused to do, and the fight went on. The enemy, in the next few hours, made several desperate charges, but were each time repulsed. At last, about four o'clock in the afternoon, they sent in another flag. We ceased firing out of respect to the flag; but Forrest's men had no such notions of honor and good faith. The moment we stopped firing they swarmed all about the fort, and while the flag was yet withdrawing, made a desperate charge from all sides. Up to that time only about thirty of our men had been hurt. But in this charge, the enemy got within the earth-works, and forthwith there ensued a scene which no pen can describe. Seeing that all resistance was useless, most of us threw down our arms, expecting, and many begging for, quarter. But it was in vain.

Murder was in every rebel heart; flamed in every rebel eye. Indiscriminate massacre followed instantly upon our surrender. Some of us, seeking shelter, ran to the river and tried to conceal ourselves in the bushes, but for the most part in vain. The savages, pursuing, shot down the fugitives in their tracks. There was Manuel Nichols, as brave a soldier as ever carried a musket. He had been a free negro in Michigan, but volunteered a year ago to fight for the Union. He, with others, had sought a shelter under the bank of the river, but a cold-blooded monster found him, and putting a pistol close to his head, fired, failing however to kill the brave fellow. He was then hacked on the arm, and only a day after died, delirious, in the hospital. Then there was Robert Hall, another colored soldier, who was lying sick in the hospital when the massacre commenced. The devils gashed his head horribly with their sabres, and then cut off part of his right hand, which he had lifted in a mute appeal for mercy. Then there was Harrison, of the Thirteenth Tennessee, who was shot four times after surrender, and then robbed of all his effects. Before I was shot, running along the river bank, I counted fifty dead Union soldiers lying in their blood. One had crawled into a hollow log and was killed in it, another had got over the bank in the river, and on to a board that run out into the water, and when I saw him was already stark and stiff. Several had tried to hide in crevices made by the falling bank, and could not be seen without difficulty, but they were singled out and killed. One negro corporal, Jacob Wilson, who was down on the river bank, seeing that no quarter was shown, stepped into the water so that he lay partly under it. A rebel coming along asked him what was the matter: he said he was badly wounded, and the rebel, after taking from his pocket all the money he had, left him. It happened to be near by a flat-boat tied to the bank. When all was quiet Wilson crawled into it, and got three more wounded comrades also into it, and cut loose. The boat floated out into the channel and was found ashore some miles below. There were, alas, few such fortunate escapes.

I was shot near the river just about dark. Running for my life, a burly rebel struck me with his carbine, putting out one eye, and then shot me in two places. I thought he would certainly leave me with that, but I was mistaken. With half a dozen others, I was at once picked up and carried to a ditch, into which we were tossed like so many brutes, white and black together. Then they covered us with loose dirt, and left us to die. Oh, how dark and desolate it was! Under me were several dead, and right across my breast lay a white soldier, still alive! How he clutched and strained! How, hurt and weak as I was, with only one hand free, I struggled for air and life, feeling my strength waning every moment! It was a strange thing to lie there buried, and yet be able to think and pray. Maybe, friend, you have known what agony was, but you never had such pains of soul as I had down there in that living grave. I thought I could feel the worms gnawing at my flesh; I am sure I had a taste of what death is, with the added pain of knowing that I was not dead, and yet unable to live in that dark, dismal tomb. So I clutched and strained and struggled on, digging upward as I could with my one puny hand.

At last—oh joy!—a faint streak of light looked in; my hand had carved an avenue to the world of life! But would I dare to lift my head? Might not some rebel, standing by, strike me down again on the moment? But I could not die there in that grave; I must escape. Slowly, painfully, I rolled the burden from my breast—he was dead by that time—and then carefully crept out from that living death. It was dark, and no one was near. A moment I stood up on my feet; then?

The next thing I remember I was in the hospital where I am now. They had found me just where I fell, and brought me to a place of safety, where, after a while, consciousness returned. I have been here a week now; and I think I shall get well.

I lie in the cot where poor Robert Hall lay when he was butchered by the rebels. They showed me, yesterday, a letter he had written the day before the massacre to his wife. He had learned to read and write at Memphis, after his enlistment, and used to send a message to his wife and children, who still remained there, every week or so. This was his letter which a surgeon had helped him put together:

"Dear Mammy"—it ran—"I am very sick here in the hospital, but am better than I was, and hope to get well soon. They have been very kind to me; and I find it very sweet to suffer for the dear flag that gives me shelter. You must not worry on my account. Tell Katy she must not forget to say her prayers and to study her lessons carefully now while she has an opportunity. And, mammy, take good care of the baby; I dreamed of her last night, and I think how sad it would be to die and never see her little face again. But then chaplain says it will be right in heaven, and he knows better than we do. And, mammy, don't forget we are free now; teach both the darlings to be worth of their estate."

That was poor Hall's letter—it had not been sent, and we have no heart to send it now. He will never see the baby's face here; but then God may let him see it up yonder!

I hope to recover and get away from here very soon; I want to be in my place again; for I have something to avenge now, and I can not bear to wait. Poor Hall's blood is crying to me from the ground; and I want to be able, sometime, to say to Manuel Nichols's wife, up there in Michigan, that his fall has had its compensation. And may God speed the day when this whole slaveholders' rebellion—what remains of it—shall be "Buried Alive!"

A Southern Scene

ANONYMOUS

"O Mammy, have you heard the news?"
  Thus spake a Southern child,
As in the nurse's aged face
  She upward glanced and smiled.

"What news you mean, my little one?
  It must be mighty fine,
To make my darlin's face so red,
  Her sunny blue eyes shine."

"Why, Abr'am Lincoln, don't you know,
  The Yankee President,
Whose ugly picture once we saw,
  When up to town we went?

"Well, he is goin' to free you all,
  And make you rich and grand,
And you'll be dressed in silk and gold,
  Like the proudest in the land.

"A gilded coach shall carry you
  Where'er you wish to ride;
And, mammy, all your work shall be
  Forever laid aside."

The eager speaker paused for breath,
  And then the old nurse said,
While closer to her swarthy cheek
  She pressed the golden head:

"My little missus, stop and res' —
  You' talkin' mighty fas';
Jos' look up dere, and tell me what
  You see in yonder glass?

"You sees old mammy's wrinkly face,
  As black as any coal;
And underneath her handkerchief
  Whole heaps of knotty wool.

"My darlin's face is red and white,
  Her skin is soff and fine,

And on her pretty little head
   De yallur ringlets shine.

"My chile, who made dis difference
   'Twixt mammy and 'twixt you?
You reads de dear Lord's blessed book,
   And you can tell me true.

"De dear Lord said it must be so;
   And, honey, I, for one,
Wid tankful heart will always say,
   His holy will be done.

"I tanks Mas' Linkum all de same,
   But when I wants for free,
I'll ask de Lord of glory,
   Not poor buckra man like he.

"And as for gilded carriages,
   Dey's notin' 'tall to see;
My massa's coach, what carries him.
   Is good enough for me.

"And, honey, when your mammy wants
   To change her homespun dress,
She'll pray, like dear old missus,
   To be clothed with righteousness.

"My work's been done dis many a day,
   And now I takes my ease,
A waitin' for de Master's call,
   Jes' when de Master please.

"And when at las' de time's done come,
   And poor old mammy dies,
Your own dear mother's soff white hand
   Shall close these tired old eyes.

"De dear Lord Jesus soon will call
   Old mammy home to him,
And he can wash my guilty soul
   From ebery spot of sin.

"And at his feet I shall lie down,
   Who died and rose for me;
And den, and not till den, my chile,
   Your mammy will be free.

"Come, little missus, say your prayers;
   Let old Mas' Linkum 'lone;
The debil knows who b'longs to him.
   And he'll take care of his own."

★   ★   ★

The Contraband's Return

HERMINE

*A Southern writer, unknown except as "Hermine," imagines a slave, referred to in the
North and South as "contraband," returning "home" from her supposedly miserable
experiences in the North and begging to rejoin her master's family. The sincerity of the
author may be doubted; the author's delusions may not.*

Don't you know me, Massa William?
   Don't you know me, Missus dear?
Don't you know old Aunt Rebecca,
   Who went away from you last year,
With Peter, Phil, and Little Judy,
   To join the wicked Yankee crew?
But I've come back, my dear old Missus,
   To live and die with you.

I never knew the old plantation
   Was half so dear a place to me.
As when among that Yankee nation
   The robbers told me I was free;
And when I looked around for freedom,
   (We thought it something bright and fair,)
Hunger, misery, and starvation,
   Was all that met us there.

How often, when we used to shiver,
   All through the long cold winter night,
I used to study 'bout my cabin,
   The hearth all red with pinewood light!
I saw they would not make us happy,
   And yet they would not let us go—
Ah! 'twas hatred of our white folks,
   Not love for us, I know.

"And Peter?" Ah! old Massa Peter
   Has gone from this cold earth away—
He was too old to be a soldier,
   They worked him hard both night and day:
He was not used to so much labor,
   And soon the poor old man broke down,
He found, alas! their boasted freedom
   A cross and not a crown.

They made my poor boy, Phil, a soldier,
   And took him from me far away;
He stood through many a bloody battle,
   Was wounded often, many a day;
He did not wish to be a soldier,
   He only wanted to be free—
They only loaded him with irons,
   Or lashed him to a tree.

Before him once, in line of battle,
   He saw our fine young master Jim,
Then dropped poor Phil his Yankee musket,
   He could not, would not, fire on him;
For they had played, been raised together,
   Young master Jim had cried for Phil—
The Yankees gave the onward order,
   But my poor boy stood still.

And then his more than cruel masters,
   White men, with hearts and deeds all black,
Struck him down with gun and sabre,
   And left him dying on their track.
O missus! my old heart is broken,
   My lot all grief and pain has been;
For little Judy, too, is ruined,
   In their dark camps of sin.

O Massa William! see me kneeling,
   O Missus! say one word for me!
You'll let me stay? Oh! thank you massa;
   Now I'm happy! now I'm free!
I've seen enough of Yankee freedom,
   I've had enough of Yankee love!
As they have treated the poor negro,
   Be't done to them above.

The Daring Spy

ANONYMOUS

This exciting story, represented as "true" but told as only fiction could, first appeared in print in 1864 in John Fitch's Annals of the Army of Cumberland.

"John Morford"—so let us call him, good reader—was born near Augusta, Georgia, of Scotch parents, in the year 1832. A blacksmith by trade, he early engaged in railroading, and at the commencement of the rebellion was master-mechanic upon a prominent Southern road. Being a strong Union man, and making no secret of it, he was discharged from his situation and not allowed employment upon any other railroad. A company of cavalry was also sent to his farm and stripped it. Aggrieved at this wholesale robbery, Morford went to John H. Morgan, then a captain, and inquired if he would not pay him for the property thus taken. Morgan replied that he should have his pay if he would only prove his loyalty to the South. Morford acknowledged this to be impossible, and was thereupon very liberally cursed and vilified by Morgan, who accused him of harboring negroes and traitors, and threatened to have him shot. Finally, however, he was content with simply arresting him and sending him, charged with disloyalty, to one Major Peyton.

The major seems to have been a somewhat talkative and argumentative man; for upon Morford's arrival he endeavored to reason him out of his adherence to the Union, asking him, in the course of a lengthy conversation, many questions about the war, demonstrating, to his own satisfaction at least, the necessity and justice of the position assumed by the seceded States, and finishing, by way of clenching the argument, with the inquiry, "How can you, a Southern man by birth and education, be opposed to the South?" Morford replied that he saw no reason for the rebellion, that the Union was good enough for him, that he should cling to it, and, if he could obtain a pass, would abandon the Confederacy and cast his lot with the North. The Major then argued still more at length, and, as a last resort, endeavored to frighten him with a vivid description of the horrors of "negro equality"—to all of which his hearer simply replied that he was not afraid; whereupon, as unskillful advocates of a bad cause are prone to do, he became very wrathy, vented his anger in a torrent of oaths and vile epithets, and told Morford that he ought to be hung, and should be in two weeks. The candidate for hempen honors, apparently not at all alarmed, coolly replied that he was sorry for that, as he wished to live a little longer, but, if it must be so, he couldn't help it. Peyton, meanwhile, cooled down, and told him that if he would give a bond of one thousand dollars and take the oath of allegiance to the Southern Confederacy, he would release him and protect his property. After some hesitation—no other plan of escape occurring to him—Morford assented, and took the required oath, upon the back of which Peyton wrote, "If you violate this, I will hang you."

With this safeguard, Morford returned to his farm and lived a quiet life. Buying a span of horses, he devoted himself to the cultivation of his land, seeing as few persons as he could, and talking with none. His house had previously been the headquarters of the Union men, but was now deserted by them; and its owner endeavored to live up to the letter of the obligation he had taken. For a short time all went well enough; but one day a squad of cavalry came with a special written order from Major Peyton to take his two horses, which they did. This was too much for human nature; and Morford, perceiving that no faith could be placed in the assurances of those in command, determined to be revenged upon them and their cause. His house again became a secret rendezvous for Unionists; and by trusty agents he managed to send regular and valuable information to General Buell, then in command in Tennessee. At length, however, in May, 1862, he was betrayed by one in whom he had placed confidence, and arrested upon the charge of sending information to General Crittenden, at Battle Creek. He indignantly denied the charge, and declared that he could easily prove himself innocent if released for that purpose. After three days' confinement, this was assented to; and Morford, knowing full well that he could not do what he had promised, made a hasty retreat and fled to the mountains, whence, some days afterwards, he emerged, and went to McMinnville, at which place General Nelson was then in command.

Here he remained until the rebel force left that vicinity, when he again went home, and lived undisturbed upon his farm until Bragg returned with his army. The presence in the neighborhood of so many officers cognizant of his former arrest and escape rendered flight a second time necessary. He now went to the camp of General Donelson, with whom he had some acquaintance, and soon became very friendly there—acting the while in the double capacity of beef-contractor for the rebel army and spy for General Crittenden. Leaving General Donelson after some months' stay, although earnestly requested to remain longer, Morford next found his way to Nashville, where he made numerous expeditions as a spy for General Negley. Buell was at Louisville, and Nashville was then the Federal outpost. Morford travelled about very readily upon passes given him by General Donelson, making several trips to Murfreesborough and one to Cumberland Gap.

Upon his return from the latter, he was arrested near Lebanon, Tennessee, about one o'clock at night, by a party of four soldiers upon picket-duty at that point. Halting him, the following conversation occurred:—

"Where do you live?"

"Near Stewart's Ferry, between here and Nashville."

"Where have you been, and what for?"

"Up to see my brother, to get from him some jeans-cloth and socks for another brother in the Confederate army."

"How does it happen you are not in the army yourself? That looks rather suspicious."

"Oh, I live too near the Federal lines to be conscripted."

"Well, we'll have to send you to Murfreesborough. I reckon you're all right; but those are our orders, and we can't go behind them."

To this Morford readily consented, saying he had no objection; and the party sat down by the fire and talked in a friendly manner for some time. Morford soon remembered that he had a bottle of brandy with him, and generously treated the crowd. Further conversation was followed by a second drink, and soon by a third. One of the party now proposed to exchange his Rosinantish mare for a fine horse which Morford rode. The latter was not inclined to trade; but objection was useless, and he finally yielded, receiving seventy-five dollars in Confederate money and the mare. The trade pleased the soldier, and a present of a pair of socks still further enhanced his pleasure. His companions were also similarly favored, and testified their appreciation of the gift by endeavoring to purchase the balance of Morford's stock. He would not sell, however, as he wished to send them to his brother at Richmond, by a person who had given public notice that he was soon going there. A fourth drink made all supremely happy; at which juncture their prisoner asked permission to go to a friend's house, only a quarter of a mile off, and stay until morning, when he would go with them to Murfreesborough. His friend of the horse trade, now very mellow, thought he need not go to Murfreesborough at all, and said he would see what the others said about it. Finally it was concluded that he was "right," and might go; whereupon he mounted the skeleton mare and rode rejoicingly into Nashville.

On his next trip southward he was arrested by Colonel John T. Morgan, just as he came out of the Federal lines, and, as his only resort, joined Forrest's command, and was furnished with a horse and gun. The next day Forrest made a speech to his men, and told them that they were now going to capture Nashville. The column immediately began its march, and Morford, by some means, managed to have himself placed in the advance. Two miles below Lavergne a halt for the night was made; but Morford's horse was unruly, and could not be stopped, carrying its rider ahead and out of sight. It is needless to say that this obstinacy was not overcome until Nashville was reached, nor that when Forrest came, the next day, General Negley was amply prepared for him. At this time Nashville was invested. Buell was known to be advancing towards the city, but no scouts had been able to go to or come from him. A handsome reward was offered to any one who would carry a dispatch safely through to Bowling Green, and Morford undertook to do it. Putting the document under the lining of his boot, he started for Gallatin, where he arrived safely.

For some hours he sauntered around the place, lounged in and out of bar-rooms, made friends with the rebel soldiers, and, towards evening purchased a small bag of corn-meal, a bottle of whiskey, a pound or two of salt, and some smaller articles, which he threw across his shoulder and started up the Louisville road, with hat on one side, hair in admirable disorder, and, apparently, gloriously drunk. The pickets jested at and made sport of him, but permitted him to pass. The meal, etc. was carried six miles, when he suddenly became sober, dropped it, and hastened on to Bowling Green, and there met General Rosecrans, who had just arrived. His information was very valuable. Here he remained until the army came up and passed on, and then set out on his return on foot as he had come. He supposed that our forces had gone by way of Gallatin, but when near that place learned that it was still in possession of the rebels, and so stopped for the night in a shanty between Morgan's pickets, on the north side, and Woolford's (Union), on the south side. During the night the two had a fight, which finally centered around the shanty, and resulted in driving Morford to the woods. In two or three hours he came back for his clothes, and found that the contending parties had disappeared, and that the railroad-tunnels had been filled with wood, and fired. Hastily gathering his effects together, he made his way to Tyree Springs, and thence to Nashville.

For a short time he acted as a detective of the Army Police at Nashville, assuming the character of a rebel soldier, and living in the families of prominent secessionists. In this work he was very successful; but it had too little of danger and adventure, and he returned again to scouting, making several trips southward, sometimes without trouble, but once or twice being arrested, and escaping as best he could. In these expeditions he visited McMinnville, Murfreesborough, Altamont, on the Cumberland Mountains, Bridgeport, Chattanooga, and other places of smaller note. He traveled usually in the guise of a smuggler, actually obtaining orders for goods from prominent rebels, and sometimes the money in advance, filling them in Nashville, and delivering the articles upon his next trip. Just before the battle of Stone River he received a large order to be filled for the rebel hospitals, went to Nashville, procured the medicine, and returned to McMinnville, when he delivered some of it. Thence he travelled to Bradyville, and thence to Murfreesborough, arriving there just as the battle began. Presenting some of the surgeons with a supply of morphine, he assisted them in attending the wounded for a day or two, and then went to a hospital tent in the woods near the railroad, where he also remained one day and part of another. The fight was now getting hot, and, fearful that somebody would recognize him, he left Murfreesborough on Friday, and went to McMinnville. He had been there but little more than an hour, having barely time to put up his horse and step into a house near by to see some wounded men, when two soldiers arrived in search of him. Their description of him was perfect; but he escaped by being out of sight—the friend with whom he was supposed to be, declaring, though closely questioned, that he had not seen and knew nothing of him. In a few minutes pickets were thrown out around the town, and it was two days before he could get away. Obtaining a pass to Chattanooga at last, only through the influence of a lady acquaintance, with it he passed the guards, but, when once out of sight, turned off from the Chattanooga road, and made his way safely to Nashville.

General Rosecrans was now in possession of Murfreesborough, and thither Morford proceeded with some smuggler's goods, with a view to another trip. The necessary permission was readily obtained, and he set out for Woodbury. Leaving his wagon outside the rebel lines, he proceeded on foot to McMinnville, arriving there on the 19th of January last, and finding General John H. Morgan, to whom he represented himself as a former resident in the vicinity of Woodbury; his family, however, had moved away, and he would like permission to take his wagon and bring away the household goods. This was granted, and the wagon brought to McMinnville, whence Morford went to Chattanooga, representing himself along the road as a fugitive from the Yankees. Near Chattanooga he began selling his goods to Unionists and rebels alike, at enormous prices, and soon closed them out at a profit of from four hundred to five hundred dollars. At Chattanooga he remained a few days, obtained all the information he could, and returned to Murfreesborough without trouble.

His next and last trip is the most interesting and daring of all his adventures. Making a few days' stay in Murfreesborough, he went to

McMinnville, and remained there several days, during which time he burned Hickory Creek Bridge, and sent a report of it to General Rosecrans. This he managed with so much secrecy and skill as to escape all suspicion of complicity in the work, mingling freely with the citizens and talking the matter over in all its phases. From McMinnville, Morford proceeded to Chattanooga, and remained there nearly a week, when he learned that three of our scouts were imprisoned in the Hamilton County jail, at Harrison, Tennessee, and were to be shot on the first Friday in May. Determined to attempt their rescue, he sent a Union man to the town to ascertain who was jailer, what the number of the guards, how they were placed, and inquire into the condition of things in general about the jail. Upon receipt of his report, Morford gathered about him nine Union men, on the night of Tuesday, April 21, and started for Harrison. Before reaching the place, however, they heard rumors that the guard had been greatly strengthened; and, fearful that it would prove too powerful for them, the party retreated to the mountains on the north side of the Tennessee River, where they remained concealed until Thursday night. On Wednesday night the same man who had previously gone to the town was again sent to reconnoiter the position. Thursday morning he returned and said that the story of a strong guard was all false: there were but two in addition to the jailer.

Morford's party was now reduced to six, including himself: but he resolved to make the attempt that night. Late in the afternoon all went down to the river and loitered around until dark, when they procured boats and crossed to the opposite bank. Taking the Chattanooga and Harrison road, they entered the town, looked around at leisure, saw no soldiers nor anything unusual, and proceeded towards the jail. Approaching quite near, they threw themselves upon the ground and surveyed the premises carefully. The jail was surrounded by a high board fence, in which were two gates. Morford's plan of operations was quickly arranged. Making a prisoner of one of his own men, he entered the enclosure, posting a sentinel at each gate. Once inside, a light was visible in the jail, and Morford marched confidently up to the door and rapped. The jailer thrust his head out of a window and asked what was wanted. He was told, "Here is a prisoner to put in the jail." Apparently satisfied, the jailer soon opened the door and admitted the twain into the entry. In a moment, however, he became alarmed, and, hastily exclaiming, "Hold on!" stepped out.

For ten minutes Morford waited patiently for his return, supposing, of course, that he could not escape from the yard, both gates being guarded. Not making his appearance, it was found that the pickets had

allowed him to pass them. This rather alarming fact made haste neces-
sary, and Morford, returning to the jail, said he must put his prisoner in
immediately, and demanded the keys forthwith. The women declared
in positive terms that they hadn't them, and did not know where they
were. One of the guards was discovered in bed and told to get the
keys. Proving rather noisy and saucy, he was reminded that he might
get his head taken off if he were not quiet—which intimation effectu-
ally silenced him. Morford again demanded the keys, and the women,
somewhat frightened, gave him the key to the outside door. Unlocking
it, and lighting up the place with candles, he found himself in a room
around the sides of which was ranged a line of wrought-iron cages. In
one of these were five persons, four white and one negro. Carrying
out the character he had assumed of a rebel soldier in charge of a pris-
oner, Morford talked harshly enough to the caged men, and threatened
to hang them at once, at which they were very naturally alarmed, and
began to beg for mercy. For a third time the keys to the inner room, in
which the scouts were, were demanded, and a third time the women
denied having them. An axe was then ordered to be brought, but there
was none about the place: so said they. Morford saw that they were tri-
fling with him, and determined to stop it. Snatching one of the jailer's
boys standing near by the collar, and drawing his sabre, he told him he
would cut his head off if he did not bring him an axe in two minutes.
This had the desired effect, and the axe was forthcoming.

Morford now began cutting away at the lock, when he was startled
by hearing the word "halt!" at the gate. Of his five men two were at
the gates, two were inside as a guard, and one was holding the light.
Ready for a fight, he went out to see what was the matter. The sentinel
reporting that he had halted an armed man outside, Morford walked
out to him and demanded—

"What are you doing here with that gun?"

"Miss Laura said you were breaking down the jail, and I want to see
McAllister, the jailer. Where is he?" was the reply.

"Well, suppose I am breaking down the jail: what are you going to
do about it?"

"I am going to stop it if I can."

"What's your name?"

"Lowry Johnson."

By this time Morford had grasped the muzzle of the gun, and told
him to let go. Instead of complying, Johnson tried to pull it away; but
a blow upon the neck from Morford's sabre soon made him drop it.
Morford now began to search him for other weapons, but before he
had concluded the operation Johnson broke away, leaving a part of his

clothing in Morford's hands. The latter drew his revolver and pursued, firing five shots at him, sometimes at a distance of only six or eight paces. A cry, as of pain, showed that he was struck, but he managed to reach the hotel (kept by his brother), and, bursting in the door, which was fastened, escaped into the house. Morford followed, but too late. Johnson's brother now came out and rang the bell in front, which gathered a crowd about the door; but Morford, not at all daunted, told them that if they wanted to guard the jail they had better be about it quick, as he was going to burn it and the town in the bargain. This so frightened them that no further demonstration was made, and Morford returned to the jail unmolested. There he and his men made so much shouting and hurrahing as to frighten the people of the town beyond measure; and many lights from upper-story windows were extinguished, and the streets were deserted.

A half-hour's work was necessary to break off the outside lock, a splendid burglar-proof one. Morford now discovered that the door was double, and that the inner one was made still more secure by being barred with three heavy log-chains. These were cut in two with the axe; but the strong lock of the door still remained. He again demanded the key, and told the women if it was not produced he would murder the whole of them. The rebel guard, Lew Luttrell by name, was still in bed. Rising up, he said that the key was not there. Morford now ordered Luttrell to get out of bed, in a tone so authoritative that that individual deemed it advisable to comply. Scarcely was he out, however, before Morford struck at him with his sabre; but he was too far off, and the blow fell upon one of the children, drawing some blood. This frightened the women, and, concluding that he was about to put his threat in execution and would murder them surely enough, they produced the key without further words. No time was lost in unlocking the door and releasing the inmates of the room. Procuring their clothes for them and arming one with Johnson's gun, the whole party left the jail and hurried towards the river. Among the released prisoners was a rebel with a wooden leg, the original having been shot off at Manassas. He persisted in accompanying the others, and was only induced to go back by the intimation that "dead men tell no tales."

Crossing the river in the boats, they were moved to another place at some distance, to preclude the possibility of being tracked and followed. All now hid themselves among the mountains, and the same Union man was again sent to Harrison, this time to see how severely Johnson was wounded. He returned in a day or two, and reported that he had a severe sabre-cut on the shoulder, a bullet through the muscle of his right arm, and two slight wounds in one of his hands. Morford and his men remained in the mountains until all search for the prisoners was over, then went to the Cumberland Mountains, where they remained one day and a portion of another, and then proceeded in the direction of McMinnville. Hiding themselves in the woods near this place during the day, seeing but not seen, they traveled that night to within eleven miles of Woodbury, when they struck across the road from McMinnville to Woodbury. Near Logan's Plains they were fired on by a body of rebel cavalry, but, though some forty shots were fired, no one of the ten was harmed, Morford having one bullet-hole in his coat. The cavalry, however, pursued them across the barrens, surrounded them, and supposed themselves sure of their game; but Morford and his companions scattered and hid away, not one being captured or found. Night coming on, the cavalry gave up the chase, and went on to Woodbury, where they threw out pickets, not doubting that they would pick up the objects of their search during the night. Morford, however, was informed of this fact by a citizen, and, in consequence, lay concealed all the next day, making his way safely to Murfreesborough, with all of his company, the day after.

★　★　★

The Case of George Dedlow

Silas Weir Mitchell

Mitchell (1829–1914), a native of Philadelphia, was a neurologist and wrote many creative works as well as important medical books on the nervous system. This fictional story may remind readers of the true tales by Dr. Oliver Sacks in its enlivening interest in the personality of the patient: "This set me to thinking," muses the limbless narrator, "how much a man might lose and yet live." When "The Case of George Dedlow" was published in 1866, readers believed it to be true, to Mitchell's surprise, and sent gifts to him and made inquires about him at the "stump" hospital in Philadelphia.

The following notes of my own case have been declined on various pretexts by every medical journal to which I have offered them. There was, perhaps, some reason in this, because many of the medical facts which they record are not altogether new, and because the psychical deductions to which they have led me are not in themselves of medical interest. I ought to add that a great deal of what is here related is not of any scientific value whatsoever; but as one or two people on whose judgment I rely have advised me to print my narrative with all the personal details, rather than in the dry shape in which, as a psychological statement, I shall publish it elsewhere, I have yielded to their views. I suspect, however, that the very character of my record will, in the eyes of some of my readers, tend to lessen the value of the metaphysical discoveries which it sets forth.

* * *

I am the son of a physician, still in large practice, in the village of Abington, Scofield County, Indiana. Expecting to act as his future partner, I studied medicine in his office, and in 1859 and 1860 attended lectures at the Jefferson Medical College in Philadelphia. My second course should have been in the following year, but the outbreak of the Rebellion so crippled my father's means that I was forced to abandon my intention. The demand for army surgeons at this time became very great; and although not a graduate, I found no difficulty in getting the place of assistant surgeon to the Tenth Indiana Volunteers. In the subsequent Western campaigns this organization suffered so severely that before the term of its service was over it was merged in the Twenty-first Indiana Volunteers; and I, as an extra surgeon, ranked by the medical officers of the latter regiment, was transferred to the Fifteenth Indiana Cavalry. Like many physicians, I had contracted a strong taste for army life, and, disliking cavalry service, sought and obtained the position of first lieutenant in the Seventy-ninth Indiana Volunteers, an infantry regiment of excellent character.

On the day after I assumed command of my company, which had no captain, we were sent to garrison a part of a line of block-houses stretching along the Cumberland River below Nashville, then occupied by a portion of the command of General Rosecrans.

The life we led while on this duty was tedious and at the same time dangerous in the extreme. Food was scarce and bad, the water horrible, and we had no cavalry to forage for us. If, as infantry, we attempted to levy supplies upon the scattered farms around us, the population seemed suddenly to double, and in the shape of guerrillas "potted" us industriously from behind distant trees, rocks, or fences. Under these various and unpleasant influences, combined with a fair infusion of malaria, our men rapidly lost health and spirits. Unfortunately, no proper medical supplies had been forwarded with our small force (two companies), and, as the fall advanced, the want of quinine and stimulants became a serious annoyance. Moreover, our rations were running low; we had been three weeks without a new supply; and our commanding officer, Major Henry L. Terrill, began to be uneasy as to the safety of his men. About this time it was supposed that a train with rations would be due from the post twenty miles to the north of us; yet it was quite possible that it would bring us food, but no medicines, which were what we most needed. The command was too small to detach any part of it, and the major therefore resolved to send an officer alone to the post above us, where the rest of the Seventy-ninth lay, and whence they could easily forward quinine and stimulants by the train, if it had not left, or, if it had, by a small cavalry escort.

It so happened, to my cost, as it turned out, that I was the only officer fit to make the journey, and I was accordingly ordered to proceed to Blockhouse No. 3 and make the required arrangements. I started alone just after dusk the next night, and during the darkness succeeded in getting within three miles of my destination. At this time I found that I had lost my way, and, although aware of the danger of my act, was forced to turn aside and ask at a log cabin for directions. The house contained a dried-up old woman and four white-headed, half-naked children. The woman was either stone-deaf or pretended to be so; but, at all events, she gave me no satisfaction, and I remounted and rode away. On coming to the end of a lane, into which I had turned to seek the cabin, I found to my surprise that the bars had been put up during my brief parley. They were too high to leap, and I therefore dismounted to pull them down. As I touched the top rail, I heard a rifle, and at the same instant felt a blow on both arms, which fell helpless. I staggered to my horse and tried to mount; but, as I could use neither arm, the effort was vain, and I therefore stood still, awaiting my fate. I am only conscious that I saw about me several graybacks, for I must have fallen fainting almost immediately.

When I awoke I was lying in the cabin near by, upon a pile of rubbish. Ten or twelve guerrillas were gathered about the fire, apparently drawing lots for my watch, boots, hat, etc. I now made an effort to find out how far I was hurt. I discovered that I could use the left forearm and hand pretty well, and with this hand I felt the right limb all over until I touched the wound. The ball had passed from left to right through the left biceps, and directly through the right arm just below the shoulder, emerging behind. The right arm and forearm were cold and perfectly insensible. I pinched them as well as I could, to test the amount of sensation remaining; but the hand might as well have been that of a dead man. I began to understand that the nerves had been wounded, and that the part was utterly powerless. By this time my friends had pretty well divided the spoils, and, rising together, went out. The old woman then came to me, and said: "Reckon you'd best git up. They-'uns is a-goin' to take you away." To this I only answered, "Water, water." I had a grim sense of amusement on finding that the old woman was not deaf, for she went out, and presently came back with a gourdful, which I eagerly drank. An hour later the graybacks returned, and finding that I was too weak to walk, carried me out and laid me on the bottom of a common cart, with which they set off on a trot. The jolting was horrible, but within an hour I began to have in my dead right hand a strange burning, which was rather a relief to me. It increased as the sun rose and the day grew warm, until I felt as if the hand was caught and pinched in a red-hot vise. Then in my agony I begged my guard for water to wet it with, but for some reason they desired silence, and at every noise threatened me with a revolver. At length the pain became absolutely unendurable, and I grew what it is the fashion to call demoralized. I screamed, cried, and yelled in my torture, until, as I suppose, my captors became alarmed, and, stopping, gave me a handkerchief,—my own, I fancy,—and a canteen of water, with which I wetted the hand, to my unspeakable relief.

It is unnecessary to detail the events by which, finally, I found myself in one of the rebel hospitals near Atlanta. Here, for the first time, my wounds were properly cleansed and dressed by a Dr. Oliver T. Wilson, who treated me throughout with great kindness. I told him I had been a doctor, which, perhaps, may have been in part the cause of the unusual tenderness with which I was managed. The left arm was now quite easy, although, as will be seen, it never entirely healed. The right arm was worse than ever—the humerus broken, the nerves wounded, and the hand alive only to pain. I use this phrase because it is connected in my mind with a visit from a local visitor,—I am not sure he was a preacher,—who used to go daily through the wards, and talk to us or write our letters. One morning he stopped at my bed, when this little talk occurred:

"How are you, lieutenant?"

"Oh," said I, "as usual. All right, but this hand, which is dead except to pain."

"Ah," said he, "such and thus will the wicked be—such will you be if you die in your sins: you will go where only pain can be felt. For all eternity, all of you will be just like that hand—knowing pain only."

I suppose I was very weak, but somehow I felt a sudden and chilling horror of possible universal pain, and suddenly fainted. When I awoke the hand was worse, if that could be. It was red, shining, aching, burning, and, as it seemed to me, perpetually rasped with hot files. When the doctor came I begged for morphia. He said gravely: "We have none. You know you don't allow it to pass the lines." It was sadly true.

I turned to the wall, and wetted the hand again, my sole relief. In about an hour Dr. Wilson came back with two aides, and explained to me that the bone was so crushed as to make it hopeless to save it, and that, besides, amputation offered some chance of arresting the pain. I had thought of this before, but the anguish I felt—I cannot say endured—was so awful that I made no more of losing the limb than of parting with a tooth on account of toothache. Accordingly, brief preparations were made, which I watched with a sort of eagerness such as must forever be inexplicable to any one who has not passed six weeks of torture like that which I had suffered.

I had but one pang before the operation. As I arranged myself on the left side, so as to make it convenient for the operator to use the knife, I asked: "Who is to give me the ether?" "We have none," said the person questioned. I set my teeth, and said no more.

I need not describe the operation. The pain felt was severe, but it was insignificant as compared with that of any other minute of the past six weeks. The limb was removed very near to the shoulder-joint. As the second incision was made, I felt a strange flash of pain play through the limb, as if it were in every minutest fibril of nerve. This was followed by instant, unspeakable relief, and before the flaps were brought together I was sound asleep. I dimly remember saying, as I pointed to the arm which lay on the floor: "There is the pain, and here am I. How queer!" Then I slept—slept the sleep of the just, or, better, of the painless. From this time forward I was free from neuralgia. At a subsequent period I saw a number of cases similar to mine in a hospital in Philadelphia.

It is no part of my plan to detail my weary months of monotonous prison life in the South. In the early part of April, 1863, I was exchanged, and after the usual thirty days' furlough returned to my regiment a captain.

On the 19th of September, 1863, occurred the battle of Chickamauga, in which my regiment took a conspicuous part. The close of our own share in this contest is, as it were, burned into my memory with every least detail. It was about 6 P.M., when we found ourselves in line, under cover of a long, thin row of scrubby trees, beyond which lay a gentle slope, from which, again, rose a hill rather more abrupt, and crowned with an earthwork. We received orders to cross this space and take the fort in front, while a brigade on our right was to make a like movement on its flank.

Just before we emerged into the open ground, we noticed what, I think, was common in many fights—that the enemy had begun to bowl round shot at us, probably from failure of shell. We passed across the valley in good order, although the men fell rapidly all along the line. As we climbed the hill, our pace slackened, and the fire grew heavier. At this moment a battery opened on our left, the shots crossing our heads obliquely. It is this moment which is so printed on my recollection. I can see now, as if through a window, the gray smoke, lit with red flashes, the long, wavering line, the sky blue above, the trodden furrows, blotted with blue blouses. Then it was as if the window closed, and I knew and saw no more. No other scene in my life is thus scarred, if I may say so, into my memory. I have a fancy that the horrible shock which suddenly fell upon me must have had something to do with thus intensifying the momentary image then before my eyes.

When I awakened, I was lying under a tree somewhere at the rear. The ground was covered with wounded, and the doctors were busy at an operating-table, improvised from two barrels and a plank. At length two of them who were examining the wounded about me came up to where I lay. A hospital steward raised my head and poured down some brandy and water, while another cut loose my pantaloons. The doctors exchanged looks and walked away. I asked the steward where I was hit.

"Both thighs," said he; "the doctors won't do nothing."

"No use?" said I.

"Not much," said he.

"Not much means none at all," I answered.

When he had gone I set myself to thinking about a good many things I had better have thought of before, but which in no way concern the history of my case. A half-hour went by. I had no pain, and did not get weaker. At last, I cannot explain why, I began to look about me. At first things appeared a little hazy. I remember one thing which thrilled me a little, even then.

A tall, blond-bearded major walked up to a doctor near me, saying, "When you've a little leisure, just take a look at my side."

"Do it now," said the doctor.

The officer exposed his wound. "Ball went in here, and out there."

The doctor looked up at him—half pity, half amazement. "If you've got any message, you'd best send it by me."

"Why, you don't say it's serious?" was the reply.

"Serious! Why, you're shot through the stomach. You won't live over the day."

Then the man did what struck me as a very odd thing. He said, "Anybody got a pipe?" Some one gave him a pipe. He filled it deliberately, struck a light with a flint, and sat down against a tree near to me. Presently the doctor came to him again, and asked him what he could do for him.

"Send me a drink of Bourbon."

"Anything else?"

"No."

As the doctor left him, he called him back. "It's a little rough, doc, isn't it?"

No more passed, and I saw this man no longer. Another set of doctors were handling my legs, for the first time causing pain. A moment after a steward put a towel over my mouth, and I smelled the familiar odor of chloroform, which I was glad enough to breathe. In a moment the trees began to move around from left to right, faster and faster; then a universal grayness came before me,—and I recall nothing further until I awoke to consciousness in a hospital-tent. I got hold of my own identity in a moment or two, and was suddenly aware of a sharp cramp in my left leg. I tried to get at it to rub it with my single arm, but, finding myself too weak, hailed an attendant. "Just rub my left calf," said I, "if you please."

"Calf?" said he. "You ain't none. It's took off."

"I know better," said I. "I have pain in both legs."

"Wall, I never!" said he. "You ain't got nary leg."

As I did not believe him, he threw off the covers, and, to my horror, showed me that I had suffered amputation of both thighs, very high up.

"That will do," said I, faintly.

A month later, to the amazement of every one, I was so well as to be moved from the crowded hospital at Chattanooga to Nashville, where I filled one of the ten thousand beds of that vast metropolis of hospitals. Of the sufferings which then began I shall presently speak. It will be best just now to detail the final misfortune which here fell upon me. Hospital No. 2, in which I lay, was inconveniently crowded with severely wounded officers. After my third week an epidemic of hospital gangrene broke out in my ward. In three days it attacked twenty persons. Then an inspector came, and we were transferred at once to the open air, and placed in tents. Strangely enough, the wound in my remaining arm, which still suppurated, was seized with gangrene. The usual remedy, bromine, was used locally, but the main artery opened, was tied, bled again and again, and at last, as a final resort, the remaining arm was amputated at the shoulder-joint. Against all chances I recovered, to find myself a useless torso, more like some strange larval creature than anything of human shape. Of my anguish and horror of myself I dare not speak. I have dictated these pages, not to shock my readers, but to possess them with facts in regard to the relation of the mind to the body; and I hasten, therefore, to such portions of my case as best illustrate these views.

In January, 1864, I was forwarded to Philadelphia, in order to enter what was known as the Stump Hospital, South Street, then in charge of Dr. Hopkinson. This favor was obtained through the influence of my father's friend, the late Governor Anderson, who has always manifested an interest in my case, for which I am deeply grateful. It was thought, at the time, that Mr. Palmer, the leg-maker, might be able to adapt some form of arm to my left shoulder, as on that side there remained five inches of the arm-bone, which I could move to a moderate extent. The hope proved illusory, as the stump was always too tender to bear any pressure. The hospital referred to was in charge of several surgeons while I was an inmate, and was at all times a clean and pleasant home. It was filled with men who had lost one arm or leg, or one of each, as happened now and then. I saw one man who had lost both legs, and one who had parted with both arms; but none, like myself, stripped of every limb. There were collected in this place hundreds of these cases, which gave to it, with reason enough, the not very pleasing title of Stump Hospital.

I spent here three and a half months, before my transfer to the United States Army Hospital for Injuries and Diseases of the Nervous System. Every morning I was carried out in an arm-chair and placed in the library, where some one was always ready to write or read for me, or to fill my pipe. The doctors lent me medical books; the ladies brought me luxuries and fed me; and, save that I was helpless to a degree which was humiliating, I was as comfortable as kindness could make me.

I amused myself at this time by noting in my mind all that I could learn from other limbless folk, and from myself, as to the peculiar feelings which were noticed in regard to lost members. I found that the great mass of men who had undergone amputations for many months felt the usual consciousness that they still had the lost limb. It itched or pained, or was cramped, but never felt hot or cold. If they had painful sensations referred to it, the conviction of its existence continued unaltered for long periods; but where no pain was felt in it, then by degrees the sense of having that limb faded away entirely. I think we may to some extent explain this. The knowledge we possess of any part is made up of the numberless impressions from without which affect its sensitive surfaces, and which are transmitted through its nerves to the spinal nerve-cells, and through them, again, to the brain. We are thus kept endlessly informed as to the existence of parts, because the impressions which reach the brain are, by a law of our being, referred by us to the part from which they come. Now, when the part is cut off, the nerve-trunks which led to it and from it, remaining capable of being impressed by irritations, are made to convey to the brain from the stump impressions which are, as usual, referred by the brain to the lost parts to which these nerve-threads belonged. In other words, the nerve is like a bell-wire. You may pull it at any part of its course, and thus ring the bell as well as if you pulled at the end of the wire; but, in any case, the intelligent servant will refer the pull to the front door, and obey it accordingly. The impressions made on the severed ends of the nerve are due often to changes in the stump during healing, and consequently cease when it has healed, so that finally, in a very healthy stump, no such impressions arise; the brain ceases to correspond with the lost leg, and, as *les absents ont toujours tort,* it is no longer remembered or recognized. But in some cases, such as mine proved at last to my sorrow, the ends of the nerves undergo a curious alteration, and get to be enlarged and altered. This change, as I have seen in my practice of medicine, sometimes passes up the nerves toward the centers, and occasions a more or less constant irritation of the nerve-fibers, producing neuralgia, which is usually referred by the brain to that part of the lost limb to which the affected nerve belonged. This pain keeps the brain ever mindful of the missing part, and, imperfectly at least, preserves to the man a consciousness of possessing that which he has not.

Where the pains come and go, as they do in certain cases, the subjective sensations thus occasioned are very curious, since in such cases the man loses and gains, and loses and regains, the consciousness of the presence of the lost parts, so that he will tell you, "Now I feel my thumb, now I feel my little finger." I should also add that nearly every person who has lost an arm above the elbow feels as though the lost member were bent at the elbow, and at times is vividly impressed with the notion that his fingers are strongly flexed.

Other persons present a peculiarity which I am at a loss to account for. Where the leg, for instance, has been lost, they feel as if the foot were present, but as though the leg were shortened. Thus, if the thigh has been taken off, there seems to them to be a foot at the knee; if the arm, a hand seems to be at the elbow, or attached to the stump itself.

Before leaving Nashville I had begun to suffer the most acute pain in my left hand, especially the little finger; and so perfect was the idea which was thus kept up of the real presence of these missing parts that I found it hard at times to believe them absent. Often at night I would try with one lost hand to grope for the other. As, however, I had no pain in the right arm, the sense of the existence of that limb gradually disappeared, as did that of my legs also.

Everything was done for my neuralgia which the doctors could think of; and at length, at my suggestion, I was removed, as I have said, from the Stump Hospital to the United States Army Hospital for Injuries and Diseases of the Nervous System. It was a pleasant, suburban, old-fashioned country-seat, its gardens surrounded by a circle of wooden, one-story wards, shaded by fine trees. There were some three hundred cases of epilepsy, paralysis, St. Vitus's dance, and wounds of nerves. On one side of me lay a poor fellow, a Dane, who had the same burning neuralgia with which I once suffered, and which I now learned was only too common. This man had become hysterical from pain. He carried a sponge in his pocket, and a bottle of water in one hand, with which he constantly wetted the burning hand. Every sound increased his torture, and he even poured water into his boots to keep himself from feeling too sensibly the rough friction of his soles when walking. Like him, I was greatly eased by having small doses of morphia injected under the skin of my shoulder with a hollow needle fitted to a syringe.

As I improved under the morphia treatment, I began to be disturbed by the horrible variety of suffering about me. One man walked sideways; there was one who could not smell; another was dumb from an explosion. In fact, every one had his own abnormal peculiarity. Near me was a strange case of palsy of the muscles called rhomboids, whose office it is to hold down the shoulder-blades flat on the back during the motions of the arms, which, in themselves, were strong enough. When, however, he lifted these members, the shoulder-blades stood out from the back like wings, and got him the sobriquet of the "Angel." In my ward were also the cases of fits, which very much annoyed me, as upon any great change in the weather it was common to have a dozen convulsions in view at once. Dr. Neek, one of our physicians, told me that on one occasion a hundred and fifty fits took place within thirty-six hours. On my complaining of these sights, whence I alone could not fly, I was placed in the paralytic and wound ward, which I found much more pleasant.

A month of skilful treatment eased me entirely of my aches, and I then began to experience certain curious feelings, upon which, having nothing to do and nothing to do anything with, I reflected a good deal. It was a good while before I could correctly explain to my own satisfaction the phenomena which at this time I was called upon to observe. By the various operations already described I had lost about four fifths of my weight. As a consequence of this I ate much less than usual, and could scarcely have consumed the ration of a soldier. I slept also but little; for, as sleep is the repose of the brain, made necessary by the waste of its tissues during thought and voluntary movement, and as this latter did not exist in my case, I needed only that rest which was necessary to repair such exhaustion of the nerve-centers as was induced by thinking and the automatic movements of the viscera.

I observed at this time also that my heart, in place of beating, as it once did, seventy-eight in the minute, pulsated only forty-five times in this interval—a fact to be easily explained by the perfect quiescence to which I was reduced, and the consequent absence of that healthy and constant stimulus to the muscles of the heart which exercise occasions.

Notwithstanding these drawbacks, my physical health was good, which, I confess, surprised me, for this among other reasons: It is said that a burn of two thirds of the surface destroys life, because then all the excretory matters which this portion of the glands of the skin evolved are thrown upon the blood, and poison the man, just as happens in an animal whose skin the physiologist has varnished, so as in this way to destroy its function. Yet here was I, having lost at least a third of my skin, and apparently none the worse for it.

Still more remarkable, however, were the psychical changes which I now began to perceive. I found to my horror that at times I was less conscious of myself, of my own existence, than used to be the case. This sensation was so novel that at first it quite bewildered me. I felt like asking someone constantly if I were really George Dedlow or not; but, well aware how absurd I should seem after such a question, I refrained from speaking of my case, and strove more keenly to analyze my feelings. At times the conviction of my want of being myself was overwhelming and most painful. It was, as well as I can describe it, a deficiency in the egoistic sentiment of individuality. About one half of the sensitive surface of my skin was gone, and thus much of relation to the outer world destroyed. As a consequence, a large part of the receptive central organs must be out of employ, and, like other idle things, degenerating rapidly. Moreover, all the great central ganglia, which give rise to movements in the limbs, were also eternally at rest. Thus one half of me was absent or functionally dead. This set me to thinking how much a man might lose and yet live. If I were unhappy enough to survive, I might part with my spleen at least, as many a dog has done, and grown fat afterwards. The other organs with which we breathe and circulate the blood would be essential; so also would the liver; but at least half of the intestines might be dispensed with, and of course all

of the limbs. And as to the nervous system, the only parts really neces-
sary to life are a few small ganglia. Were the rest absent or inactive, we
should have a man reduced, as it were, to the lowest terms, and lead-
ing an almost vegetative existence. Would such a being, I asked myself,
possess the sense of individuality in its usual completeness, even if his
organs of sensation remained, and he were capable of consciousness?
Of course, without them, he could not have it any more than a dahlia
or a tulip. But with them—how then? I concluded that it would be at
a minimum, and that, if utter loss of relation to the outer world were
capable of destroying a man's consciousness of himself, the destruction
of half of his sensitive surfaces might well occasion, in a less degree, a
like result, and so diminish his sense of individual existence.

I thus reached the conclusion that a man is not his brain, or any
one part of it, but all of his economy, and that to lose any part must
lessen this sense of his own existence. I found but one person who
properly appreciated this great truth. She was a New England lady,
from Hartford—an agent, I think, for some commission, perhaps the
Sanitary. After I had told her my views and feelings she said: "Yes, I
comprehend. The fractional entities of vitality are embraced in the
oneness of the unitary Ego. Life," she added, "is the garnered con-
densation of objective impressions; and as the objective is the remote
father of the subjective, so must individuality, which is but focused
subjectivity, suffer and fade when the sensation lenses, by which the
rays of impression are condensed, become destroyed." I am not quite
clear that I fully understood her, but I think she appreciated my ideas,
and I felt grateful for her kindly interest.

The strange want I have spoken of now haunted and perplexed me
so constantly that I became moody and wretched. While in this state,
a man from a neighboring ward fell one morning into conversation
with the chaplain, within ear-shot of my chair. Some of their words
arrested my attention, and I turned my head to see and listen. The
speaker, who wore a sergeant's chevron and carried one arm in a sling
was a tall, loosely made person, with a pale face, light eyes of a washed-
out blue tint, and very sparse yellow whiskers. His mouth was weak,
both lips being almost alike, so that the organ might have been turned
upside down without affecting its expression. His forehead, however,
was high and thinly covered with sandy hair. I should have said, as a
phrenologist, will feeble; emotional, but not passionate; likely to be an
enthusiast or a weakly bigot.

I caught enough of what passed to make me call to the sergeant
when the chaplain left him.

"Good morning," said he. "How do you get on?"

"Not at all," I replied. "Where were you hit?"

"Oh, at Chancellorsville. I was shot in the shoulder. I have what the doctors call paralysis of the median nerve, but I guess Dr. Neek and the lightnin' battery will fix it. When my time's out I'll go back to Kearsarge and try on the school-teaching again. I've done my share."

"Well," said I, "you're better off than I."

"Yes," he answered, "in more ways than one. I belong to the New Church. It's a great comfort for a plain man like me, when he's weary and sick, to be able to turn away from earthly things and hold converse daily with the great and good who have left this here world. We have a circle in Coates Street. If it wa'n't for the consoling I get there, I'd of wished myself dead many a time. I ain't got kith or kin on earth; but this matters little, when one can just talk to them daily and know that they are in the spheres above us."

"It must be a great comfort," I replied, "if only one could believe it."

"Believe!" he repeated. "How can you help it? Do you suppose anything dies?"

"No," I said. "The soul does not, I am sure; and as to matter, it merely changes form."

"But why, then," said he, "should not the dead soul talk to the living? In space, no doubt, exist all forms of matter, merely in finer, more ethereal being. You can't suppose a naked soul moving about without a bodily garment—no creed teaches that; and if its new clothing be of like substance to ours, only of ethereal fineness,—a more delicate recrystallization about the eternal spiritual nucleus,—must it not then possess powers as much more delicate and refined as is the new material in which it is reclad?"

"Not very clear," I answered; "but, after all, the thing should be susceptible of some form of proof to our present senses."

"And so it is," said he. "Come tomorrow with me, and you shall see and hear for yourself."

"I will," said I, "if the doctor will lend me the ambulance."

It was so arranged, as the surgeon in charge was kind enough, as usual, to oblige me with the loan of his wagon, and two orderlies to lift my useless trunk.

On the day following I found myself, with my new comrade, in a house in Coates Street, where a "circle" was in the daily habit of meeting. So soon as I had been comfortably deposited in an arm-chair, beside a large pine table, the rest of those assembled seated themselves, and for some time preserved an unbroken silence. During this pause I scrutinized the persons present. Next to me, on my right, sat a flabby man, with ill-marked, baggy features and injected eyes. He was, as I learned afterwards, an eclectic doctor, who had tried his hand at medicine and several of its quackish variations, finally settling down on eclecticism, which I believe professes to be to scientific medicine what vegetarianism is to common-sense, every-day dietetics. Next to him sat a female-authoress, I think, of two somewhat feeble novels, and much pleasanter to look at than her books. She was, I thought, a good deal excited at the prospect of spiritual revelations. Her neighbor was a pallid, care-worn young woman, with very red lips, and large brown eyes of great beauty. She was, as I learned afterwards, a magnetic patient of the doctor, and had deserted her husband, a master mechanic, to follow this new light. The others were, like myself, strangers brought hither by mere curiosity. One of them was a lady in deep black, closely veiled. Beyond her, and opposite to me, sat the sergeant, and next to him the medium, a man named Brink. He wore a good deal of jewelry, and had large black side-whiskers—a shrewd-visaged, large-nosed, full-lipped man, formed by nature to appreciate the pleasant things of sensual existence.

Before I had ended my survey, he turned to the lady in black, and asked if she wished to see any one in the spirit-world.

She said, "Yes," rather feebly.

"Is the spirit present?" he asked. Upon which two knocks were heard in affirmation. "Ah!" said the medium, "the name is—it is the name of a child. It is a male child. It is—"

"Alfred!" she cried. "Great Heaven! My child! My boy!"

On this the medium arose, and became strangely convulsed. "I see," he said—"I see—a fair-haired boy. I see blue eyes—I see above you, beyond you—" at the same time pointing fixedly over her head.

She turned with a wild start. "Where—whereabouts?"

"A blue-eyed boy," he continued, "over your head. He cries—he says, 'Mama, mama!'"

The effect of this on the woman was unpleasant. She stared about her for a moment, and exclaiming, "I come—I am coming, Alfy!" fell in hysterics on the floor.

Two or three persons raised her, and aided her into an adjoining room; but the rest remained at the table, as though well accustomed to like scenes.

After this several of the strangers were called upon to write the names of the dead with whom they wished to communicate. The names were spelled out by the agency of affirmative knocks when the correct letters were touched by the applicant, who was furnished with an alphabet-card upon which he tapped the letters in turn, the medium, meanwhile, scanning his face very keenly. With some, the names were readily made out. With one, a stolid personage of disbelieving type, every attempt failed, until at last the spirits signified by knocks that he was a disturbing agency, and that while he remained all our efforts would fail. Upon this some of the company proposed that he should leave; of which invitation he took advantage, with a skeptical sneer at the whole performance.

As he left us, the sergeant leaned over and whispered to the medium, who next addressed himself to me. "Sister Euphemia," he said, indicating the lady with large eyes, "will act as your medium. I am unable to do more. These things exhaust my nervous system."

"Sister Euphemia," said the doctor, "will aid us. Think, if you please, sir, of a spirit, and she will endeavor to summon it to our circle."

Upon this a wild idea came into my head. I answered: "I am thinking as you directed me to do."

The medium sat with her arms folded, looking steadily at the center of the table. For a few moments there was silence. Then a series of irregular knocks began. "Are you present?" said the medium.

The affirmative raps were twice given.

"I should think," said the doctor, "that there were two spirits present."

His words sent a thrill through my heart.

"Are there two?" he questioned.

A double rap.

"Yes, two," said the medium. "Will it please the spirits to make us conscious of their names in this world?"

A single knock. "No."

"Will it please them to say how they are called in the world of spirits?"

Again came the irregular raps—3, 4, 8, 6; then a pause, and 3, 4, 8, 7.

"I think," said the authoress, "they must be numbers. Will the spirits," she said, "be good enough to aid us? Shall we use the alphabet?"

"Yes," was rapped very quickly.

"Are these numbers?"

"Yes," again.

"I will write them," she added, and, doing so, took up the card and tapped the letters. The spelling was pretty rapid, and ran thus as she tapped, in turn, first the letters, and last the numbers she had already set down:

"UNITED STATES ARMY MEDICAL MUSEUM, Nos. 3486, 3487."

The medium looked up with a puzzled expression.

"Good gracious!" said I, "they are *my legs—my legs!*"

What followed, I ask no one to believe except those who, like myself, have communed with the things of another sphere. Suddenly I felt a strange return of my self-consciousness. I was reindividualized, so to speak. A strange wonder filled me, and, to the amazement of every one, I arose, and, staggering a little, walked across the room on limbs invisible to them or me. It was no wonder I staggered, for, as I briefly reflected, my legs had been nine months in the strongest alcohol. At this instant all my new friends crowded around me in astonishment. Presently, however, I felt myself sinking slowly. My legs were going, and in a moment I was resting feebly on my two stumps upon the floor. It was too much. All that was left of me fainted and rolled over senseless.

I have little to add. I am now at home in the West, surrounded by every form of kindness and every possible comfort; but alas! I have so little surety of being myself that I doubt my own honesty in drawing my pension, and feel absolved from gratitude to those who are kind to a being who is uncertain of being enough himself to be conscientiously responsible. It is needless to add that I am not a happy fraction of a man, and that I am eager for the day when I shall rejoin the lost members of my corporeal family in another and a happier world.

★   ★   ★

Epitaph on John B. Floyd

Anonymous

A private in Battery F, Fourth U.S. artillery, wrote about a thieving fellow soldier.

> Floyd has died and few have sobbed,
> Since, had he lived, all had been robbed:
> He's paid Dame Nature's debt, 'tis said,
> The only one he ever paid.
> Some doubt that he resigned his breath.
>
> But vow he has cheated even death.
> If he is buried, oh! then, ye dead, beware,
> Look to your swaddlings, of your shrouds take care,
> Lest Floyd should to your coffins make his way,
> And steal the linen from your mouldering clay.

The Silent March

ANONYMOUS

"On one occasion during the war in Virginia, General Lee was lying asleep by the way-side, when an army of fifteen thousand men passed by with hushed voices and footsteps, lest they should disturb his slumbers," writes William Gilmore Simms, editor of War Poetry of the South *(1866).*

O'ercome with weariness and care,
  The war-worn veteran lay
On the green turf of his native land,
  And slumbered by the way;
The breeze that sighed across his brow,
  And smoothed its deepened lines,
Fresh from his own loved mountain bore
  The murmur of their pines;
And the glad sound of waters,
  The blue rejoicing streams,
Whose sweet familiar tones were blent
  With the music of his dreams:
They brought no sound of battle's din,
  Shrill fife or clarion,
But only tenderest memories
  Of his own fair Arlington.
While thus the chieftain slumbered,
  Forgetful of his care,
The hollow tramp of thousands
  Came sounding through the air.
With ringing spur and sabre,
  And trampling feet they come,
Gay plume and rustling banner,
  And fife, and trump, and drum;
But soon the foremost column
  Sees where, beneath the shade,
In slumber, calm as childhood,
  Their wearied chief is laid;
And down the line a murmur
  From lip to lip there ran,
Until the stilly whisper
  Had spread to rear from van;

And o'er the host a silence
　　As deep and sudden fell,
As though some mighty wizard
　　Had hushed them with a spell;
And every sound was muffled,
　　And every soldier's tread
Fell lightly as a mother's
　　'Round her baby's cradle-bed;
And rank, and file, and column,
　　So softly by they swept,
It seemed a ghostly army
　　Had passed him as he slept;
But mightier than enchantment
　　Was that with magic move—
The spell that hushed their voices—
　　Deep reverence and love.

1865

A True Story, Repeated Word for Word As I Heard It

Mark Twain

Samuel Clemens (1835–1910), who became America's most famous writer as Mark Twain, wrote very little about the war. Although early on he joined a Confederate brigade in Missouri, he quickly abandoned it and went to Nevada. This story, about a former slave looking back at the war and her family's life and a happy reunion, was published in November 1874 in The Atlantic Monthly.

It was summer time, and twilight. We were sitting on the porch of the farmhouse, on the summit of the hill, and "Aunt Rachel" was sitting respectfully below our level, on the steps—for she was our servant, and colored. She was of mighty frame and stature; she was sixty years old, but her eye was undimmed and her strength unabated. She was a cheerful, hearty soul, and it was no more trouble for her to laugh than it is for a bird to sing. She was under fire now, as usual when the day was done. That is to say, she was being chaffed without mercy, and was enjoying it. She would let off peal after peal of laughter, and then sit with her face in her hands and shake with throes of enjoyment which she could no longer get breath enough to express. At such a moment as this a thought occurred to me, and I said:

"Aunt Rachel, how is it that you've lived sixty years and never had any trouble?"

She stopped quaking. She paused, and there was a moment of silence. She turned her face over her shoulder toward me, and said, without even a smile in her voice:

"Misto C——, is you in 'arnest?"

It surprised me a good deal; and it sobered my manner and my speech, too. I said:

"Why, I thought—that is, I meant—why, you *can't* have had any trouble. I've never heard you sigh, and never seen your eye when there wasn't a laugh in it."

She faced fairly around now, and was full of earnestness.

"Has I had any trouble? Misto C——, I's gwyne to tell you, den I leave it to you. I was bawn down 'mongst de slaves; I knows all 'bout slavery, 'case I ben one of 'em my own se'f. Well, sah, my ole man— dat's my husban'—he was lovin' an' kind to me, jist as kind as you is to yo' own wife. An' we had chil'en—seven chil'en—an' we loved dem chil'en jist de same as you loves yo' chil'en. Dey was black, but de Lord can't make no chil'en so black but what dey mother loves 'em an' wouldn't give 'em up, no, not for anything dat's in dis whole world.

"Well, sah, I was raised in ole Fo'ginny, but my mother she was raised in Maryland; an' my *souls!* she was tumble when she'd git started! My *lan'!* but she'd make de fur fly! When she'd git into dem tantrums, she always had one word dat she said. She'd straighten herse'f up an' put her' fists in her hips an' say, 'I want you to understan' dat I wa'nt bawn in the mash to be fool' by trash! I's one o' de ole Blue Hen's Chickens, *I* is!' 'Ca'se, you see, dat's what folks dat's bawn in Maryland calls deyselves, an' dey's proud of it. Well, dat was her word. I don't ever forgit it, beca'se she said it so much, an' beca'se she said it one day when my little Henry tore his wris' awful, and most busted his head, right up at de top of his forehead, an' de niggers didn't fly aroun' fas' enough to 'tend to him. An' when dey talk' back at her, she up an' she says, 'Look-a-heah!' she says, 'I want you niggers to understan' dat I wa'nt bawn in de mash to be fool' by trash! I's one o' de ole Blue Hen's Chickens, *I* is!' an' den she clar' dat kitchen an' bandage' up de chile herse'f. So I says dat word, too, when I's riled.

"Well, bymeby my ole mistis say she's broke, an' she got to sell all de niggers on de place. An' when I heah dat dey gwyne to sell us all off at oction in Richmon', oh, de good gracious! I know what dat mean!"

Aunt Rachel had gradually risen, while she warmed to her subject, and now she towered above us, black against the stars.

"Dey put chains on us an' put us on a stan' as high as dis po'ch— twenty foot high—an' all de people stood aroun', crowds an' crowds. An' dey'd come up dah an' look at us all roun', an' squeeze our arm, an' make us git up an' walk, an' den say, 'Dis one too ole,' or 'Dis one lame,' or 'Dis one don't 'mount to much.' An' dey sole my ole man, an' took him away, an' dey begin to sell my chil'en an' take *dem* away, an' I begin to cry; an' de man say, 'Shet up yo' dam blubberin',' an' hit me on de mouf wid his han'. An' when de las' one was gone but my little Henry, I grab *him* clost up to my breas' so, an' I ris up an' says, 'You shan't take him away,' I says; 'I'll kill de man dat tetches him!' I says. But my little Henry whisper an' say, 'I gwyne to run away, an' den I work an' buy yo' freedom.' Oh, bless de chile, he always so good! But dey got him—dey got him, de men did; but I took and tear de clo'es mos' off of 'em an' beat 'em over de head wid my chain; an' *dey* give it to *me,* too, but I didn't mine dat.

"Well, dah was my ole man gone, an' all my chil'en, all my seven chil'en—an' six of 'em I hain't set eyes on ag'in to dis day, an' dat's twenty-two year ago las' Easter. De man dat bought me b'long' in Newbern, an' he took me dah. Well, bymeby de years roll on an' de waw come. My marster he was a Confedrit colonel, an' I was his family's cook. So when de Unions took dat town, dey all run away an' lef' me all by myse'f wid de other niggers in dat mons'us big house. So de big Union officers move in dah, an' dey ask me would I cook for *dem*. 'Lord bless you,' says I, 'dat's what I's *for*.'

"Dey wa'nt no small-fry officers, mine you, dey was de biggest dey *is*; an' de way dey made dem sojers mosey roun'! De Gen'l he tole me to boss dat kitchen; an' he say, 'If anybody come meddlin' wid you, you jist make 'em walk chalk; don't you be afeared,' he say; 'you's 'mong frens now.'

"Well, I thinks to myse'f, if my little Henry ever got a chance to run away, he'd make to de Norf, o' course. So one day I comes in dah whar de big officers was, in de parlor, an' I drops a kurtchy, so, an' I up an' tole 'em 'bout my Henry, dey a-listenin' to my troubles jist de same as if I was white folks; an' I says, 'What I come for is beca'se if he got away and got up Norf whar you gemmen comes from, you might 'a' seen him, maybe, an' could tell me so as I could fine him ag'in; he was very little, an' he had a skyar on his lef wris' an' at de top of his forehead.' Den dey look mournful, an' de Gen'l says, 'How long sence you los' him?' an' I say, 'Thirteen year.' Den de Gen'l say, 'He wouldn't be little no mo' now—he's a man!'

"I never thought o' dat befo'! He was only dat little feller to *me* yit. I never thought 'bout him growin' up an' bein' big. But I see it den. None o' de gemmen had run acrost him, so dey couldn't do nothin' for me. But all dat time, do' I didn't know it, my Henry *was* run off to de Norf, years an' years, an' he was a barber, too, an' worked for hisse'f. An' bymeby, when de waw come he ups an' he says: 'I's done barberin',' he says, 'I's gwyne to fine my ole mammy, less'n she's dead.' So he sole out an' went to whar dey was recruitin', an' hired hisse'f out to de colonel for his servant; an' den he went all froo de battles everywhah, huntin' for his ole mammy; yes, indeedy, he'd hire to fust one officer an' den

another, tell he'd ransacked de whole Souf; but you see *I* didn't know
nuffin 'bout *dis*. How was *I* gwyne to know it?

"Well, one night we had a big sojer ball; de sojers dah at Newbern
was always havin' balls an' carryin' on. Dey had 'em in my kitchen,
heaps o' times, 'ca'se it was so big. Mine you, I was *down* on sich doin's;
beca'se my place was wid de officers, an' it rasp me to have dem com-
mon sojers cavortin' roun' my kitchen like dat. But I alway' stood
aroun' an' kep' things straight, I did; an' sometimes dey'd git my dander
up, an' den I'd make 'em clar dat kitchen, mine I *tell* you!

"Well, one night—it was a Friday night—dey comes a whole plat-
toon f'm a *nigger* ridgment dat was on guard at de house—de house
was headquarters, you know—an' den I was jist a-*bilin'!* Mad? I was
jist a-*boomin'!* I swelled aroun', an' swelled aroun'; I jist was a-itchin'
for 'em to do somefin for to start me. *An'* dey was a-waltzin' an' a-
dancin'! *my!* but dey was havin' a time! an' I jist a-swellin' an' a-swellin'
up! Pooty soon, 'long comes *sich* a spruce young nigger a-sailin' down
de room wid a yaller wench roun' de wais'; an' roun' an' roun' an' roun'
dey went, enough to make a body drunk to look at 'em; an' when
dey got abreas' o' me, dey went to kin' o' balacin' aroun' fust on one
leg an' den on t'other, an' smilin' at my big red turban, an' makin' fun,
an' I ups an' says '*Git* along wid you!—rubbage!' De young man's face
kin' o' changed, all of a sudden, for 'bout a second, but den he went to
smilin' ag'in, same as he was befo'. Well, 'bout dis time, in comes some
niggers dat played music and b'long' to de ban', an' dey never could git
along widout puttin' on airs. An' de very fust air dey put on dat night, I
lit into 'em! Dey laughed, an' dat made me wuss. De res' o' de niggers
got to laughin', an' den my soul *alive* but I was hot! My eye was jist
a-blazin'! I jist straightened myself up so—jist as I is now, plum to de
ceilin', mos'—an' I digs my fists into my hips, an' I says, 'Look-a-heah!'
I says, 'I want you niggers to understan' dat I wa'nt bawn in de mash
to be fool' by trash! I's one o' de ole Blue Hen's Chickens, *I* is!' an'
den I see dat young man stan' a-starin' an' stiff, lookin' kin' o' up at de
ceilin' like he fo'got somefin, an' couldn't 'member it no mo'. Well, I
jist march' on dem niggers—so, lookin' like a gen'l—an' dey jist cave'
away befo' me an' out at de do'. An' as dis young man was a-goin' out,
I heah him say to another nigger, 'Jim,' he says, 'you go 'long an' tell de
cap'n I be on han' 'bout eight o'clock in de mawnin'; dey's somefin on
my mine,' he says; 'I don't sleep no mo' dis night. You go 'long,' he says,
'an' leave me by my own se'f.'

"Dis was 'bout one o'clock in de mawnin'. Well, 'bout seven, I was
up an' on han', gittin' de officers' breakfast. I was a-stoopin' down by

de stove—jist so, same as if yo' foot was de stove—an' I'd opened de
stove do' wid my right han'—so, pushin' it back, jist as I pushes yo'
foot—an' I'd jist got de pan o' hot biscuits in my han' an' was 'bout to
raise up, when I see a black face come aroun' under mine, an' de eyes
a-lookin' up into mine, jist as I's a-lookin' up clost under yo' face now;
an' I jist stopped *right dah,* an' never budged! jist gazed an' gazed so;
an' de pan begin to tremble, an' all of a sudden I *knowed!* De pan drop'
on de flo' an' I grab his lef han' an' shove back his sleeve—jist so, as I's
doin' to you—an' den I goes for his forehead an' push de hair back so,
an' 'Boy!' I says, 'if you an't my Henry, what is you doin' wid dis welt
on yo' wris' an' dat skyar on yo' forehead? De Lord God ob heaven be
praise', I got my own ag'in.'

"Oh, no, Misto C——, I haint had no trouble. An' no *joy!*"

★   ★   ★

The Dog of the Regiment

ANONYMOUS

"If I were a poet, like you, my friend,"
    Said a bronzed old sergeant, speaking to me,
"I would make a rhyme of this mastiff here;
    For a right good Union dog is he.
Although he was born on 'secesh' soil,
    And his master fought in the rebel ranks.
If you'll do it, I'll tell you his history,
    And give you in pay, why—a soldier's thanks.

"Well, the way we came across him was this:
    We were on the march, and 'twas getting late
When we reached a farm-house, deserted by all
    Save this mastiff here, who stood at the gate.
Thin and gaunt as a wolf was he,
    And a piteous whine he gave 'twixt the bars;
But, bless you! if he didn't jump for joy
    When he saw our flag with the Stripes and Stars.

"Next day, when we started again on the march,
    With us went Jack, without word or call;
Stopping for rest at the order to 'halt,'
    And taking his rations along with us all,

Never straggling, but keeping his place in line,
　　Far to the right, and close beside me;
And I don't care where the other is found,
　　There never was better drilled dog than he.

"He always went with us into the fight,
　　And the thicker the bullets fell around,
And the louder the rattling musketry rolled,
　　Louder and fiercer his bark would sound;
And once when wounded, and left for dead,
　　After a bloody and desperate fight,
Poor Jack, as faithful as friend can be,
　　Lay by my side on the field all night.

"And so when our regiment home returned,
　　We brought him along with us, as you see;
And Jack and I being much attached,
　　The boys seemed to think he belonged to me.
And here he has lived with me ever since;
　　Right pleased with his quarters, too, he seems.
There are no more battles for brave old Jack,
　　And no more marches except in dreams.

"But the best of all times for the old dog is
　　When the thunder mutters along the sky,
Then he wakes the echoes around with his bark,
　　Thinking the enemy surely is nigh.
Now I've told you his history, write him a rhyme
　　Some day poor Jack in his grave must real—
And of all the rhymes of this cruel war
　　Which your brain has made, let his be the best."

★　★　★

A Soldier's Letter

MARY C. HOVEY

Dear madam, I'm a soldier, and my speech is rough and plain;
I'm not much used to writing, and I hate to give you pain;
But I promised that I'd do it—he thought it might be so,
If it came from one who loved him, perhaps 'twould ease the blow—

By this time you must surely guess the truth I fain would hide,
And you'll pardon a rough soldier's words, while I tell you how he
  died.

'Twas the night before the battle, and in our crowded tent
More than one brave boy was sobbing, and many a knee was bent;
For we knew not, when the morrow, with its bloody work, was done,
How many that were seated there, should see its setting sun.
'Twas not so much for self they cared, as for the loved at home;
And it's always worse to think of than to hear the cannon boom.

'Twas then we left the crowded tent, your soldier-boy and I,
And we both breath'ed freer, standing underneath the clear blue sky.
I was more than ten years older, but he seemed to take to me,
And oftener than the younger ones, he sought my company.
He seemed to want to talk of home and those he held most dear;
And though I'd none to talk of, yet I always loved to hear.

So then he told me, on that night, of the time he came away,
And how you sorely grieved for him, but would not let him stay;
And how his one fond hope had been that when this war was
  through,
He might go back with honor to his friends at home and you.
He named his sisters one by one, and then a deep flush came,
While he told me of another, but did not speak her name.

And then he said: "Dear Robert, it may be that I shall fall,
And will you write to them at home how I loved and spoke of all?"
So I promised, but I did not think the time would come so soon.
The fight was just three days ago—he died today at noon.
It seems so sad that one so loved should reach the fatal bourn,
While I should still be living here, who had no friends to mourn.

It was in the morrow's battle. Fast rained the shot and shell;
He was fighting close beside me, and I saw him when he fell.
So then I took him in my arms, and laid him on the grass—
'Twas going against orders, but I think they'll let it pass.
'Twas a Minie ball that struck him; it entered at the side,
And they did not think it fatal till the morning that he died.

So when he found that he must go, he called me to his bed,
And said: "You'll not forget to write when you hear that I am dead?
And you'll tell them how I loved them and bid them all good-by?
Say I tried to do the best I could, and did not fear to die;

And underneath my pillow there's a curl of golden hair;
There's a name upon the paper; send it to my mother's care.

"Last night I wanted so to live; I seemed so young to go;
Last week I passed my birthday—I was but nineteen, you know—
When I thought of all I'd planned to do, it seemed so hard to die;
But then I prayed to God for grace, and my cares are all gone by."
And here his voice grew weaker, and he partly raised his head,
And whispered, "Good-by, mother!" and so your boy was dead!

I wrapped his cloak around him, and we bore him out tonight,
And laid him by a clump of trees, where the moon was shining
    bright,
And we carved him out a headboard as skilful as we could;
If you should wish to find it, I can tell you where it stood.
I send you back his hymn-book, and the cap he used to wear,
And a lock, I cut the night before, of his bright, curling hair.

I send you back his Bible. The night before he died,
We turned its leaves together, as I read it by his side.
I've kept the belt he always wore; he told me so to do;
It has a hole upon the side—'tis where the ball went through.
So now I've done his bidding; there's nothing more to tell;
But I shall always mourn with you the boy we loved so well.

★ ★ ★

Carolina

HENRY TIMROD

At the end of the war, "Every man in [South Carolina] was called to arms, but the Union forces met with only a weak and ineffective resistance. On February 16, 1865, Columbia was occupied; and catching fire accidentally next day, was totally destroyed. The fall of Columbia left Charleston exposed and the Confederate troops hastened to get away while they could," writes the editor Burton Egbert Stevenson.

The despot treads thy sacred sands.
Thy pines give shelter to his bands.
Thy sons stand by with idle hands,
        Carolina!

He breathes at ease thy airs of balm,
He scorns the lances of thy palm;
Oh! who shall break thy craven calm,
        Carolina!
Thy ancient fame is growing dim,
A spot is on thy garment's rim;
Give to the winds thy battle-hymn,
        Carolina!

Call on thy children of the hill,
Wake swamp and river, coast and rill,
Rouse all thy strength and all thy skill,
        Carolina!
Cite wealth and science, trade and art,
Touch with thy fire the cautious mart,
And pour thee through the people's heart,
        Carolina!
Till even the coward spurns his fears.
And all thy fields, and fens, and meres
Shall bristle like thy palm with spears,
        Carolina!

I hear a murmur as of waves
That grope their way through sunless caves,
Like bodies struggling in their graves,
        Carolina!
And now it deepens; slow and grand
It swells, as, rolling to the land.
An ocean broke upon thy strand,
        Carolina!
Shout! Let it reach the startled Huns!
And roar with all thy festal guns!
It is the answer of thy sons,
        Carolina!

O Captain! My Captain!

Walt Whitman

Abraham Lincoln was shot on April 14, 1865, and died early the next morning. This is one of Whitman's grieving tributes.

O Captain! my Captain! our fearful trip is done;
The ship has weather'd every rack, the prize we sought is won;
The port is near, the bells I hear, the people all exulting,
While follow eyes the steady keel, the vessel grim and daring:
   But O heart! heart! heart!
     O the bleeding drops of red,
       Where on the deck my Captain lies,
         Fallen cold and dead.

O Captain! my Captain! rise up and hear the bells;
Rise up—for you the flag is flung—for you the bugle trills;
For you bouquets and ribbon'd wreaths—for you the shores a-crowding;
For you they call, the swaying mass, their eager faces turning;
   Here Captain! dear father!
     This arm beneath your head
       It is some dream that on the deck,
         You've fallen cold and dead.

My Captain does not answer, his lips are pale and still;
My father does not feel my arm, he has no pulse nor will;
The ship is anchor'd safe and sound, its voyage closed and done;
From fearful trip, the victor ship, comes in with object won:
   Exult, O shores, and ring, O bells!
     But I, with mournful tread,
       Walk the deck my Captain lies,
         Fallen cold and dead.

The Conquered Banner

<small>ABRAM JOSEPH RYAN</small>

Ryan (1838–1886) was a Roman Catholic priest from New Orleans and a popular poet.

Take that banner down, 'tis weary,
Round its staff 'tis drooping dreary,
 Furl it, hide it, let it rest;
For there's not a man to wave it—
For there's not a soul to lave it
In the blood that heroes gave it.
 Furl it, hide it, let it rest.

Take that banner down, 'tis tattered;
Broken is its staff, and shattered;
And the valiant hearts are scattered
 Over whom it floated high.
Oh! 'tis hard for us to fold it—
Hard to think there's none to hold it—
Hard that those who once unrolled it,
 Now must furl it with a sigh.

Furl that banner, furl it sadly;
Once six millions hailed it gladly,
And three hundred thousand madly,
 Swore it should forever wave—
Swore that foeman's sword should never
Hearts like theirs entwined dissever—
That their flag should float forever
 O'er their freedom or their grave!

Furl it, for the hands that grasped it,
And the hearts that fondly clasped it,
 Cold and dead are lying low;
And that banner—it is trailing,
While around it sounds the wailing
 Of its people in their woe;
For though conquered, they adore it,
Love the cold, dead hands that bore it,
Weep for those who fell before it—

Oh! how wildly they deplore it,
    Now to furl and fold it so!

Furl that banner; true 'tis gory,
But 'tis wreathed around with glory,
And 'twill live in song and story,
    Though its folds are in the dust;
For its fame, on brightest pages—
Sung by poets, penned by sages—
Shall go sounding down to ages—
    Furl its folds though now we must.

Furl that banner—softly, slowly;
Furl it gently, it is holy,
    For it droops above the dead.
Touch it not, unfurl it never,
Let it droop there, furled forever,
    For its people's hopes are fled.

★   ★   ★

Why Can Not We Be Brothers?

CLARENCE PRENTICE

Why can not we be brothers? the battle now is o'er;
We've laid our bruis'd arms on the field, to take them up no more;
We who have fought you hard and long, now overpower'd stand
As poor defenseless prisoners in our own native land.

Chorus—We know that we are Rebels,
        And we don't deny the name,
    We speak of that which we have done
        With grief, but not with shame.

But we have rights most sacred, by solemn compact bound,
Seal'd by the blood that freely gush'd from many a ghastly wound;
When Lee gave up his trusty sword, and his men laid down their
    arms,
It was that they should live at home, secure from war's dire harms.

And surely, since we've now disarm'd, we are not to be dreaded;
Our old chiefs, who on many fields our trusty columns headed,

Are fast within an iron grasp, and manacled with chains,
Perchance, 'twixt dreary walls to stay as long as life remains!

Oh! shame upon the coward band, who in the conflict dire,
Went not to battle for their cause, 'mid the ranks of steel and fire,
Yet now, since all the fighting's done, are hourly heard to cry:
"Down with the traitors! hang them all, each Rebel dog shall die!"

Chorus—We know that we are Rebels,
   And we don't deny the name,
  We speak of that which we have done
   With grief, but not with shame.

And we never will acknowledge that the blood the South has spilt,
Was shed defending what we deem'd a cause of wrong and guilt.

POST-WAR

True to the Gray

PEARL RIVERS

I can not listen to your words, the land is long and wide;
Go seek some happy Northern girl to be your loving bride;
My brothers they were soldiers—the youngest of the three
Was slain while fighting by the side of gallant FITZHUGH LEE!

They left his body on the field (your side the day had won),
A soldier spurn'd him with his foot—you might have been
    the one;
My lover was a soldier—he belonged to GORDON's band;
A saber pierced his gallant heart—*yours* might have been
    the hand.

He reel'd and fell, but was not dead, a horseman spurred his steed,
And trampled on the dying brain—*you* may have done the deed:
I hold no hatred in my heart, no cold, unrighteous pride,
For many a gallant soldier fought upon the other side:

But still I can not kiss the hand that smote my country sore,
Nor love the foes who trampled down the colors that she bore;
Between my heart and yours there rolls a deep and crimson tide—
My brother's and my lover's blood forbid me be your bride.

The girls who loved the boys in gray—the girls to country true—
May ne'er in wedlock give their hands to those who wore
    the blue.

The Confederate Note

S. A. Jonas

This poem was found, it is said, written on the back of a five-hundred-dollar Confederate note after the surrender. Jonas had been a Confederate officer from Mississippi.

Representing nothing on God's earth now,
  And naught in the water below it—
As a pledge of the nation that's dead and gone,
  Keep it, dear friend, and show it.

Show it to those who will lend an ear
  To the tale that this paper can tell,
Of liberty born, of patriot's dream
  Of the storm-cradled nation that fell.

Too poor to possess the precious ores,
  And too much of a stranger to borrow,
We issued today our promise to pay,
  And hoped to redeem on the morrow.

The days rolled on, and weeks became years,
  But our coffers were empty still;
Coin was so rare that the Treasury quaked
  If a dollar should drop in the till.

But the faith that was in us was strong, indeed,
  And our poverty well discerned;
And these little checks represented the pay
  That our suffering volunteers earned.

We knew it had hardly a value in gold,
  Yet as gold our soldiers received it;
It gazed in our eyes with a promise to pay,
  And each patriot soldier believed it.

But our boys thought little of price or pay,
  Or of bills that were over-due;
We knew if it brought us bread today,
  It was the best our poor country could do.

Keep it, it tells our history o'er,
  From the birth of its dream to the last;

Modest, and born of the angel Hope,
Like the hope of success it passed.

★ ★ ★

Rebel Color-Bearers at Shiloh

HERMAN MELVILLE

(A plea against the vindictive cry raised by civilians shortly after the surrender at Appomattox.)

The color-bearers facing death
White in the whirling sulphurous wreath,
   Stand boldly out before the line;
Right and left their glances go,
Proud of each other, glorying in their show;
Their battle-flags about them blow,
   And fold them as in flame divine:
Such living robes are only seen
Round martyrs burning on the green—
And martyrs for the Wrong have been.

Perish their Cause! but mark the men—
Mark the planted statues, then
Draw trigger on them if you can.

The leader of a patriot-band
Even so could view rebels who so could stand;
   And this when peril pressed him sore,
Left aidless in the shivered front of war—
   Skulkers behind, defiant foes before,
And fighting with a broken brand.
The challenge in that courage rare—
Courage defenseless, proudly bare—
Never could tempt him; he could dare
Strike up the leveled rifle there.

Sunday at Shiloh, and the day
When Stonewall charged—McClellan's crimson May,
And Chickamauga's wave of death,
And of the Wilderness the cypress wreath—
         All these have passed away.

The life in the veins of Treason lags,
Her daring color-bearers drop their flags,
   And yield. Now shall we fire?
       Can poor spite be?
   Shall nobleness in victory less aspire
   Than in reverse? Spare Spleen her ire,
       And think how Grant met Lee.

★　★　★

The Blue and the Gray

Francis Miles Finch

*The occasion for this 1867 tribute by New York State's Judge Finch was his learning,
on Decoration Day, that women in Columbus, Mississippi, had lain flowers not only on
the graves of Confederate soldiers but on those of the Union soldiers.*

By the flow of the inland river,
   Whence the fleets of iron have fled,
Where the blades of the grave-grass quiver,
   Asleep are the ranks of the dead:
      Under the sod and the dew,
        Waiting the judgment-day;—
      Under the one, the Blue,
        Under the other, the Gray.

These in the robings of glory,
   Those in the gloom of defeat,
All with the battle-blood gory,
   In the dusk of eternity meet:—
      Under the sod and the dew,
        Waiting the judgment-day;—
      Under the laurel, the Blue,
        Under the willow, the Gray.

From the silence of sorrowful hours
   The desolate mourners go,
Lovingly laden with flowers
   Alike for the friend and the foe:
      Under the sod and the dew,
        Waiting the judgment-day;—

Under the roses, the Blue,
   Under the lilies, the Gray.

So, with an equal splendor,
   The morning sun-rays fall,
With a touch impartially tender,
   On the blossoms blooming for all:
     Under the sod and the dew,
      Waiting the judgment-day;—
     'Broidered with gold, the Blue,
      Mellowed with gold, the Gray.

So, when the summer calleth,
   On forest and field of grain,
With an equal murmur falleth
   The cooling drip of the rain:
     Under the sod and the dew,
      Waiting the judgment-day;—
     Wet with the rain, the Blue,
      Wet with the rain, the Gray.

Sadly, but not with upbraiding,
   The generous deed was done;
In the storm of the years that are fading,
   No braver battle was won:
     Under the sod and the dew,
      Waiting the judgment-day;—
     Under the blossoms, the Blue,
      Under the garlands, the Gray.

No more shall the war-cry sever,
   Or the winding rivers be red;
They banish our anger forever
   When they laurel the graves of our dead!
     Under the sod and the dew,
      Waiting the judgment-day;—
     Love and tears for the Blue,
      Tears and love for the Gray.

The Artilleryman's Vision

Walt Whitman

While my wife at my side lies slumbering, and the wars are
    over long,
And my head on the pillow rests at home, and the vacant
    midnight passes,
And through the stillness, through the dark, I hear, just hear, the
    breath of my infant,
There in the room, as I wake from sleep, this vision presses
    upon me:
The engagement opens there and then, in fantasy unreal;
The skirmishers begin—they crawl cautiously ahead—I hear the
    irregular snap! snap!
I hear the sounds of the different missiles—the short *t-h-t! t-h-t!*
    of the rifle balls;
I see the shells exploding, leaving small white clouds—I hear the
    great shells shrieking as they pass;
The grape, like the hum and whirr of wind through the trees,
    (quick, tumultuous, now the contest rages!)
All the scenes at the batteries themselves rise in detail before me
    again;
The crashing and smoking—the pride of the men in their pieces;
The chief gunner ranges and sights his piece, and selects a fuse
    of the right time;
After firing, I see him lean aside, and look eagerly off to note
    the effect;
—Elsewhere I hear the cry of a regiment charging—(the young
    colonel leads himself this time, with brandish'd sword;)
I see the gaps cut by the enemy's volleys, (quickly fill'd up,
    no delay;)
I breathe the suffocating smoke—then the flat clouds hover low,
    concealing all;
Now a strange lull comes for a few seconds, not a shot fired on
    either side;
Then resumed, the chaos louder than ever, with eager calls, and
    orders of officers;
While from some distant part of the field the wind wafts to my
    ears a shout of applause, (some special success;)

And ever the sound of the cannon, far or near, (rousing, even in
   dreams, a devilish exultation, and all the old mad joy, in the
   depths of my soul;)
And ever the hastening of infantry shifting positions—batteries,
   cavalry, moving hither and thither;
(The falling, dying, I heed not—the wounded, dripping and red,
   I heed not—some to the rear are hobbling;)
Grime, heat, rush—aid-de-camps galloping by, or on a full run;
With the patter of small arms, the warning *s-s-t* of the rifles,
   (these in my vision I hear or see,)
And bombs busting in air, and at night the vari-color'd rockets.

Sources

Louisa May Alcott. *Hospital Sketches, and Camp and Fireside Stories*. Boston: Roberts Brothers, 1871. [LMA]

Anecdotes, Poetry and Incidents of the War: North and South, 1860–1865. Frank Moore. New York. 1866. [API]

Ethel Lynn Beers. *All Quiet Along the Potomac and Other Poems*. Philadelphia: Porter and Coates, 1879. [AQAP]

Ambrose Bierce. *Civil War Stories*. New York: Dover, 1994. [CWS]

Charles Browne. *Artemus Ward's Best Stories*. Clifton Johnson, editor. New York: Harper and Brothers, 1912. [AW]

Civil War Poetry: An Anthology. Paul Negri, editor. Mineola, New York: Dover, 1997. [CWP]

Harper's Weekly. [HW]

Julia Ward Howe. *Later Lyrics*. Boston: J. E. Tilton and Co. 1866. [JWH]

S. Weir Mitchell. *The Autobiography of a Quack and Other Stories*. New York: The Century Company, 1905. [SWM]

Poems of American History. Burton Egbert Stevenson, editor. Boston: Houghton, Mifflin Company, 1908. [PAH]

Rebellion Record: A Diary of American Events. Volumes 6–8. Frank Moore, editor. New York: G. P. Putnam. 1862–1865. [RR6, RR7, RR8]

Songs and Ballads of the Southern People: 1861–1865. Frank Moore, editor. New York: D. Appleton and Co. 1886. [SBSP]

Songs of the Soldiers. Frank Moore, editor. New York: George P. Putnam. 1864. [SS]

John R. Thompson. *Poems of John R. Thompson*. John S. Patton, editor. New York: Charles Scribner's Sons. 1920. [JRT]

To Live and Die: Collected Stories of the Civil War, 1861–1876. Edited by Kathleen Diffley. Durham, North Carolina: Duke University Press. 2002. [TLD]

War Songs and Poems of the Southern Confederacy: 1861–1865. Henry M. Wharton, editor. Philadelphia. 1904. [WSC]

Walt Whitman. *Leaves of Grass*. Philadelphia: David McKay, 1900. [LG]